STEVE HART: THE LAST KELLY STANDING

Peter Long

HAWKEYE

PUBLISHING

First published in Australia in 2022 by Hawkeye Publishing.

Cover Design by Weasley Au and Katherine Stevens

Historical records sourced from the Queensland State Archives and the State Library of Queensland.

A catalogue record of this book is available from the National Library of Australia.

ISBN 9780645502473

Proudly printed in Australia.

Hawkeye Publishing would like to acknowledge the Turrbal people who are the traditional owners of the land on which our publishing house is located in Brisbane. The Turrbal people are the original storytellers of our region.

www.hawkeyepublishing.com.au
www.hawkeyebooks.com.au

Praise for *Steve Hart: The Last Kelly Standing*

'An exciting and beautifully written novel drawn from the life of one of the younger members of the Kelly gang. The story adds well-researched and valuable information about Ned Kelly and the gang as seen through the eyes of young Steve Hart. Escaping from the massacre at Glenrowan, Steve begins a journey into the heart of Australia where he discovers its many landscapes, meets a number of its first Australians and finds himself. Steve Hart is the story of a gentle young man growing up against a tough backdrop of Australia in the last half of the 19th century. Breathtaking in its scope and strong on interesting characters, the book is a real page-turner. Peter Long's novel takes a prominent place with the best of the Ned Kelly publications.'

Maria Simms, Author.

'Peter Long is to be commended for bringing this modern, indeed postmodern love-story into the Kelly legend, which for the most part is silent on the subject of love. This is certainly a Kelly novel for the contemporary reader. One of the great gifts of the novel to humanistic understanding is its ability to bring characters to vivid psychological life – literally to give life to the individual experience. *Steve Hart: The Last Kelly Standing* brings both history and character to life through an intricately plaited series of stories which dramatise the nascent Australian national myth. But perhaps the most moving story in this polyphonic multi-faceted work, is how Steve Hart rises like the proverbial Phoenix from the ashes of what might otherwise have been a short and tragic life.'

Stephen Torre, Reviewer

'A gripping historical fiction that draws on rumours to create a gripping narrative about Steve Hart, from his start to his 'death' to his rebirth into a new self. Steve's voice is strong throughout,

This book is dedicated to Al, Hud and Ned
– a great gang who've kept me safe.

PROLOGUE

When sentencing Ned Kelly for hanging, the trial judge said,
'... now all the other members of the Kelly gang are dead.'
Ned smiled and replied, 'I've seen very little proof of that.'

1

WE arrive at Green's farm at dusk, tether our horses against the corner of the mare's yard and search on foot. The dogs bark a racket down at the house in the shadowed valley below. Someone swears at them. *Have I done the right thing agreeing to this?*

We find the mare behind some shrubs and herd her into the corner to join our mounts. My brother Dick, halter in hand, closes in, whispers sweet nothings; offers a carrot in the hope of catching her. She faces him, trembling, her eyes bulged white following his movement. Her ears point forward, flick back, point, flick, while he approaches. Gently, his hands are on her shoulder, then her quivering neck. He wraps a piece of mane around a finger, then passes a hand beneath the neck with the reins of the bridle. Once trapped, he offers the carrot, which the mare sniffs. He slips the halter over her mouth and nostrils, pulls it along her face and over the ears. He holds the carrot for her to bite; her fat teeth snap. She's caught.

'There you go, Steve, that's how it's done. Now to lift her.'

Earlier, I was the one feeling trapped, like most of us in Wangaratta, locked in to lead the same cow-like existence until death. Something gnawed at me, like a rat gnaws at a feed bag, and I was afraid I'd rupture; spill fallow upon the dark earth. My mind whispers greatness, whispers adventure, but I see no sunlight.

That day was like any, up with the sun, down to the stables, fed myself, fed, watered, groomed and exercised my share of gallopers, then home for a while, until I returned, put them to bed. I cantered across to meet my brother, Richard, to ride home to our dull family.

'Life around here is so boring,' I said.

He didn't reply. He's alright for a brother. The smart one, Pa says. But Pa doesn't see all sides to him like I do.

'There has to be more!' I said. 'Someplace where you can have all the money and all the drink you can handle. Where ya don't have ta bow down to no one.'

'That's not for us, boyo.'

'Why not?'

'We're in the middle of nowhere, that's why not! Ours is not to have the comfy life, the two-in-hand, the shiny boots.'

He kicked his horse in the ribs in an attempt to keep up with mine, taller and longer of leg.

'We could move to Melbourne.'

'Melbourne is nowhere.'

'Is too.'

'No, it's not. Not when ya listen to Pa. "Wangaratta is worse than Galway. Melbourne is a cesspool of worthless upstarts compared to London",' he said imitating Pa's Irish tones.

'What's a cesspool?'

'A stinkin' pool of shit. You'd know that if you'd stayed at school.'

'Race ya to the top o' the hill, shithead. Winner gets a shilling,' he yelled.

He spurred his bay mare with a 'giddy-up' and was already two horse-lengths ahead of me before I'd realised what he'd said. I slammed old Paleface in the ribs and shortened the reins. The chestnut pinned his ears back, cranky at the insult of running behind a finnicky mare, and dug-in with his hind-quarters for a few short but powerful strides. His enormous muscles raged beneath my skinny legs. I grasped some mane to stop me sliding from him. He reached racing speed. The wind cut tears from my eyes. We passed the mare about a hundred yards from the top and I reined-in where the slope dropped again to wait for Dick to arrive.

'You're right. He *can* go,' Dick said, breathing heavy as he halted beside me.

'Told you so. Shilling please.'

'But you're half my size. We had a massive weight handicap.'

'We'd still beat you. Shilling.' I held out my hand.

He ignored me and moved on.

At the crossroads I'd collected a sugar-bag of meat left there by the Milawa butcher shop, where I had worked as a butcher's boy following school. The owners continue to allow us a discount as a tribute to my former service. I slung the bag across Paleface's withers and the idiot shied, nearly dislodged me, then settled and we walked in silence.

I thought of Mrs Gardiner, the butcher's wife. Beneath her loud comments and raucous laugh, marinated from years of tobacco smoke and hard grog, resided a capable woman. With flashing eyes, hair teased high, gypsy-style clothes, ankles and wrists rattling with bangles, she couldn't help but draw attention.

'Thanks, Steve,' she'd said one evening after I'd carried one of her sleeping babies home from the shop for her. 'You're a good lad, and loyal, but you're so like a sapling bending witless with the breeze. Careful you not be too easily bent for another's purpose, my boy. You might live to regret it.'

I still don't quite know what she meant, but I was fearful she may have peered into my murky future.

'Would you get on with your story, Steve,' she'd say. 'You speak so slowly the horse of your story has bolted.'

While I'm quick of action I'm not of words. She warned me that people might think me slow-minded because of my slow speech.

She did something else.

She grasped my right hand, turned it palm-upwards, then ran her finger slowly along the lines separating the puffy mountains on its landscape. My backbone wanted to curl up like a cat as the wondrous sensation moved from hand to backbone. Her face puckered in concentration.

'The other. Give me the other.'

She clicked her fingers impatiently, grasped my left hand, examined it. She held my palms level with the floor, like the nuns would do before thrashing them with the cane if we misbehaved.

'If I'm not mistaken, you'll have a very dramatic life. A very dramatic life indeed… You have a broken life-line and, whatever it is that is to happen, will occur at a young age.'

This is a horrible thing to tell a child. It set a worry ticking, like a wobbly chronometer inside my tiny heart.

'Will I die?'

I searched her face for any attempt on her part to lie.

'Not necessarily, but something will happen and you'll never be the same again. It'll be as if you had died; stepped from the fire like a phoenix; or been reborn like the priest requires; or you'll be killed and people will remember your spirit. I just can't tell.'

She had squeezed my fingers too hard for my liking, as if she wished to wring the vision from her mind. She drew me into a hug and kissed my forehead before releasing me into the night.

I've never spoken about it and certainly can't with Dick, who'd ridicule me. Not sure why the memory resurfaced now.

Me and Dick crossed the creek at the ford, the water no higher than our horses' knees, and argued our way up the hill. At the crest a paddock rolled out before us down into the valley.

'Talkin' about horse-flesh, look at the mare… over there… in Green's place.'

I looked and saw a fat, glossy-coated grey grazing alone.

'Just about to drop a foal I reckon,' I said, then twisted to face Dick. 'Don't change the subject. My shilling!'

'Yeah, I reckon so, too,' he said, ignoring my request. 'Greeny has that stallion Pontius Pilate standing at stud. Now, if that foal was to him, it could be worth a fortune.'

We rode past.

'Yeah, the foal could be a fast yearling… fetch a high price.'

'We could lift her… the mare,' he said.

'And do what?'

'Report her missing, then seek a reward for "finding" her. That's what the Clancy's do.'

'Ah, good one.'

'Better still, we could hide her up on Pa's block in the Warby's until she foals, then slip her back after six months… without the foal. Could even claim a reward then, for findin' her. Two for the price of one, eh?'

Pa has two-hundred-and-thirty acres of undeveloped country up near the Warby Ranges, as well as the home block near town. I looked over at the Warby's, glowing purple along the horizon.

'Stupid idea. I'm not a thief.'

'You said you want the high-life. You're never going to get it without doing something to take it… Do a couple of lifts and it can set you up for life. There's an opportunity staring you in your stupid face.'

We rode on.

'You could buy a fancy saddle to impress ya Greta mates. Throw a few coins around at the shanty to attract the girls. Girls love a generous fella; someone who'll show 'em a good time,' he said.

'Hard to show 'em a good time in gaol.'

'They love a risky fella though. Can't help themselves.'

'That's me all right – daring… but not a crook.'

I chortled and hoped he'd shut up.

'Ya won't be a crook. We'll borrow her. That's all.'

'Well, do it yourself.'

'I need ya ta help me collar her. I can trust you.'

I rode along quiet, thinking, for half a mile.

'Well? Ya in… or ya out?'

His eyes implored me. I didn't really want to, but I said, 'Alright, if you believe it'll work.'

He's my older brother. I'm barely seventeen and he's twenty. I always go along with him and so far he's managed to keep me safe and out of trouble. He's worked with horse dealers O'Brien, Monaghan, and the Clancy's, so knows his way around, does Dick.

'Let's go home, grab a bridle, slip back later and "borrow her".'

'Borrow!'

I chuckled on for a moment or two.

❖

I look around nervously. I'm scared Green might see us, especially now the trapped mare and our horses are snorting. Down at the house the dogs bark; perhaps they smell us. I hear the trapped mare stamp her feet.

'Come on mate, the fence.'

'Alright, hold ya horses.'

Even under pressure I'm a laugh.

A male's voice echoes from below. 'Fer God's sake, shut ya barking.'

I undo the wires from the corner strainer and pull them back to the next post where I've banged a short stick into the holes where the wire runs to keep them taut. Dick leads the mare through the gap onto the road.

I peer down at the house. A man stands in the yard, addresses the dogs. Jesus, he can't not see us.

'You piss off in case he's onto us,' I whisper.

I restrain the wires, check my handiwork, peer down at the house in the failing light. The man stares up the hill. The dogs bark like crazy. What will he do? I mount Paleface and dash to join Dick.

We canter home in the blossoming darkness, then drop the mare in our neighbour's holding-yard where we'll leave her until the weekend, when we're not working and able to transfer her to the Warby Ranges away from prying eyes.

'That went well,' says Dick.

'As long as we don't get caught.'

'We won't get caught. Greeny won't even know she's missing until she's long gone.'

Kookaburras rattle in the dusk; first one then another, round after round of choruses roll in from various angles around us.

'Hope ya right, 'cause ya know who Pa will blame?' I say over the din.

'That's right… you… It's 'cause he knows I don't never do wrong. I don't cheek him,' the smart-arse replies, even laughs at his own joke.

'That's 'cause he thinks the sun shines outa ya arse, ya bastard.'

It's true. Pa idolises him. He never did take to me. Dick is well-built and cheery-faced, just like Pa. I was born a runt and bandy-legged, second in line of five boys and eight girls and had to fight for every bit of space just to survive.

Whenever I went to show or explain anything to Pa, or even seek his advice, he'd move me on, interrupt me or brush me aside.

'Look Pa, I've got this beetle.'

I'd get an 'Uh huh,' and he'd continue to carve the roast, or do whatever it was he was doing.

'It seems to have legs that are different sizes,' I would say, holding it up close to his face.

'That's good, boy. Run along now.'

'Pa, would ya help me saddle old Paleface, he won't stand still while I lift the saddle?'

'Not now, Steve, I don't have time for that.'

I would start to stutter. He would stutter back to tease me out of it.

'C-c-c-c-c-come on S-s-steve.'

I would see red and fly into a rage. Once he did it in the crowded General Store. He bent over and put his sneering face level with my eyes.

'S-s-s-s-s-spit i-i-i-i-i-t o-o-o-out S-s-steve.'

My eyes blurred over. I raced at him and pushed, and pushed

again, at his stomach, hard.

'Pa, you are a bbbbad man, a bbbbbad mmmman,' I screamed.

He held me at arm's length. I kept swinging, desperate to get at him. When he thought I'd calmed down, he lowered his hands, embarrassed because everyone was watching.

Free of his grip, I flailed into him again, oblivious to everything, but this time I struck him in the mouth. He wiped his lips and any sense of geniality with it. He pushed me backwards with such force I fell onto the floor, splitting my head. Then he reached down and dragged me by the collar out of the shop like a dead ewe, a trail of blood following after me on the floor.

'When you learn to talk properly you can come back.'

I hated him from that moment.

Ma knows what it's like to be the butt of Pa's anger. When it was really bad, I'd hide in her bed between her bedclothes, her pyjamas over me and draw the comfort of her odours.

It was her persistence that helped me overcome my stutter.

'You're rushing and you're jumbling ya words, Steve. I like to hear your words and how you say them.'

Dick and I arrive at our farmhouse at Three Mile Creek on the southern edge of Wangaratta where I've lived since my birth in 1859. It sits stark upon the fifty-three-acres, which Pa paid for after his emancipation, transported here for pickpocketing. It's good land, formed by the joining of the two mighty rivers, the Ovens and the King, and the rich sediment deposited when they flood.

The house lies in darkness, so we sneak our horses into the house paddock, unsaddle and carry our kit into the lean-to beside the hay shed. Dick drops his gear onto the pile of rubbish on the floor, but I hang mine on a hook as I've been taught by the stable-hands where I work. We creep into our beds and I sleep in my clothes to reduce any noise, which might wake Pa.

2

I wake, dress and ride in the half-dark of morning to the split-timber racing stables located near the racetrack just past our place. I'm beggared as if I never slept.

I've frequented these stables since I was eight years of age. I helped the owners muck out or groom their horses until, over time, they grew to trust me and give me more interesting chores, like lunge them in the round yard. The stables have five boxes plus a few holding yards, and small tackle room with an open fireplace to boil the billy and keep the cold winters at bay.

Many a morning I've sat here listening to the stable hands and jockeys weave their tales. I suck in the affection wafting among us.

'Venables escaped again last night.'

'Whose job was it to check?'

'Marcia's. You checked the gate didn't you, Marcia?'

'Of course. 'E must have jumped out.'

'You didn't let him out did ya, Steve? You were the first 'ere.'

'No, I'm the one who returned 'im. It's the third time I've done it this week.'

'He must have jumped. Anyone want this last piece of toast? No? I'll 'ave it then.'

'I'd like to see him jump.'

'I'd like to be on him when he jumped. How good would that be?'

I love it. I must admit that, at first, I used the stables to escape home, but I found I loved being around the horses, and the carers. Horses don't hear your stuttering; don't keep account of your weaknesses. They take you for who you are – how you treat them.

One morning, a year in, the owner, Mr Clarke, a swarthy old chap with a bent back and a permanent worry-frown beneath his receding hair-line, led out a saddled horse, which was strange for that time of the morning, so close to knock-off.

'Here, Steve, 'op on him.'

'Sorry Mr Clarke, I don't know how to ride.' I couldn't lie.

'I know you don't, laddie.' He adjusted the pad's stirrups. 'This is a good time to start. I'll teach you. You can't work 'ere and not ride.'

I saw he meant it, so hesitated no longer. He legged me up and showed me where to position my legs and how to hold the reins to control the horse and look tidy.

'Walk around the yard for a wee while, until you've learned to steer, then we'll ferry the horses to the track.'

After a month of riding at every opportunity, and with his occasional oversight, I was comfortable enough to ferry horses and undertake trackwork alone.

Mr Clark appeared to enjoy watching my progress; his eyes sparkled beneath those silver eyebrows when he swapped the saddle over to a new racer. I just loved being the subject of his gaze.

'Aye, laddie, you're a natural at this game.'

I thrilled at the feel of a horse beneath me and the powerful surge of energy as they dug in for a track gallop. It raised me from a mere mortal to a God. I don't know how to explain it, but I imagine it's like the feeling the celestials on the gold fields get from the opium they smoke. I couldn't get enough of it.

Of course, being competitive, I made sure I learned everything I could about horses and their care, even had a few solid busters; one at speed against a tree from a bolter that busted my leg, but I learned.

One afternoon a blazed-faced galloper named Paleface was led to the stables with a shocking limp. He hopped on three legs and dragged his off-front as he moved. My heartstrings wrenched because I loved Paleface and his grit as a racer. I heard mutterings of 'putting him down', heard discussions that he 'had no future'. I thought he must have broken his leg but learned that a large piece of his hoof had pulled away at the heel and exposed the soft inner-hoof – serious, but something he could survive.

Mr Clarke approached with a rifle.

'You can't shoot 'im.'

'Got to laddie, I'm afraid!'

I didn't know what to do. I teared-up.

'Step aside.'

'No. S-s-shoot me instead.'

'Can't do that. Any other ideas?'

He slammed a bullet in the chamber.

I moved to stand between Paleface and the trainer.

'I'll look after 'im.'

'Can't have him eating feed while not workin'. Stand aside.'

I'd never seen this side of the industry. He cocked the rifle.

'I'll buy him.'

'What with, laddie? You've no money.'

'The money you pay me. You keep.'

He lifted the rifle towards his shoulder.

'Where will you stall him? Costs a lot to feed a racehorse.'

'I'll take him home. He'll heal there.'

Mr Clarke's face softened.

'All right, five shillings. You can pay him off over time.'

'Oh, thank you, Mr Clark. That's so good.'

I hugged him and watched his neck flush red like an ember.

I gathered Paleface's lead and secured him in a shady spot. My eyes seldom left him throughout the day. After work I found some discarded horseshoes and, with the help of an experienced stable hand, tacked a shoe on his damaged hoof and led him home, where I copped a clipped ear from Pa for being late.

Six months free of mud and damp it took for him to recover and walk unfettered. I changed the shoe often to provide added support and learned so much I was tasked with shoeing other horses. I earned more money and repaid my loan sooner than I ever imagined.

Once he was fit, I rode him at every opportunity, sometimes on long treks to the Warby's where I tested our boundaries. Occasionally, Dick and I took rifles and hunted.

❖

I've mucked out the stalls and groomed my mounts and it's midday, two days after we lifted the mare. I'm confident that Dick was right. I had worried unnecessarily.

'Steve, there's someone to see you,' sings a voice from the stable entrance.

I'm confronted by Dick on horseback, arms behind his back, led by two uniformed, mounted police 'traps'.

One blocks my path.

'Come 'ere, Steve, we want a word,' commands Sergeant Steele, who knows me from skylarking with the Greta Mob.

My eyes dart like a dog nabbed in a chook house. I don't know whether to approach or scarper. I turn to Dick for instruction. He's hung his head, offers no advice. Out of loyalty to him, I can't flee. Besides, to run I would appear guilty. I approach with my chin up.

'What do ya want, S-s-sergeant?'

'Do you know anything about a stolen mare left at your neighbour's place?'

'N-n-no Sergeant, nothing.'

'That's strange because Dick just told us you and he left it there.'

'Did he?... Oh, that mare?'

Why did he lag me?

'Yes, that one.'

'Yeah, I might remember, now ya mention it.'

'Your neighbour says you left it there.'

'Did he?'

'Yeah.'

I try to catch Dick's eye but he stares between his horse's ears.

'Well, that's right, we did leave it there. It were dark and we didn't know who owned her.'

'The brand is David Greens of Winton.'

'Ah, is it?'

'Yes, and we already checked with him. There're no fences down where she could have escaped, but he showed us where the fence was opened, and also, your tracks.'

I shrug my shoulders, try to get my thoughts in order.

'Cuff him, Constable,' says Steele.

Constable Bracken dismounts and cuffs me, hands in front.

Mr Clarke appears around the corner of the stable like an ornery bull. His face is flushed, his shoulders are rounded as he charges us.

'What's going on? What's happened?'

He bundles into us, separates me from Bracken like he would tear hay from a bale.

'And who might you be?' Steele asks.

'I own the stables. Steve works for me.'

'We caught these two rascals stealing.'

'What, here… at the stables?'

'No. Out towards Winton.'

'Not Steve? I can vouch for Steve. I don't know the other one.'

He looks at Dick as if he's horse shit on his nose. It breaks my heart to see Mr Clarke's faith in me being destroyed, torn apart like carrion in an eagle's beak.

'He and his brother there stole a horse.'

'No, Steve wouldn't do something like that. Not steal.'

'Borrowed,' I say.

Mr Clark's face winces as if I've gut-punched him.

'A lark. It were a bit of a lark.'

I don't think there's a horse alive could jump the disappointment I see in his eyes. I'm gutted. I mount Paleface and I'm led away trailing Bracken.

3

BIG brave Dick, apple of Pa's eyes, won't hold my stare as we ride to town. What is he concerned about? What can the traps prove? Nothing. I'm on a winner, won't even have to raise the whip. Free by nightfall!

In town I feel each passing eye bore into me. *Thieving convict's sons. Dirty Catholic trash*, I imagine most, especially the Proddie's, think. I stare at them defiant, but feel anxious, hollow inside.

Three or four blocks in, we approach St Augustine's; the Catholic school we attended. It's built of sandstone blocks with a modern galvanised-iron roof, giving off a horrible air about it, like a nunnery with nary a tree to grace it. It felt like it was a gaol when I was there.

Unlike my life at the stables in the half-light of mornings, life in the full glare of day at St. Augustine's was not nearly as exciting. For some reason, my competitive nature never required me to excel at school in the same way it drove me to horses. School life dragged. I avoided attending at every opportunity, and from a very young age.

'Did you get to school today?'

'Yes, Ma.'

'Mr Solomon says he saw you swimming at the creek.'

'That was after school.'

'Are you sure? I didn't get that impression.'

'Yes, Ma.'

There was one incident involving Sister Patricia, my year-four teacher. She was my parents' age and her flushed, slightly overweight cheeks puffed out as she breathed and her chest thrust forward like a bronze-wing pigeon.

The *incident* occurred a week after our term-three exams, as we were winding down for Christmas break.

'Children, a piece of paper with the exam results has been stolen,' she complained. 'Open your desks now, so I can inspect them.'

She sauntered, grim-faced, to the rear of the room and worked her way along the back row of desks until she reached mine. The file sat on top.

'Alright, I've found it. You, mister, will stay behind after class for detention.'

She swiped her hand across the back of my head enough to make me yelp and my eyes wobble. Some down the front, who hadn't seen the swipe, giggled.

After class she chalked 'I must not steal', on the blackboard and pointed her finger at me, as God must have to Moses, to portray her wrath.

'You'll not leave until you've written that line one-hundred times and you'll do it every afternoon this week.'

She slumped behind her desk on the raised platform, drew her starched tunic up to her hairy knees and, glum as a frog without flies, stared at me.

I wondered a lot about boys and girls. Why we were different. Why we boys couldn't wear colourful clothes, couldn't snuggle up to our mothers. I also thought about the priests with their long swirling robes, and rich colours. How they weren't allowed to marry as if marriage was below them. A nasty sin. I wondered, as I sat angry before sister Patricia, a bride of Christ, if a nun was a woman? Her legs were solid, practical like Pa's. My legs had far less hair. Did they have female parts, or had they been born without, like the blessed virgin, Mother Mary? What would it be like not to have a part, where there should be one? What would it be like to have one? Why was I a boy and not a girl? Sometimes, I couldn't tell the difference in my thinking, confused like the church.

I always remember that day. The list informed my parents that I had failed all my exams that year. It caused holy hell at home.

The traps dawdle. It takes an age to pass the school. It's as if the horses have sensed my reluctance. I run my eyes over the playground, see where we played marbles, where we lined up in class groups each morning, forced to sing God Save the King – even us Irish. I catch a whiff of the school toilets as a breeze brushes past. I see where I stubbed my bare toes on cold mornings on the stones placed on the footpath beside the buildings.

A sadness pervades the place.

While I acted-up at home, at school, I just failed to co-operate. I spent days staring out the window, feeling I didn't belong. I was less twitchy by then, able to sit still for a while, tired from early morning starts at the stables, invisible to teachers. I neither asked questions, nor answered any. To the teachers I was a lead-weight – a cynical clown, a wise-cracking midget in the back row, a pigtail-pulling pest, the fool who, if kept in after school, pissed in the slate's cleaning cloths to register my protest, rather than complain.

This continued until I was ten or eleven years of age. I remember the letter:

Dear Mr Hart

We are disappointed neither you, nor your wife, have been able to meet with us to discuss Steve's future.

We suggest, due to his lack of interest and diligence, that he no longer attend.

The Principal.

I couldn't believe it, my dream solution: freedom! My parents, worn down by my relentless drag against the bit, agreed with the school, and I quit. My father was so resigned to the prospect of my failure that, to my great surprise, he didn't even lecture me.

I thought I could work at the stables but there was no vacancy. I was fortunate to score the job at the Gardiner's butcher shop.

We ride along Norton St. towards the police barracks and courthouse, like a Saint Patrick's Day parade, and pass the massive steel gates out front of the brand-new railway station, built when the rail-line to Wodonga was completed.

'There's a rumour about you and these gates, Steve,' Sergeant Steele says. 'Must have been bullshit! Like everything else you do.'

I don't reply, nor react. The other traps laugh like music-hall clowns.

My bandy legs make me slow of foot, but on a horse, I grow wings. Those of us in the Greta Mob – Tom and John Lloyd, Joe Byrne, some hangers-on – gathered at the railway station one afternoon after a picnic race-meet. We rally around a love of horses and horse racing, and dress in flashy clothes. Our strapped moleskins, high-heeled boots, and sash, is a type of uniform. We wear the chin-strap of our ribbon festooned cabbage-tree hats beneath our noses to look sharp. We have a merry time.

I had a lot of grog on board and laughed so much I thought my sore ribs would never recover. I heard someone comment.

'You know, they say there's not a horse that can jump these gates.'

'Oh, I don't know,' I said.

Tom Scanlon snorted.

'What, your horse can?'

I hate being derided. I don't say much but what I say, I mean.

'No, but there's a horse, Venables, at the stables could jump 'em.'

We'd proven Venables had jumped out of his stable, and from a standing start.

'What, not a trained jumper?'

'No. But 'e could do it.'

'Bet he couldn't.'

'You're on. Who's going ta back me?'

'You'll break ya stupid neck,' Tom said.

Many indicated they would bet on it. I sized the gates up close. They were huge! My bravado galloped away and I buckled a little at the knees. Yet I rode to the stables, saddled Venables and returned – at a far slower pace than I'd left. I couldn't chicken-out now, even if I wanted to.

My mate, Joe, the unofficial bookie, took the two-shilling wager off all present and placed the coins in my hat. At his nod, I rode to the fence and threw my jacket across the top rail.

'Unfair,' someone yelled.

'Horse needs a sight-line,' I said, disregarding the jibe.

Because the gate was hung high, perhaps I should have put something on the ground as well, to help Venables estimate where to launch, but didn't, for fear of an uproar.

I fired Venables with a dig in the ribs and, after a short settling-canter, showed him the gate, thirty yards out; let him have his head to attack. His ears flicked forward, then folded back, stayed there. The sound of hooves on blue metal rang like a miner's sluice in the now quiet space.

'Come on old fella, we're in this together,' I urged, more to comfort myself than Venables.

At a point in his charge, I wished he'd baulk and bail, because the fence looked so bloody high. There's no way the poor beast could make it. I prepared for the worst, attempted to breathe, but couldn't. I felt Venables gather himself, barely a stride before he would smash the gate, then launch, clearing it like it was a fallen log. Somehow I clung fast.

The crowd clapped. I raised my finger to my forehead as if it was all so predictable it didn't deserve mention.

'Told ya it could be done,' I yelled.

My reputation as a horseman was sealed. Even the traps were aware.

❖

I steal a glance at the gate and thank the good Lord for grog. I don't think I could jump it now, stone-cold sober. I refuse to chat with my captors, as if there's nothing wrong, acting like we're all mates on a joyride. I pretend I don't hear their sarcasm.

We continue along Ovens Street and then Faithful, until the Courthouse appears in the distance. I lose some confidence, pant like a cat. Townsfolk, people I recognise, step to the street to watch us pass; make comments.

'What have they done, Sergeant?'

'Have they bailed someone?'

'Well done troopers. About time someone put these bludgers away.'

We front the Police Barracks and Courthouse. Both are timber buildings, the barracks, shingle-roofed and the modern courthouse, iron, and set further back. The horse stables complete a courtyard behind.

They help us from our horses and prod us up the stairs because the painful leg-irons slow us. We are locked in separate holding pens, and not permitted to speak. Dick remains sheepish and I can't figure-out why. After two hours, I'm handed papers.

'Fill these in. The Magistrate will need them.'

I see there is space to write my name and I imagine the other space is for my address because it has letters which, sounded-out, make that sound – a dress. Stupid language. Do I wear a dress? The rest is just way too hard. I wish I could read better; that I had taken more notice of schoolwork.

One of the constables completes my paperwork, then collects

Dick's, which he's completed himself. Later, the constable returns with another piece of paper, which he makes me sign.

'It's a record of what you told us about the stolen mare.'

I sign as best I can and he takes pages over to Dick, who appears to read, then alter.

The constable shakes his head like a willy wagtail.

'You can't change it, boyo.'

'Well, I didn't say it. I didn't never say I stole the bally horse. I said we found it. Change it to what I've writ and I'll sign it.'

The constable concedes and returns later with two pages, which Dick signs.

'The Magistrate will deal with you both in the morning.'

I watch Dick in the other room. For a twenty-year old he's taking this badly. His whole body shakes.

4

MID-MORNING and after a long night of broken sleep I listen to the traps dining. They're certainly noisy. I entertain myself guessing accents. There're Irish and Welsh lilts, sprinkled amidst the local drawl of the cornstalks. I hear the posh English voice of the officer-in-command, and laughter, which I don't appreciate, given the mess I'm in.

The chatter stops, and not long after, Sergeant Steele and Constable Bracken appear.

'Alright you two, on your feet, turn and place your hands behind your back,' commands Bracken. His shirt pulls at its buttons, sweat darkens a swamp beneath each armpit.

I stand, as does Dick. Handcuffed leg and wrist, we are released from our cell and fall-in behind the policemen to shuffle-march like hobbled horses across the parade-ground into a court waiting area, with bench space for twenty-odd persons.

'Sit there until your case is called.'

We perch upon a rough wooden bench designed for about six bodies. The two traps sit beside us and shuffle the papers they hold, fidget like they're nervous. I should be the one who fidgets.

Clerks move along and across the hallway as if they're on life-serious missions. Time drags. Other victims sit, like us, awaiting their fate; perhaps horrific. If I'm found guilty, I can kiss goodbye to becoming a jockey. It sucks.

Steele and the constable, though, sit without a care. The constable hums an English tune I've heard before but can't remember where. It contradicts the beat of my heart; mashes my senses.

27

Further along the hallway a door creaks open and a clerk signals a group waiting on a nearby bench. A man white of flesh, soft of hands and muscle, cloaked in a long gown, files past, the swish of the fabric as he passes, lingers. I admire the way the cloak falls from the shoulder and swirls across his buttocks, to hover mere inches above the floor. *Bit girlie*, I think. Clean, crisp and noble, he guides the others through the door, which creaks shut.

I glance at the constable who's leaned his head against the sandstone wall, eyes closed. I wonder what my chances are of wrestling his pistol and making my escape. But then I'd be a real criminal; a fugitive, so, desist.

I've remained silent too long, so ask Bracken.

'Do we get one of them blokes in a dress?'

I point at one standing across the aisle talking seriously to another waiting family. Bracken laughs.

'No, not unless you're rich as all hell.'

'Who are they?'

'Lawyers. People use them for more serious matters.'

Ah, I think. *Our matter is not really serious. Great, probably get a warning at worst.*

The door from the courtroom opposite us rattles open. A man in waistcoat and spats, his pomade-slicked hair parted in the middle, and ears covered by his fluffed-up sidebars, emerges.

'You're on next, Constable. The Magistrate's ready.'

'Come on boys. You're up!'

I rise fast, rattle my leg-irons by the action. Bracken grabs me by the elbow and steers me through a door into the courtroom, all rough-timber furniture, and a sawn-wood ceiling. I see Ma and Pa seated in the second row. I try to catch their eye but they refuse to meet mine, as if they're ashamed. The Police Magistrate faces us from behind a raised platform and Bracken guides us into a long bench to the side.

'Constable Bracken, what do we have here?'

'We have brothers, Richard and Steve Hart, charged with stealing horses, Your Honour.'

'How do they plead?'

'They plead guilty, Your Honour.'

'It reads here they plead guilty to *borrowing* a horse, Constable, not stealing.'

'It does, Your Honour but, when we checked their scrub-block in the hills, we found another twelve horses with dodgy brands.'

'Are they your horses, sir?'

The magistrate's question is directed to me. I swallow.

'N-n-never saw them b-b-before.'

Bracken interrupts.

'The brother, Richard, says he thought they may have been Steve's. It's in Richard's statement.'

The prick. Why would Dick say that? He's set me up. No wonder he wouldn't look at me. The horses must be his and his dealer mates.

'W-w-were the brands mmm… were they mine?' I ask Bracken.

'No.'

'Then they c-c-can't be m-m-mine.'

Oh my god-forsaken voice. It fails me when I most need it. I need to show I'm not as dumb as I appear.

The Magistrate smiles.

'The defendant will only speak when he's requested to.'

'Is the paddock m-mine?'

'That's you, sir – the defendant. Be quiet or I'll lock you up, regardless.'

I shut up even though my dander is up. I sit with mouth open, disgusted at how the truth is twisted and at my inability to set it straight.

'Does the paddock belong to him, Constable?' continues the magistrate.

'No, your honour.'

'Does it belong to the brother?'

'No, your honour. It belongs to their father.'

'So, you have nothing. The twelve horses may have wandered there. Someone else, the father perhaps, could have placed them there.'

'But he didn't. We have tracks from where the horse was stolen at Green's, leading to where the horse was later found, then leading to the defendants' house. We have a confession that they took the horse,' the Constable said, voice rising.

'One horse?'

'Yes, your honour.'

'Fair enough. We're talking about a single horse and no confession. Is this correct?'

My eyes sparkle. We're going to be let-off. Stupid traps have pissed-off the magistrate. I shoot a look of glee to Dick before I realise, I'm not talking to him. No matter, I'm so happy.

The Magistrate writes in a large book and ignores us. He can write all he likes, we're free! He raps his gavel.

'The Court will note, in spite of the false charge, this is still a serious matter. In light of the evidence, I find both boys guilty, not of stealing, but of illegally using a horse.'

'But your honour,' shouts the constable, clearly rattled.

'Quiet! I have ruled. It's a serious offence but the Crown's case lacks sufficient evidence to be classed as stealing. I commit you both to twelve months hard labour at Beechworth Prison, to commence today.'

What the? I wait to give him an angry glare, but his head is stuck in a document, and his hand traces ink patterns with a quill. My arms are cuffed but I manage to give him the finger.

'Next.'

My heart stops like a cricket stops when you crush its little body between your fingers: it writhes but cannot function. My life is stuffed. I'm a crim. It's all I can do to bring myself to look at Dick; I'm so angry. He glances at me but refuses to check-in. I glance at Ma and Pa, two rows from the front. Ma's cheeks glisten with tears. Pa's hatred of me is scrawled across his crusty face.

'Look what you've done, now, Steve, you useless bastard,' he says, loud enough for me, and others, to hear.

Sweat oozes across my brow. The handcuffs and leg-irons are heavier, and far tighter.

5

WE bounce and bump in the wooden prison cart the twenty-five miles to Beechworth. The gold town fairly rollicks as miners attend to their busy lives and I catch glimpses of rows of tents, joss houses and bullock drays through the tiny, barred window. I've visited Beechworth often, but it feels different this time. Sadder. The cart stops in front of the gaol's arched-granite gateway where the gates groan open. I recall Pa's harrowing stories of convict life. For the first time fear is physical; grasps me by the throat and shakes me like I'm a rag doll.

We creak into the main yard. Men line the fences in the holding yard and cheer when we jump down. I'm still not used to the leg-irons and stumble.

We're escorted past a crowded yard, towards a door with a blue and white sign above it. *Administration.* Inmates shout comments through the fence.

'Where ya from boys?'

Wolf whistles rise from everywhere, at once.

'Hi gorgeous. I've got the little one. Sweet meat.'

'What ya in here for?'

I lower my eyes as we pass through the brick entrance. I swagger in a display of bravado that I don't feel.

'Okay, strip, chaps and empty anything from your pockets or bags,' orders a guard in a black uniform with solid cap.

Four officers inspect us for lice, wounds and I suppose, hidden weapons or drugs. We're sent into the showers. I'm not used to being naked in sight of others and feel totally exposed, vulnerable.

'Whew. This is torture. I'm freezing,' I say, despite my promise to remain silent for the next twelve months.

'Be thankful. Some places don't have a shower,' the supervisor says.

We are issued prison digs – rough, canvas worker's wear – then lined up against the wall to be photographed. I can't believe I'm going to be captured for all time in such ill-fitting, dun-coloured clothes. My skin fairly crawls at the thought.

Clothes are important. With prison garb in hand, I recall an evening, years earlier, when I was at the butcher's house to feed their animals while they visited friends. I noticed a floral-patterned, sleeveless dress draped across their bed. In the lamplight the vibrant pink and green fabric shone and appeared to leap from the pale bedcover to possess me.

As if in a trance I slipped my hands beneath the dress's waistline, lifting it as if a body still inhabited it – legs one side of my hands, head and chest the other. I stared at it for ages as if frozen, before I gently scrunched it and held the soft fabric against my face to draw in its exotic scents. I wondered, despite knowing I shouldn't, what it would be like to wear such a delicate object. I imagined wearing it to a posh dinner in a grand house with art on every wall, lush drapes framing every window, silver service upon the table, as if I'd, once, inhabited such a universe.

My dream-like state continued while I removed my bloodied Bluchers and discarded my grey butcher's kit, to stand pale and naked before the dress in the flickering lamp-light. I caught my wavering reflection in the cracked sideboard mirror. Before me stood a bloodless creature from another world, a creature with few attractive features, barren of pride, and so very, very needy.

I slipped the delicate dress over my head and watched it shiver down my body. My flesh reacted as if shot with the charge from a Morse-code transmitter, it went into such a spasm. I couldn't believe that something so delicate, so light, something so soft and sensual against my skin, could cause such a reaction.

I paraded in the mirror as I had seen the young ladies in the butcher shop parade: swinging their hips, weaving their tails like sensuous cats, holding their hands with fingers alert, at a line to attract my eye to their shape and pouting their lips like a Murray River Cod. I did all this and it felt so natural. I was no longer colourless but a splendorous being.

My father was not a man to express his finer feelings but as I stared at myself, I recalled watching, unobserved, my mother parading nearly naked in front of him in their bedroom, exactly as I just had. His comment made her smile as wide as a slice of watermelon, and he pounced on her from behind, laughing loudly, while she giggled like a schoolgirl. Never had I witnessed them display such fun and affection. I wondered if I would have that effect on others: turn rock into animal, salt into sugar? I believed I could.

I paraded for ages, until I realised spectators, attracted to the lighted window, might spy me. It would be a shocking sight. I undressed, tidied the room, donned my butcher-boy gear and escaped into the darkness.

I thought about nothing else the next day and did my chores as if I were an automaton. I imagined wearing the dress again. I checked each woman who entered the store to see how she moved, how she held her hands, her lips, the angle of her head.

'You're looking pretty today, Mrs Kent. Did you buy that dress in Town?'

'No, I got this in Melbourne two years ago, Steve… for the cup.'

'My, my, Trudy, you're dolled-up this morning, love your shoes.'

'Why, thank you Steve, I wasn't convinced they went with this outfit. Nice of you to notice.'

I realised I'd always noticed; I just wasn't aware of it. I sought to remember each gesture and each moment of the previous evening. At the same time, I felt a shame creep between my joy: a dirty feeling that tinged the pleasure, like a stray gumleaf in the quart-pot destroys the salving taste of tea.

The next evening, I returned to the house, convinced my modelling would never, could never, occur again but, against my will, I found myself repeating the previous events. This time I rummaged for underwear and located exotic finery, lingerie the type of which I was totally unaware.

Now Mona, what shoes should I wear with this outfit? I said to myself.

I had to be satisfied to pose resting my over-sized feet on top of the only dress-pair in the cupboard.

Again, the excitement pulsed but this time I was conscious of its physical dimension. Perhaps the taboo of femininity, the secrecy, the glow of the lamp, the preening of self, heightened my awareness.

I may have portrayed a woman on the outside but my prick strained, curved upright against the fabric at my groin. It was so sexually strange. I repeated the activity for the two nights before the Gardiner's return, as if drawn in by a magnet, despite my shame.

When the family returned, I soon bent to my old ways, but the experience never left me. I thought about stealing the dress to keep it close in order to fulfil my newly aroused passion, but good sense prevailed. I told no one.

It wasn't long after I'd discovered this other me that I became impressed with the Greta Mob and their snazzy dress.

By day, I was in a bleak underworld of carcasses and sawn bones wearing blood-splattered clothes and boots. But after work, I'd hang out in the street or hit the pubs, dressed like a toff. Our external coverings tell us everything about what is beneath; about who we are, while at the same time, tell us nothing.

'How'd ya hurt ya leg?' the superintendent asks, after the photograph is taken. One leg is bent out of shape, bowed.

'Smashed into a tree, chasing horses.'

'Sir!'

'... Sir.'

'It's a wonder you can walk, boy.'

When that's completed, we are escorted to separate cells but in the same cellblock. I don't sleep.

When the cell doors clang open in the morning, I follow the crowd to breakfast. The wide hall is crowded with men packed tight along wooden tables. I'm overwhelmed with the rumble of male voices and clattering plates. I take a tin plate and mug off a pile, draw cutlery from a bucket, join a line and receive the slops offered.

I locate Dick who makes space for me to park myself.

'You all good?' he asks.

'Yeah, fine!'

We eat in partial silence. When most have eaten their meals and space appears at the table, various inmates, people we know from around the district, drop by.

'Heard you'd joined us. Horse stealing, wasn't it?'

'Yeah, one of Greeny's mares. Don't know how he twigged,' Dick says.

'He'd know where his first florin was hid, would Green. Let us know if we can be any help,' says one old lag. 'I've put out the word that you're alright. You should be safe.'

It's nearly comforting.

❖

Before me is a pile of rocks and I'll use this hammer breaking them for the next eight to ten hours. It has taken a week to get into the swing of it, but I'll use the opportunity to build my body, get fit.

I'm not attractive, or a large man who attracts physical attention, positive or negative. I keep low. I'm humorous and can imitate people; staff usually, clever enough to get a laugh.

'Now, you, that prisoner with the turnip under 'is arm,' I'd say, in my scratchiest voice to impersonate Mister Weldon, the Welfare Officer. 'Are you growing it there, lad, or did it just stick there by chance, as you walked past?'

'Oh no, boss, I'm just returning it. I noticed it walking out of the kitchen,' I'd reply in Dick Turner's high-pitched voice, a lag well known for stealing fruit to fire up the prison hooch.

My audience usually laughs.

As someone who's young and entertaining, I'm allowed to pass across groups, which acts to keep me safe.

I can do this gaol thing.

6

I watch two prisoners step down from the enclosed prison cart. One captures my attention. He's young, a boy like me, and he's striking – dark-haired and physically well-proportioned like a lean, native cat. I wish beyond hope that we might be friends.

He scans his surrounds. Takes tentative steps, not yet used to the gaol yard legs-apart-shuffle required to prevent the steel anklets and the linking chain from hurting bones, cutting flesh. He grimaces with each step. Neither does he have the thousand-yard-stare needed to transport himself from his present hell to somewhere no one can quite touch. He stares at people, other "cons", the authorities. He doesn't look down or appear mentally vacant and that, too, is dangerous. He needs to learn fast or he'll die.

He needs to learn that gaols are run by gangs, which act to, among other things, protect their members. While you have to qualify for membership, the gangs choose you. They assess your suitability through various means, such as your reputation, the way you behave, your age, size, background, who you know, and they control you through intimidation.

Sure enough, after passing through reception and settled in his cell block, he's soon bailed-up by Drag, the leader of the gang at the top of the block pecking order, flanked by three of his Drongo sidekicks. I've learned the new lad's name is Danny.

Drag's hairline recedes through the middle of his head, leaves a dark ring of hair around the edges. His long neck, sharp jaw and protruding nose make him appear like a goanna. His tanned body is muscled, like most of us in the hard-labour section. He sports a horrendous scar across his left eye and cheek, as if he's been struck by a sword. It's why he's called Dragoon – a swordsman – shortened to the handle Drag. I once looked into his eyes and it's what I couldn't see there that chilled me. It's like looking into the yellow eyes of a soulless reptile. There's nothing to appeal to.

Drag towers over Danny, pokes his finger into the poor lad's face and speaks loudly.

'Get this inta ya thick head, pretty boy. In this block, nothin' happens without me knowin'.'

'Why do you need to tell me that?'

'Because you look like the type who thinks he's too good to take orders.'

'From them who've no right to give me orders, yes, I am.'

'There ya go. You're just lippy, aren't ya?'

'You'll see who's lippy soon enough if you keep talking like that.'

'Before you leave here, I'm gonna make a little slave bitch out of you, pretty boy, and you're gonna thank me for it.'

Danny looks agitated. If he reacts it will either get him killed, or a month in solitary. If he keeps his calm the bullying bastards will depart as quickly as they've appeared, yet cause more trouble for Danny later. He keeps his calm.

On cue I notice the gang, for no logical reason, depart. He believes the threat averted; feels safe to resume his business. The poor lad is unaware that a fag is posted to report when he enters the showers, where his real initiation will begin. I've seen the bully game often enough to know how it ends. For some unknown reason I can't stand by and watch it happen to Danny, such is my infatuation with him. But what can I do?

I loiter around the communal area and when I see him ready his clobber for a shower, I hide in the far toilet cubicle hoping, somehow, I can protect him.

I hear him enter and set clothes aside. The shower splashes on the concrete, upon a body. Moments later more footsteps, the violent sound of flesh-on-flesh, grunts, the sounds of struggle.

'What do ya think now, tough boy?' Drag's voice echoes around the barren enclosure.

A groan, a defiant sound from a choking Danny.

'Not so full of lip now, are you? You're gonna get to like this, or every day someone is gonna bash ya until you do.'

I leave the cubicle and slide behind Drag bent over the struggling Danny. I swear I don't know what possesses me, but I kick the dog between his spread legs. I feel my boot connect with his groin; hear a horrible sound as he sucks in air. Then, as he half-turns and bends further to protect his aching groin, I kick him in the head. He has no idea what's hit him, topples backwards on the stone-flagged floor with a sickening thud, where his blood mixes freely with the shower water. He's unconscious. I can't believe it. Danny stands shock-still and stares at me open-mouthed.

'Turn off the shower, mate. Leave and don't say a word, or ever mention that I was here. They'll think you dropped him yourself and leave you alone in future,' I whisper and offer a weak smile.

All he can do is stare, open-mouthed like a riled frilly lizard. I return to the cubicle.

I hear him leave the block. For minutes, all is quiet except for a dripping tap. Then I hear the fag, who was posted at the door to block intruders, call for Drag through the doorway.

'You OK, mate?'

No reply.

'Drag, you alright?' A little louder.

Moments later I hear the fag's footsteps enter.

'S--t... Drag?' he says, as if the goanna is awake, fear and surprise washing in his voice.

The fag retreats without checking further, doesn't want to be implicated. I sneak past the unconscious thug and cockroach my way to my cell, hoping I haven't been sighted.

I'm not being heroic. By helping Danny, he's in my debt. It's a type of reverse intimidation tactic. I get to decide whenever it's time to call in favours, how he can repay it. I never planned it, but it's a fact. It's a dirty society in gaol. No one is clean – we're in it together. We all try to survive as best we can.

Back in my cell, I worry that I may have killed Drag and be locked in here for life. I race to the hole in the corner and chuck my guts up with the terror. But if no one saw me enter or leave the showers, then the guards, based on the fag's say so, will blame Danny. How can I have been such an idiot?

I hear a scream. Someone's discovered the creepy bastard.

'Guards, guards… quick! Drag's hurt!'

Immediate lock-down of the Block. There's a continuous clatter of footsteps on the steel walkway; guards coming and going, and through my cell door peephole, I spy a stretcher arrive. *Come on, is he alive or dead?*

'If anyone knows anything about this incident, knock on your cell door,' booms the Warden's voice.

Everything is silent. Not a knock, while we wait for the next boot to drop…

'Rot in hell, then. You'll stay in your cells on bread and water until I get an answer.'

God, more days to sweat. I wish I'd thought more about the consequences. I'm not sure I can stand it. Each time I think about it, I seize in panic. Each hour draws itself out like a day.

Two days later the doors open as usual for breakfast. I track Danny down and sit beside him.

'Jesus, mate, I'm so pleased to see you.'

'Oi'm pleased to see you, too. You're Steve, right?'

I sense a hint of Irish accent.

'Yeah.'

'Thanks for what ya done.'

'Mate, I'm not sure I done you a service. If the fags let on to the Warden, you could be in a lot of trouble. Go up for murder.'

'Self-defence.'

'Doesn't count for much in here. Serious business for you and, I guess, for me also.'

'If ya think I'd lag you, matey, there's no fear of that.'

I believe him. Just by the way he says it. We lock eyes.

'Nah, I don't think you will… Is he dead?'

'No idea.'

'Chriiist, how stupid am I?'

'It'll be alright, mate.'

He turns to the others at the table.

'Anyone know what we was locked in for?'

'They found Drag hurt in the shower block.'

'How d'ya know?'

'Terry the "Trusty" told me.'

'What happened to him… Drag? Did he have a fall? A heart attack?'

'No idea.'

'Is he dead?'

'No, he's holed-up in the hospital, but touch and go.'

I breathe in. There's hope.

I hear applause. Sporadic at first, then picked up by all along the cell block. Drag is led, nearly carried, back to his cell by two guards. His step is spastic. It's been two weeks and word is about that he has brain trouble, can't remember much, has limited movement. News has also caught up that Danny's brother was a long-term inmate and a tough guy, which builds on Danny's reputation for having bashed Drag.

That night I learn Danny's only fifteen years old. He's so young. I'm seventeen at least. We're barely shaving, let alone standing on our own two feet.

I notice the world differently since his arrival. I watch a tiny green fern struggle to gain a hold on the bare, granite prison wall; a willy-wagtail build a nest under the guard's parapet; smell the scent of perfumed soap waft from the superintendent's family quarters; hear the tinkle of the chapel piano visit us in the lockdown darkness of night. Things once hidden to me. Everything is special since Danny arrived.

I rush to find him each morning, like a magpie to its nest, to share a food morsel with its chicks. I enjoy chatting while he showers, observing his slim body, his wispy beard, the pattern of dark moles clustered across his back. I like the feel of his shoulder brushing against mine at the dining table, and how his eyes hold mine when we talk. It's not only overwhelming: it's weird. I'm uncomfortable about my feelings but at the same time, I'm thrilled; the happiest I've ever been.

We look after each other, he and I, and I enjoy the fact he's outspoken, rough, fearless, in contrast to my quiet ways.

I've never felt as deeply about another human being. I've met very few people worthy of my respect and have seldom felt admired. Apart from having rescued him from a poor start to prison life, Danny appreciates the fact that I'm a good listener.

Turns out we share friends back home. I tell him about the Greta Mob.

'We just hang out and get up to mischief. Mostly drinking and horse-riding tricks. We practise new tricks all week to surprise each other on a Saturday night.'

'Saturdays in Greta... not the centre of the universe.'

'No, but people line up to see our tricks. You... you should see us when there's a dance on. We dress fancy and enter the hall together. We look a treat. Everybody is interested in what we're up to. The fun we have, drives 'em envious.'

'Are they all from Greta, the mob?'

'Mostly, but I'm not, for instance. Tom Lloyd comes in...'

'Tom Lloyd? He's a relative.'

'True? Get him to bring you along when we get out. You'd love it.'

I watch his face alter as he locks in the idea.

'Shh,' I say and place a finger to my lips as a sign of silence. Someone is finishing a yarn.

'So, we're in the barn and I was convinced the farmer's daughter were a chaste young thing, and I the devil. I had let my hands play lightly with her flesh thinking I'd be swotted aside but she chased my hand and I had to get serious.'

'Darby Earl is telling a story. You'll love this. Loved his last one,' I whisper to him.

The storyteller has stopped. Those gathered around lean in to better hear him, or to encourage his effort.

'She says, 'Darby Broom, are you gonna do something, or am I going to die waiting'? Then she reached out and moved real close. I mean close.'

'Oh, for real?'

'For real, fellas. Then, the language on that girl would have done a bullocky proud, as she urged me on. I tell ya me boys, those quiet ones have the real passion.'

Every listener laughs and cheers, and even I can visualise the scene.

Neither Danny, nor I, have any experience to draw upon, so it's an exciting and strange world they describe. It's a world on the outside so far away, and it adds to the inside longings we have for pleasures denied.

Some men, like Drag, will never be released, meaning the world of family, soft women and normal niceties, is now unavailable to them. So they take an interest in other men for comfort. They attempt to entice others into their world and many inmates will "play for the stay". It's quite easy to cross over if you're forced, or if you're out of your mind on prison hooch.

Strong partnerships form and petty jealousies, or serious ones, flare up all too often into serious conflict, which affects us all. It's a frightening part of prison life. But partnerships also act to protect a couple from unwanted attention and I think ours acts like that – to protect us. We're both very young and vulnerable, so our bonding may have kept us safe.

But all things cannot last. I farewell Danny. His four-month prison-term is up and I shudder to think that from March until June, I'll be left here in Beechworth's hellhole by myself.

'I'll find you, as soon as you're released, Steve.'

'You do that… make sure ya track me down.'

We hug in the holding yard. I tear-up like I got Bindies in my eyes and I'm sure I see a tear in Danny's eye as he walks through the gate to freedom.

Danny's here. It's July. I had to rely upon his promise to find me because I couldn't locate him. No one could.

I've been back in Wangaratta since June, having promised myself and Sergeant Steele I'd behave. The four months of gaol without Danny dragged like a heavy chain around my spirits. I threw myself into the rock-breaking task, determined to build my muscles, if nothing else, to help it pass. I learned leatherwork and a range of arts and crafts to avoid feeling so wretched. I plaited belts and whips for Danny. I gained comfort from the repetitive action, enjoyed the way the individual strands wove and clung together, flexible yet strong. Many viewed this as being a sissy but I didn't care.

I rush to him and we hug. Our fingers weave together. I hold him at arm's length.

'Where have you been?'

'Hiding with me brother after a run-in with a policeman, back in April. Me poor mother has been gaoled three years for a crime she didn't commit.'

To associate with known felons is absolutely the wrong thing for me to do. I see pain in Danny's eyes.

'Oi'm not guilty of the things they accuse me of, either.'

'I believe you. It's real crook.'

I have both his hands in mine and I'm peering into his troubled eyes, like Mrs Gardiner peered into mine after she'd read my palm.

'Yeah, fookin unfair and fookin inhumane, that's what that is.'

'Okay mate. I'll think it over. I'll have a think if I should join you.'

'You do that. Oi'll understand if you don't. No one wants to go back into that hellhole.'

I do think it over. It's Danny after all. How can I live without him? If I am caught associating there may be a penalty but, at this point in my life, it's worth it. It'll be fine. Life without him is very dull, so very dull indeed.

Chances are, though, his troubles will blow over, they'll release his ma and we're no longer in trouble. So, goes my thinking, over and over. What will I tell Pa?

Someone once said there's no good time to pass on bad news.

'Pa? You're not gonna like what I got to tell ya,' I say.

It's three days following Danny's visit.

'Well don't say it.'

I suspect he knows what's coming, having seen Dan and I talking.

'I'm over this. I'm not gonna keep at this life anymore. I want some adventure and have been offered a job shearing. I'd rather have a short but merry life than this drudge, workin' for someone else.'

Pa's face does a backflip, his right fist tightens and his arm cocks ready to strike. Jeez he's pissed. But I'm older now and quite bulked from breaking rocks, so I see him check himself, put his fists away.

'You might think you're clever follerin' them skylarks, boyo, but you'll be livin' on borrowed time... All that glitters is not gold, you know. You'd be better getting a backbone of your own and settling down. There's no price that you can put on your liberty, and I speak from experience,' he says, so close to my face I feel his warm breath batter my flesh.

I realise there is no point talking further, so I push him. He takes a step backward, fuming. I walk away, mount my horse, and launch into the unknown – an adventure.

7

I ride to meet Danny. Riding, first, to the Wombats and then west, off the track into spectacular country.

I wind through narrow creek cuttings, pass wallabies munching along high paths trodden through scrub that reaches up into the razorback ridges. From below, beside the river, I strain in the saddle to sight the different eucalyptus trees along the ridges, like the sweet-smelling peppermint gums, so good for making tea in a billy can over a campfire. I see stringybarks with long strands of bark drooping from their smooth, pale trunks. The white branches of the candle gums remind me it is still early spring. On a sunny day these trees help my spirits soar, but on a rainy or overcast day their ghostly presence cloys my soul, hammers it into the surrounding rock.

At a point in the journey, a distant peak appears between two buttes on the canyon wall opposite. I make my way uphill, into a barely penetrable patch of scrub. Dan says the boys use a different route each time to avoid creating a pathway making it difficult for anyone other than a blacktracker to find them. I'm about three horse-lengths away from missing the opening when luck has me stumble upon it.

I frighten a young bloke when I appear from the dense scrub into a grassed clearing surrounding a hut. The poor blighter stands shirtless against a ramshackle alluvial mining-race, and ten yards from the pistol I see glinting in the sun. He's as stunned as a startled wallaby.

'Top a the morning' to ya. I'm lookin' for Danny?'

I watch his clever mind work overtime, his eyes, black wasps, thrash about above his dark beard, race from me to his pistol, from his pistol to me, then back again.

'Why? Who are you? A fookin' trap?'

'Nah, mate, I'm a friend of Danny's.'

'The hell you are. How'd you find us?'

'Danny told me you were up this way.'

'Hey, Steve, you made it.'

It's Danny's voice, thank Christ, but I can't see him. I'm not sure what this crazy-eyed bounder in front of me is going to do. Then I glimpse Danny moving around from the side of an old mullock heap.

'Did you give this prick permission? Directions?' the big fellow shouts over to him. The wasps don't lose track of me for a second, nor I of him.

'Yeah, you said we needed help.'

The cunning fellow slides closer to his pistol as we talk.

'It didn't cross ya wombat mind ya should mention it to me?'

'Oi didn't know if he would come.'

I expect to like the brother after all the stories Danny shared about him in gaol but I quickly wonder if it wasn't just younger brother "idol worship" if this crazy is his brother. I sense he doesn't take to me either and by his behaviour so far, I think he, also, is a bit of a prick.

'I'm Steve Hart,' I say, staring down on him from my horse. I nod in Danny's direction. 'We was friends in Beechworth.'

'Yeah, Ned Kelly,' he says, reluctantly.

'I'm here to work,' I add, in an attempt to impress. I wasn't aiming to be a burden.

'Ya are, are ya?'

I nod my head.

'Good. It's not a fookin holiday home. Ya won't be here to rest. And his name's Dan, not Danny.'

'I won't be restin', and I brought whiskey with me,' I say, as if that will solve everything.

Later, Dan confides that Ned thinks I'm a sheila with my chin-strapped dandy hat, my city riding pants and fancy boots. It's me Greta mob, goin'-to-town outfit.

That night, we're on the grog. I notice Ned is still wary of me.

The hut is a solid log-cabin, not the usual wattle-and-mud daub humpy. It's topped with a brush roof. Each wall has vertical slits for windows like a fort, to enable defenders to shoot out all sides in the event of an attack. The logs have been adzed flat on both tops and bottoms, to ensure there are no gaps for attackers to sneak up and shoot at exposed defenders.

'Harry Powers built this hut, years before I met him, as a safe house,' Ned explains. 'I hated it then because the bastard had me holed away up here for months on end. I couldn't care how safe it was; it kept me away from Ma and the family.'

Danny smiled.

'Love it now, instead of goin' back inside, don't you brother?'

Ned nods, swigs on the bottle and watches sparks from the fireplace fly into the sky. The hut contains a few bunks, a table and a fireplace. Outside, there's a cleared area with a lean-to for meal preparation in summer and when it's dry.

The lads can down some grog. The level falls rapidly and as the night wears on, our tongues loosen. Dan regales us with stories of the Greta Mob. He joined following his release and describes to Ned the incident with Drag and how it led to meeting me.

The brothers then explain the recent incident that has them on the run. Their version differs from that of the policeman, Fitzpatrick, who had come to their house to arrest Dan on a supposed warrant for horse thieving.

They are agitated and, as far as I'm concerned, have every right to be.

I'm not large of build, but very fit, and hardened from a year busting rocks with a sledgehammer in prison. I set-to assisting with the digging at a pace equal to the Kellies. It yields a handy packet of gold dust and a few substantial nuggets, despite the lease having been previously fossicked.

Sometimes circumstance drives an idea or an invention.

'We're out of grog.'

'We can't be, we just bought a packhorse-load-full a week ago.'

'We need to make our own. That's what we need to do to keep outa the trap's sight… earn some money.'

'Easier said than done,' I reply, thinking she's a hare-brained idea. They convince me of its merits.

The next time we do a supply run we pick up materials to fashion a still, along with the ingredients to make whiskey. We try to live legally but by God it's difficult.

Some afternoons we target practice; shoot at clay bottles with our pistols and rifles. We treat this serious because the traps hunting us are trained marksmen and we are mere youngsters, after all. At other times it's quite a hoot.

'Got him,' Ned shouts above the gunfire.

'Got who?'

'Constable Lonigan.'

'Why him?'

'He's the one who squeezed me testicles while Fitzpatrick held me, when arresting me for ridin' me horse on the footpath at Benalla that time.'

'Now he's got no testicles,' says Dan, pointing to the broken bottle – once the poor constable.

'Shame, 'cause I aimed for his face,' Ned says, and we fall about laughing.

It appears I pass muster with Ned because after a few weeks digging, I feel his critical eye soften. I'm careful not to overstep the mark with either Dan or Ned, or to become a wedge between them, but to become a key ingredient in the family mix. It's not easy. I desperately want to spend as much time as I can alone with Dan; time not available due to the nature of the life we're living.

I often bite my tongue because Ned is self-opinionated and talks over Dan. He's not a blowhard but he brooks no argument with his point of view.

'We should run a shaft through this part of the river before we continue, Ned,' says Dan.

'So, we're a mining engineer now are we, boyo? We'll continue as we have been,' Ned decides.

'On the farm we ran mainly horses by the end,' says Dan.

'No we didn't, ya idjit, we had all them dairy calves down the back paddock,' Ned corrects.

'Well, they still wouldn't have amounted to more than the horses.'

'But them horses weren't ours. They'd be borrowed,' he raves on.

I want to pull them both up, because I know how Dan idolises his big brother and how much Ned is grinding him down by ridiculing him in front of others, but it wouldn't pay me to interfere. Ned, with his flared beard, shining teeth and waving arms is the main attraction, and we're the support rails. My opinion is seldom sought. So far, I've hobbled me tongue and we get along fine.

After a month, Dan says, 'See Steve, Oi told you life would be sweet if you stuck with us. We're going to be rich and happy. You mark me words.'

I believe him. He has his arm along my shoulder as we walk from the sluice to the hut. With his arm around me I believe anything. Dreams of fame and fortune can come true.

8

THE world must have flipped a page because, after weeks of cold and sleet-filled rain, we get to enjoy three days of splendid spring weather with blue skies. It's late in October 1878. I've been with the boys at the hut for a few months.

I slip out of bed and kick the ends of smouldering logs together in the fireplace. They smoke-up, sting my eyes and make it difficult to see. I slip the tin billy along the hanging rack to sit within the fire then retire behind the hut to piss.

I stand there concentrating, directing my yellow stream over this leaf, and that ant, when I notice the crows have stopped their banter, and the magpies' carolling is barely evident. A shudder races along my backbone to such an extent I nearly piss down my leg.

After a minute or two of silence, convinced that all is normal, I move inside to lace my boots. The billy hums and bubbles. I notice that Ned has his eyes open but has not spoken. I think Dan also might be awake but playing 'doggo', to avoid having to meet the cold air or do chores. Joe Byrne, who rode in the night before, is genuinely asleep. He's tired from days of serious drinking and shagging a Beechworth barmaid. I lace my boots and stand to throw tea-leaves in the billy.

I hear a rifle discharge nearby. It's unmistakable. Its echo runs on for moments and seizes my chest tight. I straighten. Ned sits up, then Dan. Ned cocks his head to listen.

'Rifle fire,' he hisses.

Joe's news from Beechworth was that traps are using search parties to hunt the Kellies, and lug body-straps on pack horses for their corpses. They aren't intending to just scare us if they find us.

The thought of how close they might be chills my bones, and I don't think I'm on my Pat Malone feeling it. We throw a boot at Joe to wake him.

'Traps,' says Dan when Joe opens his eyes and he's up and dressed in seconds.

We saddle-up and ride a mile down-stream towards the mountain spring and its shingle-hut. The boys are armed but I'm not. Joe thinks he can smell smoke, perhaps from a campfire. We dismount and sneak to the hut amidst the stringybarks. Ned ducks for cover in the tree ferns, waves us down.

'Traps!'

They're so close to flushing us, I tremble.

Their lean-to is sited in a clearing, horses tethered to a log. Stringybark Creek mumbles nearby. Smoke from their campfire drifts past the hut, while two traps go about their ablutions. It's all so peaceful.

'That's bloody Lonigan and McIntyre,' Joe whispers.

'I think we should bail 'em up and even ransom them, to get Ma released from gaol,' whispers Ned, outa the blue.

'What? Now?'

'Yeah, now.'

He stands without waiting for agreement.

'Bail up, you bastards,' he shouts.

Lonigan goes for his gun. Ned shoots him and the trap falls. Ned swings his gun at McIntyre.

'Stand, ya bastard.'

'I'm unarmed,' he replies, as he raises his hands.

Ned's out there as quick as a snake to cover McIntyre, removes his rifle and throws it to me.

'Move over and sit on that log by the fire, Constable. Jump to it … Joe, check Lonigan… where are the others?'

McIntyre's in shock, as am I. I haven't moved within the cover of the tree-ferns. I'm now armed. McIntyre never sights my face.

'He's dead. Lonigan's dead,' says Joe.

I start to tremble.

'I asked you, *Where are the others?*' repeats Ned, poking the trap hard in the chest on each word with his rifle-barrel.

'Th-th-they're up the creek lookin' for tracks,' says McIntyre.

I'd stutter too if it were me. Ned lowers the gun, slightly.

'Then sit there quietly, ya bastard, until they return. Don't move and you'll be safe. We don't mean to harm you. I was out to hold you for trade, except stupid Lonigan thought he were smarter.'

McIntyre sits, shakes visibly. The boys back-out of the clearing to the cover of the ferns, where I've remained. I move into the tent.

'Lonigan is the one was so brutal to me as a youngster,' Ned explains. 'He got his just desserts.'

Dan's face is pale as flour. We wait in silence staring at McIntyre's back, each in a world of our own. It's a beggar of a position to find ourselves. Finally, Scanlon and Kennedy ride up to, but not into, the clearing. They call to McIntyre stuck on the log. He doesn't reply.

'Bail up,' shouts Ned, perhaps fearing they might scarper.

Both traps shoot and dismount fast. They use the cover of trees to attack. Their bullets concentrate on Ned, tear up dirt and bark around him.

Meanwhile, Dan advances on Kennedy's flank only to be shot by the trap, who leaves cover. From my hide in the tent I take a bead on Kennedy, he's dead in my sights. I sweat at the thought of killing him, can't pull the trigger. Ned takes a shot at him.

'Shoot a Kelly will ya?' he screams.

Kennedy drops his gun from the bullet's impact and attempts to run but, realising how hurt he is, stumble-turns to surrender. Ned finishes him off. It's a gruesome sight.

I'm wounded. Must be a shot from Scanlon. Shit it stings. I see Joe Byrne aim and wing Scanlon, then both he and Ned hunt him down like a wounded wallaby and execute him: put him out of his misery with gory attention.

In the confusion, McIntyre mounts Kennedy's horse and gallops away, gaining too great a lead for Danny or I to catch him. Who knows what the consequences of that will be?

The thought dawns on me like a cinder in the eye. I'm now part of the Kelly Gang – outlaws at large. A criminal, responsible for a capital crime – murder – while still a teenager and not having murdered anybody. It's the same for Dan, but he's even younger. When the shock of the gruesome events hits him, he blubbers like a child and strides away from Joe and me in the hope we don't notice. I want to race after him to give comfort but Ned rushes out of the long grass, having just checked on Kennedy.

'Where's Dan?'

Ned's boots and trousers are splattered in blood and gore. Joe points up the creek.

'He pissed off… to the creek.'

Gun in hand and sensing something amiss, he rushes towards the creek after his brother, calling: 'Dan, where are you? Here… come here.'

He finds him. I can't see them for the large stringy barks and ferns growing along the creek bank, but I make out Dan's voice.

'Stay away from me. Oi don't want to talk to you.'

'Dan, come here… this moment.'

Dan, teary-eyed, reappears through the reeds heartbeats later and storms at pace past Joe, and me, as he heads uphill to the old hut. He waves his wounded and bloodied arms about, throws his hands in hopeless gestures to the heavens.

'Dan, get back here, I tell ya!'

Ned sounds like he's calling a cattle dog back from the herd.

'Why? Ya gonna shoot me too, now Oi'm wounded?'

Ned rages past us up the creekbank in fast pursuit of Dan.

'He asked me to matey. He begged me ta finish him off. Put him outa his misery… Ya know I'd never hurt you.'

'Look what you've got us into?'

'It were a fair fight. They coulda surrendered.'

'Fair? There were four of us.'

'There was four of them.'

'You know what Oi mean. Now McIntyre's escaped and they'll know exactly who killed them. We're doomed.'

'It's best the government knows the Kellies aren't to be messed with.'

'Messed with, is it? Messed with? They'll just send more of them and we'll end up a bloodied, maggoty mess like this lot lying there. Mark my words.'

They argue back and forth. They say if the Irish argue all ya can do is hold their hat. It's like that with the Kellies. Joe and I potter about, going through the traps' kit, until the boys are ready to leave.

The killings are grizzly. Having been a butcher's boy, blood doesn't worry me but it shocks Dan. Fresh from Beechworth, Dan was looking past an open gaol cell towards a free life. Now he sees only the terror of the cell-door slamming shut and the hangman's noose, waiting for him through the gore. Ned appears to be at a loss for how to comfort his baby brother and follows him around like a curious puppy, while Dan lets it all out.

But what about me? It's far worse for me. It isn't even my fight. It isn't my family who's been harassed. It isn't my ma rotting in prison. I didn't even take a gun to the gunfight. I didn't kill anyone. In spite of all that, I'll still swing for the hangman if they capture us. I feel right shafted.

With Dan more composed and his wound bound, we cover the bodies with blankets, steal their weapons and ammunition, then ride a long route back to our hut to lick our wounds.

'You two lads should scarper. Especially you, Steve, this isn't your fight. No one will know you were here.'

'O'im goin' nowhere,' declares Dan. 'It's my ma and Oi'll fight for her.'

Ned nods his head at me.

'What about you, Steve?'

I'm out of my depths and part of me wants desperately to run but they're my mates after all and 'in for a penny, in for a pound' as the saying goes. This isn't the 'merry life' I'd planned but I'd hate for them to think I was gutless, especially Danny.

'I'm in.'

Later, lying quiet in my swag, I feel Missus Gardiner's fingers trace along my palm and attempt to remember her words.

9

DAYS later and now living rough about a half-day's ride from the hut, we meet Kate Kelly, who brings food and tobacco. She's a striking woman, dressed in skirt and blouse, and seated astride rather than side-saddle. She has the rations in saddle bags but she's also cooked a mutton pie, which smells delicious, slung in a muslin bag over her shoulder.

'The traps is everywhere. They're watching like a hawk. Tried to follow me until I went cross-country for a while and lost 'em,' she says, puffing from the ride.

She moves closer and Ned's face lights up.

'Gosh that smells good, Katie.'

She rolls the pie bag from her shoulder.

'It might be the last home-cooked meal you get for a while.'

'True lass, true.'

'No, it's real serious. It's in this poster they've pasted across the district.'

She waves a piece of paper at us but it's too dark to see, except we can make out an imprint of Ned's face.

'What's it say?'

'It says ya can be shot on sight by anyone with a mind to it. That's what it says.'

'What the hell?' says Joe.

'And it allows the government to gaol your supporters, and there's a £1000 reward each, for information leading to your arrest.'

'Jesus… we're being treated like dingoes.'

'What's worse is, they've added more than two hundred extra police and a party of blacktrackers from Queensland, to hunt you day and night until captured or killed.'

Even the horses appear to listen. The thought of blacktrackers runs a chill down my spine. Kate hasn't finished.

'Only way you'll survive is by relying on family and friends for even the food on your table. But the trouble is they'll get locked-up, now, if suspected of helping you, as many have been already.'

She reaches across her horse and touches the blood-stained cloth over Dan's wound.

'You all good?'

'Yeah, nearly healed, just may never play piano again.'

She laughs.

'Ma sends her love. I visited her in gaol last week. She says she won't let the blighters get her down and for you all to stay safe.'

The boys are obviously pleased. She straightens her back.

'I best run or it'll be milkin' time before I get home.'

She jogs off into the night and we sit until the silence wraps its warm breath around us. We return to our camp and eat like it's our last supper, each fully occupied with the task of calming the raging pain in his gut.

❖

Some nights we go visiting: a town here, a shanty there; a friend's hut in another valley. We procure food, we meet friends, we grog on. Travelling is always a lark. When I first joined the boys, before Stringybark, I followed meekly as we moved across country. Ned rode his marvellous colt. He loved to apply pressure, did our Ned, so always stretched the pace rather than call an all-out race and I soon realised he didn't like to be beaten.

When you're a small chap like me you seldom compete head-on, and while Ned was a good horseman, he wasn't alone. I took some satisfaction in staying with him on the steepest slopes or across the highest sliprails, or over the tallest fence, or through the deepest river. It niggled at him but it earned me his grudging respect.

One night I peel off and get home before him. When he arrives, he says, 'Jesus, that horse can move. It's a lot further that way. Well done.' Solid praise from Ned Kelly.

'I was a jockey, you know?'

'No, I didn't.'

'Well, I was… after I left the butcher shop. The prison term put an end to that.'

'I guess!'

'Yeah, believe it or not, in the end, I won a number of races at meets in Benalla, Beechworth, Wangaratta and other small communities around home.'

'Ah, you're a bit of a dark horse, orright!'

'Yeah, but not sure we can count on outracing the traps as a ticket to freedom.'

Next morning, I hide the boys over at the Warby's. Truth is, being cornered like rats in a bucket, we are at wit's end and desperate, needing to raise money to survive. We're stuck for an answer.

10

WE'VE set up base at a sheep station at Faithfull's Creek, outside Euroa, where we can rest our horses. We're holding twenty-two residents hostage, under Joe Byrne's care, while Ned and Dan drive hawker, James Cloister's borrowed cart, to town to rob their bank. It's close to Christmas '78. I've ridden my bay mare in ahead of the others because I'm not yet recognised as a Kelly gang member and I'm having a meal while checking out the town to ensure all is as planned. When the boys' cart, finally, rolls into town, I saunter across to meet it.

'You made good time.'

'Didn't feel like that. It was a dawdle. Hope we don't need to escape in a hurry or it will all be over, we're so slow,' says Dan.

'All quiet here, I'm pleased to say. Barely anyone has moved into or out of town all afternoon.'

'Good,' says Ned, real peaceful-like.

I point at a small gate beside the bank.

'The bank residence is around the back.'

'Great. You and Dan secure the family before we raid the bank proper. In the meantime, I'll stay here with the cart.'

I help Dan break into the manager's residence and we muster the manager's wife, her mother and children, and lock them in a room festooned with Christmas decorations. I hear footsteps descending the stairs above and panic, falsely believing we'd secured everybody. Is it a guard? I turn this way and that like a butterfly behind glass.

Dan freezes and I push against the wall as the footsteps leave the stairs and move towards us along the corridor. We're goners. It's now or never. I step out, pistol ready to bail whoever it might be. It's a maid about my age!

'Steve Hart, what are you doing here?' she says.

Oh Christ, this is the worst that could happen to me. Fate is a bitch.

'Ah… hi Fanny… y-y-ya not going to believe this, but I'm here to r-r-rob the bank.'

I can see she's surprised, perhaps shocked.

'Oh, is this your game now?'

'Quick s-s-step in here, out of danger,' I say, grabbing her by the shoulder.

I sweep her into the room with the others, and without explanation, lock her in. Dan looks at me, inquisitively.

'Who the hell is that?'

'Fanny Shaw. I went to school with her.'

'You're lagged now, mate. They've put a name to the fourth man.'

I feel something lock tight inside, as if it will never be free again. Perhaps it's hope I've imprisoned? I can't back out of the gang now even if I want to. My options are shot. I hate it. Perhaps I could shoot her. Jesus, what have I got myself into?

We signal Ned, then quietly relieve the bank of two-thousand-odd pounds in cash and gold. We return slowly by cart to Faithful Creek then dash away on rested horses. Sergeant Steele and his traps arrive next morning, we are told, but there are so many tracks around the homestead, they can't follow us.

We distribute the money across our sympathisers, who need it for bail or to pay off debt caused by the new laws. Given that I earned about a pound a week when I worked, the ten pound and more that we've gifted most is fair compensation.

I'm a Kelly now.

The government has posted military guards on all Savings Banks across northern Victoria in an attempt to prevent us ever repeating our success. The trap is closing and we feel it tighten like a rough noose around our necks.

'Where'd the money go?' Joe asks.

Ned starts, as if he hears criticism in Joe's tone.

'We gave most of it away.'

'I know that but we must have some left?'

'Bugger all.'

'So, we starve while you play "good guy" to the colony?'

'I'm not playin' good guy. We can't afford for our supporters to be tempted into lagging us.'

'If we starve it will have the same effect.'

'We won't starve. We'll bail another bank.'

'Where? They've got troopers guarding every bank for five-hundred miles from here.'

'Across the border. We'll bail one there. They won't expect us, and we won't be shot on sight, either.'

Which bank and how to bail her still requires some thinking. We're sitting around the campfire after dinner with a large bottle of whiskey between us, while Ned and Dan tell humorous stories to do with their father, Red. I stand amid the laughter and move outside the circle of firelight to piss. The whiskey plays hell with my kidneys.

'Remember when we found his stash out in the shed?'

Dan nods.

'Yeah, hidden in the saddle bag, wasn't it?'

'True, hanging off the top rail, so Mum couldn't reach.'

'What stash?' I ask, over my shoulder, while I continue to piss.

'A red dress, a bonnet and some women's under-gear?'

'What?' I screech in mock shock.

'Yeah. Women's clothing.'

I return to the fire, fumble with my buttons.

'What did he use the clothes for?'

'He rode off in them so no one would recognise him.'

Ned shakes his head.

'No, he didn't, he was a bum-duffer… He went to meet his mates.'

Dan won't have it. They continue to argue.

'Maybe he wanted to go places unnoticed,' I suggest. 'I do that sometimes. Dress as a woman to disguise.'

It goes over like a lead balloon with Ned. I can tell by the tight cut of his mouth.

'My sister suggested it and it works like a charm,' I lie.

Ned goes quiet and looks at each of us in turn. Checks to see if there is more to it, or if we are taking-the-piss. I fear he'll think I'm a sheila, or a poof.

'You could check on the traps for us, then? See where they is coming and going?' he asks.

'Yeah, for sure. We need to lift a side-saddle from somewhere. Makes it even more convincing. We can all dress if it comes to that.'

I think it passes muster.

On the afternoon of February eight, 1879, I'm checking Jerilderie in New South Wales, wearing a woman's dress in case my description has been circulated, with a view to robbing its bank. All seems peaceful, and the bank, as described by Joe and Ned after their scouting visit yesterday, appears to take numerous large deposits, if the number of duffle bags delivered is any gauge. I re-join the boys on the edge of town at sundown, where we'll wait until midnight.

'Okay boyos, remember how well Euroa went. We don't want any rough stuff, so stay calm and it'll all work in our favour,' says Ned, after the town clock strikes twelve. 'Remember what the papers say. We are respectful in spite of the traps makin' us out ta be wild dogs. We'll try and trick the traps to give up without a fight.'

He taps his pistol to the side of his hat as a sign we should use our noggin.

We ride the deserted main street in the foggy darkness. Our horses' hooves click on the odd flagstones and echo a rhythm. Ahead of us, the police station is silhouetted against the fog by a halo of light above its entrance. I swallow hard when we reach the door and dismount. As bold as brass, Ned knocks on the solid door and shouts.

'Wake up. Wake up. There's been a horrible murder. Wake up, please.'

A constable in night-shirt appears, holding a lamp. He's half asleep and cranky. Joe steps behind him and places a pistol to his head.

'Make a noise and you're dead.'

Using the trap as a shield we push our way into the barracks. The smell of cramped humanity offends my nose, reminds me of gaol.

'Come on lads. Wakey, wakey, hand off snaky,' says Joe, and we herd all the traps into the cell.

The next morning, Ned, Dan and Joe, wearing police uniforms with one of the traps in hand to allay suspicion, walk like cock roosters through town. Dan returns all excited, and relays the events that occurred.

'The locals never twigged… were friendly and greeted us as if we were their own.'

Morning Constables, they said.

Morning Ma'am. Lovely fruit you have displayed.

'Then we gathered mail from the post office, bought a new surcingle from the stock and station agency, and visited the bank.'

New men on the force, the local trap explained. *Just familiarising them with the security measures for those times they replace us… when we take leave.'*

'Ned fronted the bank manager, Tarlton.'

Do ya regularly check your pistol?'

'Tarlton looked sideways behind the teller's stand, perhaps the pistol's location.'

Aye. We fire it once a month as per bank rules, he said.

'No one was any the wiser.'

He laughs at their audacity, quite smug that they had pulled it off.

When we enter the bank soon after, Tarlton isn't present. Ned jumps the counter and grabs the teller's pistol. I storm upstairs into the manager's residence and spring him bathing in a large tin-tub.

'Ya better dress fast or I'll drag ya downstairs so all can see ya big fat shiny arse,' I threaten.

As he dresses, I pray that when I'm older I never look as ridiculous naked as him. We join those downstairs. I spy a fob-chain hanging from one poor chap's vest-pocket.

'I'll relieve ya of that burden,' I say, yanking a large gold watch out and holding her up to my ear to see if she's working.

'Sir, I'm but a poor clergyman and that fob was my father's, and his father's before him. I beg you not to take it.'

I'm tired and cranky from life on the run; hiding out, and stressed by dawdling here too long. I don't intend to concede anything. I throw the watch in the air and catch it before disposing of it in my pocket.

'Well, Reverend, God musta meant me to have it, or he wouldn't have put it in me way,' I say, then give the old fella a hard-luck grin, before I stroll back along the counter to cover the entrance.

Ned growls, confronts me, his face a dark storm cloud.

'Give the Reverend back his watch.'

'No, piss off.'

'We don't steal off the regular people. Give it fooking back or I'll take it off ya.'

My hand hovers over my pistol. Who does he think he is? I'm so on edge and so riled at his ordering me about, that I'll shoot him. Then, I think, through clenched teeth, he's right, why fight? I dig back into my pocket and find the watch. I pretend it is all a joke.

'Ha, Reverend, did ya think I meant it? Here… catch.'

No one is fooled.

As we did in Euroa, to prevent news leaking, we round townsfolk up as hostages and herd them into the Royal Mail Hotel, beside the bank, where we intend to hold them until Monday evening. I watch Ned write a note about creating a Republic of Northern Victoria.

I think he's stepped beyond his station due to the attention the Council now pays us, and the injustice inflicted on his ma. We're in the newspapers; on the tip of everyone's tongue. I'm agitated about spending so much time exposed like this in town. I'm on a hair trigger, ready to explode. How are we to know that someone hasn't squeezed through our net and is not, right now, rallying the traps in the next town? We don't need this grandstanding.

Yet, like at Euroa, we act the part of perfect gentlemen. You'd swear Ned were a diplomat or a politician the way he panders to them folk. Big hero Ned!

'Dan, you and Steve do a bit of fancy riding… entertain the folk,' Ned says.

Dan agrees and we mount up like trained monkeys and amuse the mob with some of our riding tricks. Dan is excited by the attention. As a finale, I gallop past, lying horizontal along the side of my horse, making it a shield between me and the watching crowd, and I pretend to shoot Ned with me pistol beneath its neck. I wouldn't have missed had I pulled the trigger.

Letter written; Ned decides he's had enough. He locks the hostages in the hotel then we mount and spur our horses to canter along the track out of town. Whew.

Even Joe has concerns.

'This will piss-off the government well and truly, Ned.'

'Good. One day they'll learn not to mess with us. They picked the wrong man to mess with when they picked me.'

We return to our hideout and distribute the massive two-thousand-pounds takings to our sympathisers to win loyalty, and assure our freedom. Ned promises this time he'll hide some of the spoils as back-up.

The press goes into a frenzy about the robbery and highlight how I'd been a scum to lift the watch and how Ned made me return it, and suggest that we are fighting amongst ourselves. It's not true. It was merely a quirky day, I tell myself. We all lift personal pieces. It was just Ned wanting to make a big hero of himself. Joe Byrne wears a ring he stole off a hostage – Ned would never chip him. Why me?

The traps search for us day and night. It's relentless. We spot their parties in the distance, hear them, sometimes, very close, and keep relocating to foil the unremitting blacktrackers. The traps harass our sympathisers hoping either to starve us out, or get intelligence as to our whereabouts. It's wearing me down and I can speak for the others as their nerves too, are on a razor's edge. The chill weather, the rough sleeping, the starvation is too much. So, we head to the Bogong high plains to lie low.

TO pass the time we play cards, practise shooting – although we have to be careful not to run out of ammo – and, I spend time leatherworking, with a view to earning a bit of honest money.

Bare-knuckle boxing – to keep fit – also helps pass the time. Each week we have a 'bout' with a different gang member in the bare patch outside our bark lean-to. The Kelly boys and Joe are gluttons for punishment – tough nuts – and a spar is a bloody affair. I do one circuit of boxing with each, and cop multiple hidings.

I often dress as a woman and visit a town ahead of the boys, to check if it's clear for us to enter, or to get information from one of our cockatoos about trap search-parties.

It's ploys like this that allow us to leave our hideouts to meet up with friends. We visit Melbourne, where a specialist checks my feet, which are more troublesome as a result of hard living and my bandy legs. We paddle in the ocean at St Kilda, something I'd always wanted to do. It's hard to imagine the ocean until you see it; its vastness wraps around me.

I also visit my family during this period, which I thought I may never do. I feel a need to, now that life is so wobbly. I've never declared that I'm an outlaw, and worry about their reaction. We're sitting in the dining room and I'm licking mutton fat off my fingers, when Ma surprises me.

'I read in the newspaper, that Fanny Shaw believes you are the fourth member of the Kelly Gang.'

'Does she?'

'Don't play idiots with me, son. We didn't raise you to end up like this,' she says, and starts to sniffle.

'I know, Ma. Alright… I did see her at Euroa. I couldn't avoid it.'

'Fancy, involving women and children in your godless games.'

'It's not as it sounds, Ma,' I argue. 'The Police just hound the Kellies and now we'll be shot on sight. There's no other way for us to make a living, or defend ourselves, except to do the robberies. Besides, we give our money to our sympathisers.'

'What do you say, Richard?'

She still speaks to him as if he's her teenage lover.

'Leave me out of this, woman,' he says, and fumes away at the end of the table. He won't look at me, and sighs a lot, bashes his spoon on his cup until our Ettie, my sister, fills it again with tea. But for my ma, and my love of her, I wouldn't have bothered returning.

After Ma's declaration, I feel it's fine to bring Dan and Ned home one evening. It's awkward enough. Pa isn't an angel, having been transported as a convict, but, as far as he's concerned, I've taken an evil arc he'd predicted since I was but a wee child. Ma is convinced I'll end up on the pointy-end of a bullet, or at the end of a noose, especially after being charged with murder following the Stringybark Creek balls-up.

I arrive with the boys in tow and front the darkened doorway. My hand shakes as I fumble the latch, swing the door. It feels like I'm introducing a future bride. The light spills briefly over the stoop and we enter to see the family seated around the table loaded with Ma's best finery. Pa rises to meet us. His chair scrapes loudly on the polished-mud floor.

'P-p- pa, M-m-ma – this is Ned Kelly. Ned… Richard Hart.'

Ned cracks one of his famous smiles and shakes Pa's hand vigorously, then moves around and kisses Ma's. She swivels her backbone ever so slightly when his lips brush her knuckles.

'Ya not as big as I imagined,' says Pa.

'No?'

'No. I'd imagined you'd be bigger, given you beat wild Wright.'

A reference to a widely advertised formal bout between Ned and Wild.

Ned grins.

'Lucky blow, Richard, that one.'

'… and this is Dan Kelly, Pa. W-w-we met in Beechworth.'

'Hello Mister Hart, Missus Hart.'

Dan shakes Pa's hand then acknowledges Ma from a distance.

I point my finger at the youngsters, my brothers and sisters.

'And these are the little Harts.'

I see Ettie's face sour and pick up on the fact she's now a teenager.

'And, our Ettie… of course.'

She basks in the fact that the boys single her out with a nod. I've brought gin, so I find pannikins, pour a drop, pass the pannikins around and we older ones drink, then sit down to eat. Pa warns us he's heard that visiting them isn't such a wise idea because the traps watch both our farmhouse, and the bridge, which crosses the river at Beechworth, in the hope of trapping us.

'Ya can't take on the system and hope to win,' argues Pa.

Ned sits forward as if he's loading an argument.

'It's not just us agin the police. There are thousands of countrymen agin the injustice we're fighting. If we can squeeze the Legislative Council, we may not only get the police cleaned up but, also, change the Council and the laws, to give the little man a fair go.'

The girls and Ma are all ears, as are most audiences when Ned speaks. They remind me of the sixty-odd souls we'd held captive in the Royal Mail Hotel in Euroa, listening to him read his letter to the politician, Cameron. The thinking behind it, a republic of northern Victoria, is an angle on the story unknown to most.

I scan Pa's face; see he's breathing it in. Later, he breaks open a port and pours Ned and Dan, but not me, a drink. He raises his glass and clinks theirs.

'To your cause,' he toasts. 'Take care and look over each other.'

That's the closest he's ever come to endorsing my behaviour. Thankfully, it's before my death, not after, so I got to hear it.

Ma notices that I wasn't offered a drink, so moves behind me to massage my shoulders, while they carry on. I feel her tear, then another, spill warm across my neck. Someone cares for me, knows I have feelings, when all the world considers me an animal. Am I?

IT'S not long after the family dinner that Dan informs me Ned is infatuated with our 'Ettie', a delicate blonde with a soft heart and eyes as blue as Dan's. It's late 1879 and I realise my sister, overnight, has transformed from a girl to a woman.

Ned attracts women like honey attracts flies. He has the gift-of-the-gab, is witty and eerily direct. It's said he has ongoing love interests in his cousins Mary Miller and Kate Lloyd, along with Bridget Conway, the Greta publican's widow. He does love his cousins and they him. When they were young, he explains, they experimented as many youngsters do, and growing in a close community they had each other's back. That's where the seriousness ended. Apart from that, they socialise together and dance when there's a need, and as Ned says, 'have a gay old time of it'.

Bridget is a different matter. She knows what it's like to have mature wants and to have them satisfied, and Ned is eligible, but not interested in settling: exactly the type of fellow she seeks.

'Why aren't ya interested in me, woman?' he enquired across the bar one evening as we drank.

"Cause you're like all the other men in here, Ned. Ya see me as a meal ticket.'

'There's no other man alive like me,' he'd blathered in his blarney-stone cocky manner. 'I don't see ya as a meal ticket, or wife. I see ya as a woman who needs cheerin' up.'

'Oh, it's cheerin' up I be needin', is it?'

'Yeah. Cheerin' right up.'

And he dragged her to her feet and they danced the quadrille at a wicked pace.

Ned entertained her in her widowhood, but didn't demand a material change in her lifestyle, or a commitment to involve either her child or hotel.

Many a night he failed to return to camp, having drunk long into the evening with her, and friends, after the doors closed, spending the remainder of the night in her arms. She was loud and blousy, kept the gin flowing and, if she were a man, she'd be on the road liftin' stock and bailin' cattle. She was so brave, and so like her clientele. She and Ned teased and challenged each other, and she was perfect for him, for the type of life he leads.

'The poor widow has needs and who's the man could deny the wants of a grieving woman, now? You tell me?' he says.

But now, it appears, she is no longer enough.

Soon after Dan alerts me to Ned's interest in my sister, Ned appears at the Oxley bakery where Ettie works.

She says he walked bold as brass into the shop, overflowing with customers like cream from a jam tart. She looked up as Ned entered and her face turned crimson at the sight of him. He asked if he could meet her after work and she agreed. From that moment, like most people who meet him, she was captivated.

Ned and Joe often visit their girlfriends in town. Sometimes, Dan accompanies them to meet up with family. I hate it. I wish I could be with Dan every moment. Some mornings they reek of drink, make cracks about trollops present, and it's all I can do not to demand more details. I'm jealous but back-off. They're my mates.

Ned confides in me his feelings for Ettie and asks what I think about the union.

'It's alright by me. She's all grown now… It will be a hard road for Ettie, though, if the traps catch you. Have you discussed that with her?'

'Aye, I have and, if you have no further objections, I intend to get the local priest to marry us next week. There'll be no guests apart from her best friend, Nancy, as witness.'

'Is she mad? Ma will be so disappointed at not being invited.'

'When this dispute with the Police is finished, and it will be, then we can celebrate more publicly. At the moment, we can't afford to have Superintendent Hare and his men spoil Ettie's big day now, can we?'

What can I say?

They slip over to Moyhu on the Ovens, a ride of a few hours from Wangaratta, and marry in the fledgling Catholic church, outside the gaze of the ever-frustrated traps. They spend the honeymoon night in a sympathiser's cottage, on the condition they be gone by sun-up.

❖

The love story is but an 'interlude', as the music hall people say. The traps are still hammering us. Superintendent Hare has replaced Sergeant Steele, who was accused of incompetence, having failed to capture us. I assist the boys stay on the loose, and frustrate the traps, through our move from the Wombat Range to the Warby Ranges, my old stomping ground.

Ned's frustration with the traps rises. It builds upon his inability to free his mother, Ellen, and pokes that scab further. He wrote the 'Jerilderie Letter' at Euroa and in it, outlined the idea of a Republic. This fuels his idea for revenge; launches a daring plan to ambush police and perhaps spur an uprising.

We're as drunk as parrots, on home-made grog, when Joe raises an idea close to his heart.

'Ya know, our biggest weakness is so few of us and so many of them.' He plays his eager eyes across us. 'Am I right, or am I right?'

'Well maybe,' says Ned.

'The next weakness is we can't afford to be wounded, because we can't go to the doctor, because he has to report us under the Act. Am I right?'

'Right.'

'Well… why don't we make ourselves some armour?'

'Armour?'

'Yes, armour.'

'Like King Arthur?'

'Well, I was thinking like the Chinese emperors, really.'

'Same thing.'

Ned being a know-it-all.

'Can you imagine the plod traps wondering why we can't be felled? They'd run, right? I'm correct, right?'

Joe has celebrated many Chinese festivals at Beechworth; seen replicas of the suits.

'I'm thinking we could use the same principle to hang rows of steel plates off our shoulders down to our knees, use a steel helmet, with a flap, to cover our neck.'

He draws his idea in the dirt, where we squat and play with the notion. Later that night we agree to it.

Tom Lloyd assists us to locate and mould the plough-shares required to create our version. The first set is curved, beaten while red-hot over a green tree, in a paddock near Moyhu. Ned and Dan are eager to see if the chest-plates can deflect a bullet.

'Here… lean them against this tree stump and we'll test,' I suggest.

They shoot at them with their pistols, laugh like drunken Jackasses, listen to the ricochets ping off into the distance.

'You idiots you've barely hit the target. Concentrate,' I say.

They fire another volley, then another from rifles. We race to the armour, keen to see if our gamble has paid off. While the plates are dented, there're no holes.

'Woo hoo, it's worked.'

We feel safe in the suits, perhaps invincible. Dan grumbles, nevertheless.

'They might protect us from bullets but they're a bitch to wear. They're so damn heavy.'

'Can't walk or run to save ya self, either,' says Ned, his voice muffled by the helmet.

Each set weighs the equivalent of half a three-bushel-bag of wheat. Dan points to his front.

'Can only see straight ahead through the visor. Be easy for someone to jump ya.'

I sneak behind him and bang his helmet with my pistol butt. He shakes and his legs buckle as if he's about to fall with shock. Bloody annoying when it happens to you; it's like your head is stuck inside a chiming church bell.

We evade the traps for months. While we have many sympathisers, the longer we hold out the greater the chance some will turn to support the authorities, through trap intimidation or the rich reward.

Joe stares into the fire, speaks absent-minded.

'Aaron has traps stay at his place. Says the government forced them to let them stay.'

The fire crackles and spits. Ned clears his throat.

'Kate says many of the women are agin us because they're forced to work the selections, while the men are locked-up for supporting us, or we demand goods, when the family hasn't enough for themselves.'

Ned, always conscious of neighbours' hardship. Dan speaks for all of us.

'Got that way Oi'm not sure who to trust no more.'

Ned nods, faces Joe, bites his lip.

'Speaking of trust, our Kate says that's bullshit about your mate, Aaron.'

There's a chilling pause.

'Is that right?'

'Apparently, Ellen, his pimply, fifteen-year-old wife, told the grocer that the traps pay rent, and that Aaron's laggin' us. The traps wait for you to lead them to us, after you've visited.'

'The bastard. I had it out with him about gettin' close to some traps, last month. He says he's just suckering them.'

'Not what Kate's heard… she says Aaron hates me for drawing you away from him – jealous I got between you and him. Says he's going ta 'shoot me, then fuck me while I'm warm'.'

He makes eyes at Joe.

'That's not very neighbourly of him, now, is it?'

Joe squirms, struck by the comments.

'Look,' Ned continues. 'It's been seventeen months of hiding and I think we're ready to give the traps a huge surprise, but Joe, you and Dan need to check the rumour about Sherritt, and deal with it, if it's true. Can't afford to have traitors go unpunished.'

There it is! It's worrying if someone, as close to us as Aaron, can be turned. I'm wary of elaborate plans which require us to involve others. The chain of trust is stretched too far.

I'm naturally anxious but, on this occasion, when it comes to taking on the whole bloody Victorian police force, I'm even more anxious. It's like I'm always waiting for the other boot to drop since Mrs Gardiner read my future in my palm.

Because Ned had reservations about me, I've never raised a doubt, nor stalled in doing anything he demands, but this time I do. While Dan and Joe attend to Aaron, Ned and I ride to Glenrowan to trick the traps into an ambush as they rush to capture us after Joe's visit to Aaron's. The armour is on the pack horses, so we mean business. I warn Ned.

'I have a bad feeling about this one, mate.'

'Why? What makes you say that?'

'Not sure I can explain it. In the first place, there's too many people turning against us. If the traps can turn Aaron… they can turn anyone.'

'That snake? Joe'll fix Sherritt… But, why the concern? Who can know what we're up to next?'

'Well, for starters… one hundred and fifty sympathisers, who'll be in Glenrowan to watch the fireworks.'

'Oh, them? They'll be fine. Come on, mate. Have some guts. No guts, no glory.'

'It's not about guts, mate, it's about brains. I've got a feeling that's all.'

'Ya can't listen to the little people at the end of the pasture, boyo.'

It's his favourite way to ridicule doubt.

'Lay off, mate,' I snap.

'You worry too much. Have I led you astray before? We're going to change history; you and I. Australia will be the better for it, and will thank you.'

I can never argue him, except in my mind.

We top a rise and, below, squats the town of Glenrowan, nestled in the valley beside the rail-line, its sprinkling of yellow lights contrasts against the dark clouds gathered low along the ranges behind.

Ned pulls his oilskin closer around his neck in an effort to keep out the cold breeze. I shudder inside mine.

We ride down the ridge to, in Ned's words, change history.

13

TWENTY-EIGHTH of June, 1880, it's dead cold. Ned and I ride to the rail-line bordering Glenrowan.

Our plan is to use Aaron's demise to draw the traps here, then ambush them. After that, we will change the government or, at least, the savage policies that put gold in the pockets of the squatters and harm us poor settlers. We will establish a republic.

After an hour's labour and unable to dislodge the tracks to derail a trainload of traps, we seek help from local rail fettlers.

We bust into a hut only to find the fettler in bed laying rail into his woman. He takes exception to Ned poking him in the arse with a pistol and draws one of his own we didn't notice, so busy were we taking in other scenery. He pulls off a shot, which misses, and Ned wrestles the gun off him.

The blighter fights, pushes Ned aside.

'Torna indietro, stupida troia!'

Ned backhands him.

'Shut up.'

The young woman screams. Ned turns his pistol on her.

'You too, we're not here to hurt you… either of you. Quiet! I need your help.'

Now the alarm's raised and the traps, possibly, warned. We cut the telegraph lines soon after. I nab Constable Bracken then round up sixty townspeople and hold them in the Stationmaster's house, while Ned ensures the rails are uprooted. I get bored and move all our hostages to Annie Jones' posh, Glenrowan Inn.

We party with the hostages while we wait for the train to arrive. Joe and Dan have just joined us, reporting that they've shot Aaron at point-blank range for lagging us, and that a bunch of traps were hiding under his bed. The boys got a neighbour to call him outside and, in front of his wife and children, shot him. It was as if he knew Joe was after him. They challenged the traps to come out and fight but they wouldn't. I can't imagine how tough it must have been for Joe to shoot Aaron, a boyhood friend.

I remind myself we're not here to party but to put an end to those corrupt traps who bully poor souls in our valley and beyond, through false arrest, and imprisonment for associating with us; destroying their livelihoods, and separating families on the mere hint of helping us. They've hunted us like pack-dogs for weeks and placed a bounty on our heads, a King's ransom, for information leading to our capture or death.

Where are the traps? They should be here by now. We put money on the bar and nobody is without a drink. We play games and dance – the fun calming the hostages. It isn't like we've mustered them for rape and torture, but to hold them so they can't warn the traps. Apart from the cranky old publican, Anne Jones, everyone else appears happy.

Oh, she's a tough one alright. Years earlier, she'd lagged Ned's mum for selling sly grog, so I'm surprised Ned has cosied up to her after their little spat. Through the half-open rear door, I watch the two of them outside, lounging against a split-rail fence, away from public view, talking earnest, and smoking, while we rabble on inside.

Ned slides closer to her and runs the back of his hand across an ample breast. She pushes her head back and flashes her eyes, smiles all coy. She can't resist, rolls across to lean upon him, face to face, then pushes apart at the hips, to stare at Ned's groin, as if to say, 'Oh my, Mr Kelly, what have we here?'

She squirms her buttocks ever so slightly, but deliberately against him, discards her cigarette. She takes his chin between her fingers and kisses him softly, then passionately.

He swivels them so she is against the fence; pushes. I see her raise a leg and wrap it behind his. He fumbles with his fly and they thrust at each other until there's no movement. They stand motionless but locked, for a long moment, then unravel, straighten their clothes, lean beside each other on the fence to get their breath. Ned returns inside, checks if he was missed. Our eyes meet and he pretends they haven't. He walks to the far end of the bar.

I'm partly excited, part-scared as if I've just witnessed an accident. I'm aroused but my gut swirls as my imagination grips me, puts me in Ned's place, puts me in Annie's; feels their enjoyment. I'm confused.

Annie's in her fifties, yet Ned always says, you can get more out of a broke horse than a witless yearling. I feel wretched for our Ettie.

I've drunk too much, too soon. Young Jane Jones, Anne's daughter, claims a bench and I recline along the space remaining. She draws my head upon her lap, wipes my brow and strokes my hair, so I close my eyes. I believe women find me unattractive so I'm surprised, later, when I open my eyes, that her face is only inches from mine.

'This is all so exciting, don't you think?'

The party swirls around us – laughter, clink of glass, the smell of booze, the memory of watching her mother.

'Far too exciting,' I reply.

I'm still apprehensive about the traps but her clear breath blows away my fear; lifts my spirits.

'Fancy… riding with Ned and Dan Kelly, and having the newspapers writing about you every day,' she continues, twirls her hand with a flourish. 'And, here I am with one of the most dangerous men in the world, a puppy in my lap.'

She taps her pinky upon my nose as she says it.

'I'm not a puppy.'

She teases, bares her teeth and snaps like one.

'What are you, then, a dog?'

'I'm a man. I breathe and bleed like the next.'

'You need to be bold like Ned – that's a man.'

I'm cut. Will no one ever see me as a man?

Later, Joe chips me. 'Mate that Jane is hot. I would have rolled over and ploughed her juicy furrow with me nose, it was so close.'

'You don't know what we got up to, Joe,' I reply, implying I'm ahead in the sexual game.

To be frank, the idea never enters me head.

We believe the train must be close, so don our armour, ready for battle. The moment resembles the end of a warrior's ceremony, where we drink too much to the Gods, play as if there's no tomorrow, then within a moment, turn solemn and prepare for glory, or death.

Ned suits-up first and parades about like a fashion model, the dress-like iron top and skirt shake about him while he walks. The hostages cheer and laugh, while a number run their hands up under his steel skirt as he wanders past. He turns and tousles their hair.

'Ned… Ned,' they chant while he continues to pose.

He places the rounded helmet over his head, where it takes on the force of a mask, hiding his identity, while at the same time creating another; covering him but, also, covering the way we watch, so as to entice our imagination.

'I am a knight of the people,' he booms from behind his iron mask.

He takes the form of the hero. Oh upright, rigid, iron man/woman figure of knighthood. We all, every man and woman in the room, allow him to transform: push him up like a rider on a metal spear in a Greek festival.

Joe dresses and poses beside Ned, while Dan and I stand either end of the line with our helmets under our arms. We're perfectly posed for a poster to lead the revolution were there a camera to be had.

'To the republic of northern Victoria!' shouts Ned, who hasn't touched a drop of grog for the entire time.

'Three cheers,' shouts the crowd, their glasses raised, while Dan and I lean towards the bar to find a spare grog. We are immortal, that's what we are – freakin' immortal.

Earlier in the night Dan insisted on dancing with Curnow. There were women to dance with – 'cranky Annie' for one – her daughter, Jane, for another, but he preferred Curnow. He waved his pistol.

'Dance with me, man, come on.'

'Give it up, sir,' said Curnow.

'Oi want to dance with you real bad,' said Dan, leering at him like he were gaping at one of those French postcards we'd seen at St Kilda.

Curnow pushed him away.

'I can't dance with these boots. Ask the girls to dance.'

'Oi prefer you, cock,' insisted Dan, attempting to put his arm around Curnow's shoulders while playing with the teacher's dandy red scarf, a match for Dan's colourful hat ribbons.

Curnow pushed at Dan. Ned stepped in, challenged the teacher, who feathered up like a cock rooster.

'It's not too much to ask, is it? To dance? Don't worry about the boots. Dance with the boy.'

Curnow sensed the threat in Ned's tone and danced with Dan around the room. The crowd thought it were hilarious, but I knew, for Dan, it was no joke; no joke at all.

I was pissed with him, for dancing with another. Why aren't questions asked about his manhood, or Joe and Aaron's, or Ned's for that matter? Curnow was livid that his man-up had been challenged.

It's strange but Ned, now, allows the school teacher to leave, in order to attend to his sick wife. I think Curnow is so angry he'd do anything to jag us at this stage. But Ned is always open to flattery and the teacher praised him earlier, on his inspirational political ideas. Curnow leaves the Inn; limps home with his scrawny missus.

I need to find my hat, which I think I've left at the stationmaster's house, so I remove my armour, then head out to find it, while at the same time aim to have a squint along the train line to see if I can spot anything strange. The train is hours overdue.

I watch Curnow and his missus disappear into their house, which I pass as I move onto the trainline by the Station and see no signs of a train. I search the house and find my hat, then set out for the Inn. The cloudless night sky, the brisk air, the noise and laughter from the Inn, the night odours, I breathe in to clear the sickly feeling of too much whisky. There's something magical about the whole evening; it contradicts the deadly intent of our visit.

I gaze at the Curnow's house wondering if I should perv through their lighted window. Not that I can imagine too much exciting happens between the scrawny couple. It's then I catch movement by the scrub, near the rail line. It's Curnow and he's swinging a lamp, bold as brass, as he walks. The bastard intends to warn the traps: stop the train.

I rush across the paddock on his tail. I'm not fast of foot but neither is the injured Curnow. He's entered the scrub and I don't want to lose him.

I hear the urgent pant of an approaching train. I jog towards it and my leg bones fairly hurt. I brush against trees, into shrubs, stumble over undergrowth then break onto the rail-line, where it curves into Glenrowan. I'm a hundred yards from where we ripped up the rail. The steam train's head-lamp pours along the track, lighting it up like a vaudeville stage. Curnow, further along, with his lamp covered with a red scarf, signals the train to stop. Its wheels squeal as it brakes – throw golden showers of sparks.

I back off the track into cover. Traps pour from the train's bowels even before it stops. I see against the headlights their black cut-out shapes weave between the escaping steam. Our ambush has failed. I make Curnow out, in stark contrast against the light, as hordes of traps gather around to hear his story.

I raise my pistol to shoot the prick, but think better of it. I should return to the Inn to warn the gang. My bandy legs are not used to so much exercise, they're sore and tired, but they answer my call and I run blind through the scrub until I break into fields, and sight the inn's yellowed lights.

I hit the veranda and rush to Ned.

'The ambush has been sprung. Bloody Curnow has waved the train down and it's around the corner, undamaged, with all traps aboard.'

'Shit! Suit up boys, we're in for a fight.'

14

IT'S Johnny Jones, Jane's baby brother, who raises the alarm.

'The police are here.'

By Christ, he's right.

I peer across the veranda towards the train station and sight a long line of traps; some in their dirty uniforms; others in civilian clothes, jogging our way. I guess I never connected a train-load of traps with an actual number, counted how many snakes were intent on harming us. There were at least ten, armed to the teeth in the first line, with rows of traps following close behind, eager to join battle.

It isn't supposed to be like this. I slam the helmet on my worried head.

'Kelly, release the hostages or we shoot,' comes the warning from some trumped-up frog in a dark uniform and a peaked hat. It may be Superintendent Hare, who I've never had the privilege to meet, even though he is hell-bent to shorten our careers.

'Shoot all ya like ya miserable dogs,' replies Dan, not believing they will, on account of the hostages.

'Don't say youse weren't warned,' the trap shouts – his last word smothered by the roll of gunfire as those to the left, and right, of him, fire.

Joe fires first, then Dan. Ned and I join in moments later.

Shoot, those bastards have no respect for life or limb, nor for innocent or guilty. Shoot first, talk later, is their motto when it comes to dealing with us. I hear a bullet whack into leather.

'Oh, fook, I'm hit. It's me foot,' says Joe, as he staggers back inside the inn, where Dan and I have already retreated.

'Ungh,' says Ned, like he's been kicked in the cods. He bends and sucks air, shot in numerous places. Flares cast a ghostly glow over the rows of traps and bounty hunters closing on the pub. Ned's face is pale.

'I'll warn the others,' he says through gritted teeth, as he ducks around the corner away from the streaming bullets.

Ned's cousin, Jack Lloyd, has mistakenly fired two flares from the McDonnell's Railway Tavern opposite. They were meant to alert sympathisers hiding on the outskirts of town, that our ambush was successful. Ned now must warn them that, despite the flare, both the derailment and ambush have failed.

More traps join the turkey shoot, and all hell breaks loose, as they unleash fusillade after fusillade at us. It's as if the Inn has been wrapped in a large packet of firecrackers. Glass and wood splinters spit around us. It's a hell of a racket.

'Get down… on the ground,' shouts Dan.

Men, women and children hit the wooden floor. Some pray aloud to the Saints to save their lives. My pores gush sweat, and my gut wants to hurl all the beers I've sunk, so horrifying is the situation. Hostages still standing are hit and fall.

'Help, I'm shot… Help,' someone in the other room screams.

'Muummmy, mummy!' screams another: an adult.

I crawl across and drag a wounded bloke towards the cover of the fireplace. The hail of bullets continues, relentless. It's bedlam and horrific. We curl up and sweat it out.

Three hours later, Joe fills a glass with whiskey to toast the Kelly Gang's success at keeping the traps at bay.

'Here's to the bold Kellies.'

The armour prevents his neck swinging back to swig, so he lifts his front-plates to allow it. I raise my eyes when I feel whiskey spray on my hand, to watch Joe slide down the wall onto his arse, where the armour props him up in a strange arrangement. I slide to him. His head is cocked back as if he's staring at the ceiling.

'You alright, mate?'

'No, I'm done.'

He lifts his head so it will fall forward, to check his wounded thigh, and he says 'Dionysus Phallus'. Mandarin, I think. I remember the words as if they're painted on my brain.

I stare where he's staring: at his thigh, high up in the groin. A dark puncture wound pumps blood to his heartbeat. I place my butcher's-boy-fingers over the hole, but the blood swirls around them and pools between his legs. I grab a cleaning cloth off the bar and jam it into the wound. He shivers, uncontrollably, his teeth clack, rattle like a stick along a picket fence.

'You in pain?'

'No, all good. Can't feel a thing.'

I wonder if the opium he pumps into himself still surges through his veins, kills the pain. Two bullets whoosh past my ear and sink into the bar beside him. The traps are spreading out. I roll back like a rabbit to the fireplace beside Dan but he, too, is dead-still, his face as white as the ash in the stove's hopper. At first, I fear he's been hit, hurt, then I see he's breathing fine. I shake him.

'Come on mate, snap out of it. Time to fight.'

'Poor Joe.'

'Yeah, he's past saving. Nothing we can do.'

Bullets pour through the building. My skin curls up tight over my soft bones. We let loose with an ineffective round or two out the windows. We drag young Jane Jones over towards us to give her cover. Her mother, "Cranky Annie", sees her posh furniture and fittings shredded by bullets.

'Look what you animal Kellies have brought on me. I wish I'd never heard the name,' she screams at Dan.

'Keep ya trap shut, ya moll,' he replies. 'You was all happy to help the traps when they was hunting us. Making your rooms available to the bounty hunters. See what it feels like now, at the other end of police business.'

It's not our intention to harm hostages: Jerilderie and Euroa are proof of that.

'I don't know where the hell Ned is, Dan, but it's totally unfair to have the hostages face this… totally,' I yell.

'If we let them go, boyo, we have no bargaining chips.'

'The traps don't appear to give a fig about them.'

It is during a lull, many hours into the siege, and after many arguments, Dan agrees to free the remaining hostages. Shouts, 'Hey Hare, we're going to "bush" the hostages so you wombats don't cause them more harm… They're innocent.'

'They're sympathisers or they wouldn't be there,' the superintendent replies.

'They're folks from the town. They don't know us from a bar of soap.'

'It's on your head, boyo, for hiding like girls behind innocents.'

Wrong thing to say to Dan. It pisses him right off. He changes his mind. He'll hold them.

I don't want their blood on my hands. 'Come on, let 'em go. He's right, ya know. We gotta think of the women and children.'

He ponders for a moment and, probably because of a firing lull, nods to let 'em loose.

They run. In spite warning the traps of our intention, Sergeant Steele from Wangaratta deliberately shoots at Mrs Reardon carrying her baby. An idjit trap shoots at and kills Cranky Annie's son, Johnny Jones, a mere child. Daughter, Jane Jones, who'd held my head only hours before, is shot in the face as she flees.

Hostages escaped, Dan and I step over two dead bodies, innocents, as we move into the rear room, hoping the ball-shot cannot pass through two sets of walls. Thousands of rounds are fired at us that night. The walls are peppered with holes. Dan puts his lips to my ear.

'We gotta get outa here!'

I don't know how we can.

'If we get the chance, you go first,' he says.

It seems as if the firing will never let up, so relentless is the shooting. Then, as in a dream, bullets no longer pour into the Inn. It's like the wind has died during a storm. It goes from bedlam to stone-cold-silent in seconds. It's eerie at that time of the morning. The bar clock ticks, shows it's approaching four o'clock. I feel my aches and pains surface with the silence.

After my ears stop ringing, I hear a commotion and gunfire outside but no pellets passing through, and risk a peek through the window. All the traps are focussed on nearby scrub. I turn to Dan.

'I don't know about you, matey, but I'm outa here – let's move.'

Dan nods. I plunge out the back door and chance escaping scot-free, or dying with my boots on. I dive into the field behind the inn, keep low as I crawl in the main furrow that lies beside the road.

Not a shot is fired my direction. Not a person is on this side of the tavern in spite of all the troopers. I crawl like a frightened dingo pup until I reach the other side of the gully and hide my sorry arse behind some logs.

I lie there, heave for breath, wait for the chase, or Dan, but neither arrives. I raise my head above the logs and see traps, focussed on a metal-like object, shimmering in the misty light of dawn. I realise it's Ned.

I thought he had escaped. I really did. Having warned his supporters to stay away from the inn, he must have returned. I hear him swearing.

'I'm gonna send all you traps to hell.'

What a debacle. He's called all the fires of hell upon himself. Through the cannonade of gunfire, I hear the ping and zing of their bullets as they ricochet off, and all around, him. It was planned that we all would escape – why has he come back? Perhaps he couldn't find us at the horses? Perhaps he's trying to distract the traps so we can scarper, if we haven't already, or to rescue Joe Byrne who, God bless his handsome soul, is already dead? Ned's act is a brave, but tragic case of love.

They rush him. He doesn't return fire. I think that he must be dead. I hear them shout.

'It's Kelly!'

The mongrels race in for the point-blank kill. Constable Bracken gets between them and poor Ned's body.

'Leave him alone.'

I see them arguing. Is he alive? Is he dead? *Dead*, I think.

The sight of Ned's felling fills my throat with bile, and for the first time in months of defiance, and continual hounding, my legs buckle and I wish to curl up against that log, and surrender. But the bile turns to a scorching anger. I use that distraction, and my anger, to allow me to piss-off through the morning mist, out over the rail-line, towards the horses.

As I run, I think. *Go back Steve, ya mate needs you.* Then I think, *I'm more use to him alive than dead.*

'You gutless prick, Steve,' my accusers say, my defence screams, the members of the jury scream. *'You gutless prick.'*

But run I do. I feel a rush of blood to my brain saying, *You're free, mate. You're free. Get out of here!*

As I run, I realise it's not mist but smoke. Something must be alight. I see a figure disappear into the timber at the other end of the paddock. Is it Dan?

I never quite reach where we'd tethered the horses because I see something ahead, flickering white in the mist. It's a pale apparition dancing ghostlike between the trees.

My heart stops. Perhaps I've died? But no, my body aches too much to be dead.

Christ, no… let it not be traps! Is it Dan? Have I jumped out of the pan, into the fire? Are the horsemen of the apocalypse on me? My legs seize. I'm ready to surrender.

I make out… see it's… a horse, a riderless horse: Joe's grey mare, "Music", all a panic, having pulled free of her hitching. She tears about like a white banshee in the mists of hell. Her reins drag and catch in the fallen branches. She bashes through shrubbery with eyes splayed wide in fear.

'Whoa girl, whoa, hold up, now. That's a good gal!' I move towards her, hold my arms out like I'm herding chooks, not a horse.

I trap her; take my time (although my heart wants me desperately to rush). I rub her neck with my trembling hand to calm her, to warn her I'm about to make a demand of her petrified soul, then, as gently as I can, I roll onto her back, dig spurs and gallop with my back to Glenrowan, intending never to stop.

15

I'VE ridden all day, to reach London Rock, our meeting point, near our old Bullock Creek bush camp. I'm absolutely exhausted.

I light a fire with my flint, ready a brew with the tealeaves in Joe's quart pot, then lie back against a tree, take a huge breath, close my eyes and relax. Minutes later I sip the brew and touch my side where it pains. Sticky. Blood on my fingertips. I lift my shirt and find a wound oozing blood down my side. Ah Christ the Redeemer, it's a gunshot-wound. I seize up inside, steel myself to look further.

The bullet has passed through my stomach, just above my hip and, in the excitement, I've barely noticed the pain. Funny that, eh? The hole's shit ugly and bruised, but the bleeding's stopped. I'll survive. I rumble through Joe's saddle bag to see if he has any opium to dull the pain. Nothing. I notice a bullet has passed through Music's rump and feel a twinge of guilt.

I fall asleep in the scrub. Is it shock... exhaustion? I have no idea, but my body draws that sleep in, like a dry-sponge seeks moisture from a wet glass.

I wake into darkness with my half-finished brew in hand. My teeth chatter from the June cold, and ants swarm all over me like I'm a warm turd.

What woke me... I've no idea.... and I won't breathe because I can hear... footsteps. Is it the traps? Have they tracked me already? I make out the shape of a human figure against the moonlit sky. Feel for the pistol on my lap, cock it to shoot. The steel-on-steel click it makes strikes like a bell in that silence.

'Don't shoot. It's Dan... ya prick. It is you, isn't it, Steve?'

'Yeah, Dan, me darling... Ya frightened the bajeezus outa me. I never heard you. I thought you was dead!'

Dan stumbles closer. I make out his shape and his fine features in the glow of the fire's embers. I uncock my pistol.

'Oi left close behind you, but I didn't know where you went. Then I realised the traps were fussin' over someone else.'

'It were Ned,' I say. 'He come back and the mongrels shot him. They continued shooting even when he was so badly wounded, he couldn't return fire. I seen it.'

Dan buckles to his knees.

'Ah, Jeezus. My brother, the poor bastard. I thought it were you, Steve, because it was all coming from the other direction. I thought they'd spied you and had gunned you down like a helpless wombat… so, Ned … Why didn't he run while he had the chance?'

'Only the Saints know.'

'Anyway,' Dan continues, 'while everyone was fussin' over Ned, someone snuck up and put a fire under the bloody Inn… she were well alight when I last looked.'

'Bejeezus, what a way to go. Grilled,' I say.

'Can't imagine. The thought sickens me – we'd blister like pork.'

He shudders like a bullock shakes free of flies.

'Imagine doing something like that to another human being? Thank Christ we slipped out,' I add.

'Thank Christ for Tom Lloyd. He and some relatives were watching from the reserve. They smuggled me through the cordon, dressed me wounds, lent me a horse.'

'Shit, will they lag us?'

'No, they're good folk. Our secret will die with them.' He stands there, that beautiful man, all a tremble.

'Come here mate. I'm shot, wounded. Lie beside me,' I say.

I reach out. He slides under my arm, and rests his face against my chest. While I feel an overwhelming sadness at the loss of both Joe and Ned, I feel for a moment like God smiles upon me. I have Dan with me, and can face the Devil's minions with his help.

16

WE'VE holed up at London Rock for a day or two, a bit witless about what to do next. We managed to shoot a possum for one meal and a duck for another, but it barely calmed our hunger. Months of being chased by the traps, living hand-to-mouth, has already torn the flesh from us and, being only jockey-size myself, I'm now skin and bone. Dan isn't a big lad, either, unlike Ned or Joe. Some whisper he is effeminate in shape and style, but not to his face. The portrait photo he carries on his person shows how fine he is.

Across the campfire I see tears rim the lad's eyes. My cheeks sting as I feel his pain.

'Ya say you seen 'em bring Ned down?'

I nod.

'Oi can't get my head around it – his death.'

'Me neither.'

'What am I gonna do? How can I live without him?' His chin trembles, lips flutter. 'He were a father to me, after Pa left us, when Oi were but a wee one.'

The tears roll out of him. It was a shock for a lad barely seventeen. I've lost a cobber in Ned, but the lad has lost family and, as he says, a father figure. His father, Red Kelly, was odd and his mother, Ellen, lived with a herd of men in her trail, none of whom led the boy – so it was down to Ned.

'Well, there's only us, now. We're nearly family,' I say.

I hope it's true, that we will be together for life. I stand with some difficulty, the wound in my side having stiffened me greatly. I draw his sweet head, with its curly locks, tight against my waist. He sobs and sobs. I've no idea what to do with him, but to hold him.

I grow sadder by the moment. His being is my being. My stomach drags as if a large bag of corn weighs it down. My cheeks burn, as if what I'm feeling inside wants to squeeze from my face as tears, but I can't be soft while he's being so.

'What will become of us, Steve? What can God have planned for us, having chosen for us to live and others to die?'

'Maybe we're meant to give up this life and turn over a new leaf. Make a fresh start… in Queensland or over in Western Australia.'

I've given it some thought, even before Glenrowan.

'No fookin' way. Not me! Oi'm gonna go back to hunt down that cur Curnow and stuff him in his grave, the two-faced prick.'

'Dan, look…'

'No, I promise you, I'm gonna do it… and Superintendent Hare, and that murdering bastard, Sergeant Steele… I'll gut them while Oi'm at it, too. Not only did they fook us but they killed those hostages. There was no need.'

His face is rage-red and my heart races heavy at the thought I might have to back him in what he wants. Ned and Joe were our mates, after all, and should be avenged, but the odds are stacked heavily against us.

'Well, instead of pissing off from the Inn, it sounds like we should have charged them wombats, then and there? You weren't so keen yesterday morning.'

I was winding in a slippery argument like I would an unbroken colt.

'Don't start, Steve. Don't be a smart arse, like Ned says ya are. We'll track 'em down like blacktrackers and knock 'em over, one by one, on the QT. We gotta do it. And, let's face it – Ma is still in prison… all this sacrifice for nothing.'

I push back.

'How will we live mate? Where will we go? Who's going to look after us now that we can't lift from the banks to pay the supporters? Who'll back us now that Ned is dead? Anybody with any brains can see that the Police have won the day and killed off the insurrection. It's as plain as the nose on ya face.'

He's stubborn is Dan. We've argued for days. Back and forth. In the end he agrees that it's too soon to avenge the boys and that it would be better to let the smoke settle before we attack. I also argue that the first place the traps will search will be our old haunts, like the Wombat Ranges, and that we should move out as soon as possible.

We head north towards Queensland, for as sure as whiskey is our saviour, once the traps realise we've escaped the siege fire, they'll be after us. We leave without telling anyone, believing that's the safest thing for us and our families, given the Victorian *Felons Apprehension Act* could put them in gaol if they help us.

Christmas Eve, we risk a drink in an isolated shanty, near the New South Wales – Queensland-border town of St George.

We've ridden for many months, through NSW, and out through Dubbo, north into south-west Queensland, doing odd sheep and cattle-work, afraid to join polite society in case we expose ourselves. When we camped for a month or two beside a large billabong, I salted, dried and tanned cow and kangaroo hides. Thereafter, beside the campfire at night, I plaited belts and stockwhips. It calmed me. We sold them to selectors, or to stockmen we met. I made enough for food as long as we lived off the land to back it up.

We always act sober, and never *lift* anything, in order not to draw attention to ourselves. We sneak, now and then, into a pub, or a shanty like this, to quench our thirst, and hear the voices of fellow souls.

I have three finely plaited kangaroo skin belts and a greenhide whip on the table beside me, in the hope that someone might wish to buy one. I stroke the soft plaits and marvel at how close Dan and I have woven together over the weeks on the run. In spite of the shock of recent events I feel stronger as a result of our bonding.

A red-faced old codger, with a lot of drink on board, shuffles across to speak to us. He slides his skinny old arse into the vacant seat beside Dan. I think he wants to inspect the goods.

'You look, to me, like a couple of shady characters,' he says.

I freeze like a stunned bandicoot and stare into my drink to hide my panic. He extends a sun-ravaged hand to Dan.

'Me name's Henry.'

Dan shakes his hand and says poker-faced, 'Yeah, we're what's left of the Ned Kelly Gang.'

I shake my head in disbelief. What an idiot.

'Well, that you're not,' the old chap says, with confidence, peering up from beneath hooded eyelids.

'Why's that?' challenges Dan, stern faced.

'Because you're roasted meat, mate.'

Dan's face twists like a question mark. 'Roasted?'

'Yeah, mate, scorched black. I'll show you the photos of that pair, if ya aint seen 'em.'

'No idea what ya talking about, old fella, no idea.'

Henry shuffles to the bar and retrieves a neatly folded newspaper from a pile of papers on a stool. He flicks to an article reporting our death at the hands of police, with photographs of Joe hanging lifeless off a doorknob at the Benalla lock-up, and our scorched bodies outside the charred remains of the Glenrowan Inn. They look like the blackened, blistered kangaroos you see roasted on a blackfella's fire. My supposed corpse has lost its legs and is barely recognisable as human.

'How could they tell from those bodies? They could be anyone!'

Henry snatches the paper from us and scans the article.

'It says here,' he points to the article, 'a Catholic priest, Father Gibney, raced into the burning building and identified them.'

Dan and I exchange glances. I don't know Gibney. Those poor blighters in the photo are just charred blobs of burnt flesh: men caught up by circumstances. The Devil's trade: a criminal for an innocent soul. What had they done wrong in the eyes of God, eh? Makes ya wonder, it does.

'Ah, well, you got us there, cobber,' I say. 'We didn't think anybody would have heard of Ned Kelly out here.'

'There's been an enquiry and sixty thousand petitioners across Victoria wrote in seeking a stay of Ned's execution. Everybody has heard of Ned Kelly,' he replies, licking his blistered lips. 'And a couple of pretty boys, such as yourselves, would no more be part of that gang, than fly. I knew you was lying, straight up.'

In other circumstances, I would have been tempted to pistol-whip him for insinuating I'm a "fancy man", but I choose not to take umbrage. I smile and whack knees against Dan's to calm him down.

'So, Ned's alive?' Dan whispers. His lower lip trembles. His eyes blink too fast as he searches for the truth in the old codger's face.

'No. He survived the siege, but faced Court and was hung.'

I move me foot over, to rest against Dan's.

'Just surviving is enough, you'd think. Newspaper reckoned one-hundred-and-fifty police and bounty hunters shot fifteen thousand rounds into the place before they burned it. Credit to Ned to walk out of the place,' Henry adds.

We don't answer but the numbers register – fifteen thousand rounds! Silence pervades and an opportunity to change the topic.

'We're on the hoof, Henry, looking for work. We hear everyone who's able has left for the gold fields.'

'Bell Ridge starts shearing on Monday if ya lookin' for work,' the old fellow says. 'The shearing gang left yesterday. If you head off at dawn, you'll be there Monday.'

'Shearing, eh?' says Dan.

'Yeah, there's always work there. Tell the boss, Henry Olsen sent you.'

'We might just do that,' Dan says. 'What'll you have, Henry? Beer?'

'Rum, mate, rum. Can't get the beer cold here.'

Henry prattles on. We're barely aware. Ned lived. Perhaps we could have sprung him, had we stayed. Joined up with the Lloyds, O'Brian's, brother Dick, and young Byrne, and played havoc. I dread facing Dan alone, given I'd enticed him to go on the lam, rather than terrorise the traps.

I can't delay the inevitable and we leave the pub to join our swags. To my surprise, Dan, though sad, is quite settled about the matter. The past months seem to have matured him.

'If he faced Court, at least he had a chance to call out the police corruption. He'd be pleased about that.'

'Hope he spoke out about them traps shooting hostages.'

'Oi hope so too.'

'What do you think about Gibney, the priest, sayin' it was us what was burned? Why would he do that?'

'He's Catholic.'

'So what?'

Dan stares at me in disbelief.

'He sees all the hardship the 'Proddies' cause us – the rich landholders, the Governor, the Council – hears all the hate in the community.'

'Truth is on our side.'

'Ned putting three hundred pounds in the poor-jar after Jerilderie helps of course.'

'Yeah, and the priest might of assumed it was us, because I threw my armour over one of the bodies.'

'Me too.'

We stew it over until we hit our swags.

That night I wake drenched in sweat with my heart racing. I dream Dan is encircled in fire and I can't reach him; can't save him.

'Dan, Dan, don't leave me. I'll see you on the other side,' I shout.

I wonder how long it will take to wipe the grizzly photographs from my dreams.

17

BASED on Henry's advice, we'd eaten, saddled our horses and departed for Bell Ridge Station before sun-up. We'd ridden two days in featureless country to get here. It's amazing how fate works. As we approach the shed boss, Dan freezes.

'Jesus! It's Kerry Lingard.'

'Does he know you?... Let's scarper.'

'Nah, he's alright, Kerry.'

We approach. He glances at us, then double-takes when he recognises Dan, looks around to check we are alone.

'Shit, Dan, a ghost. I thought you were killed.'

'Walking dead, mate. We need some work and a place to lie low.'

He was a drinking mate of Ned's.

'Happy to help out,' he says.

The shearing shed is a large two-storey affair, using the modern galvanised-iron sheeting, strapped to a bush-timber frame. Beneath the shed and surrounding it are wooden sheep yards, whose rails are quite low for us boys who are used to horse or cattle yards. Dan swings his leg over the top rail.

'That old horse of yours, what's his name, would struggle to jump out of this pen.'

'Venables? Yeah, you're right.' I smile at the stupidity of the statement. Venables would do it in his sleep.

We explore the shed and pick a preferred stand to shear in, meet the rest of the gang over dinner, and move across to the shearer's quarters, where rows of bunks lie tousled along each wall.

'We better grab a bunk and prepare for tomorrow,' Dan says and I don't need encouraging.

My apprenticeship with those maggots – sheep – begins as the sun cracks the horizon.

'Come on you blighter.' I can't wrestle my first ewe out of the pen. The other shearers laugh. Some are on their third beast. Kerry pops into the yard.

'Here, grab it like this.'

He shows me how to pull its shoulder backwards into my body so I can reverse drag it into the area before the shearing stand. There are some jumbucks that come along quietly and lie back to welcome the clicking shears, as if it's a duty best done quickly. But there are others who, from the moment you touch them, buck, kick and pull away, even when they're on their backside on the floor, trapped under your arm. They're real pests.

'Oh shit… she's bleeding.'

The shearer beside me notices and demonstrates on his jumbuck.

'You can't help but slice them if they move, but they bleed over the fleece, and ya don't want that happening too often. You've got to press down on them here, to stiffen the leg, or stretch them to straighten the wrinkles on their neck, to reduce the injury.'

I hear 'Tar here tiger' and the roustabout scrambles in with a pot of black tar to dab on the wound. If the bludgers stayed calm their life would be easier. At times, though, I find myself siding with these rebel sheep, admiring their resistance.

Shearing is non-stop until the mob is shorn. It pays shearer and cocky to get the job done as quickly as possible and leads to competitive tallies of more than three-hundred per day being racked up and moved into legend. The gold rush has torn apart most of the old shearing gangs, so there's many a hard-luck story amongst our sorry mob. If the truth be told, Dan and I are not the only ones on the lam, so few personal questions are asked.

Sunday afternoons we have a few hours to relax, have a grog or two, a clean-up, repair our kit and write letters if you can write. Some guys kick a footy made from a sheep's bladder. I've spent a few Sundays hanging out at a loose-end like this, but today I've saddled old 'Music' and ride into the wilderness to remove that "penned-in" feeling. I return and do trick-riding past the huts – standing on the saddle at the canter, or performing Indian mounts from side to side – for a bit of a laugh. Another fellow grabs his mare and canters past, hangs sideways off his saddle, then backwards over her tail, with his head mere inches from her flying hooves. It's most impressive.

The yarding ganger meets me next morning. He's the stockman of the team and obviously a rider. He knows me by the name Fred Layton.

'Jesus, Fred, you can ride. You have that horse bouncing out of his skin.'

'I spent most of my days upon a horse as a youngster,' I say. 'We had competitions on who could do the wackiest things.'

'I never figured guys down east could ride, for some reason. You know, just toy blocks those little farms.'

I smile.

'Lot of rough country down our way. You might only have a thousand acres on the flat but it might be five thousand when you take the mountains into account. I even won the 'Benalla Handicap' one year,' I add, and immediately wish I hadn't.

Being only jockey size, I earn respect through horsemanship, rather than through my fists or feats of strength. But my bragging got me into trouble as a youngster and I need to give it away, or the same will happen. Dan and I will never be "gun" shearers but we don't care. It's enough to have three square meals cooked for us, a roof over our heads and to feel safe.

We've sheared for months; got the hang of it. The mob will finish by week's end and conversations centre around 'what next'. Most of the gang will continue shearing, but some talk about joining the gold rush. New finds are reported monthly, mostly in northern Queensland, and stories of unimaginable riches circulate.

It's humid and my shirt sticks with sweat. Dark storm clouds gather along the western horizon, sending gusts of hot wind across us.

On the pretence of a smoke, Dan and I move from the cookhouse outside to a log near the woodheap, in search of a breeze. Three freshly slaughtered sheep's carcasses hang on a timber gantry beside us, their garish frames swing with the storm's breeze.

We discuss the possibility that the traps might tail us, that the odds are high even though the newspaper says we're dead. We think it might be a ploy to put us off our guard.

A lop-eared shearer, who'd arrived at Bell Ridge soon after us and who, for some unknown reason, I just don't take to, sits on a log beside us and points a tattooed finger at the wad of tobacco we've left open on the log.

'Mind if I borrow the makin's?'

I nod. 'Help yourself.'

He pulls off a fig and kneads it into his palm, fits it loosely in paper, seals it with a lick, draws heavily as he sets it alight. An arm covered in amateur tattoos makes me wonder if he's done time.

'You fellas say you're from Victoria?' he asks, in a raspy cigarette voice.

'We didn't say,' I mutter, cigarette smoke curling from my lip. 'But, yeah, down that way.'

'Didn't ya say you'd won the Benalla Cup? That's down that way.'

Shit, here we go, I think. *Me and my need to big-note myself.* Sweat bubbles down my backbone.

'Yeah, you're right.'

'I been wondering where I seen you fellas. My family's down that way.'

Smoke puffs from his nose as he speaks. Behind him the

carcasses swing rhythmically with the wind, their bloodied flesh highlighted with each lightning flash. Dan twitches and shuffles his feet, as if he wishes to run. In my mind I hear him bawl me out for failing to keep my trap shut.

'So, where do ya think it was you seen us?' I say, my voice as hard as armour.

'I thought I might have seen you on a postcard.'

Dan and I laugh.

'A postcard? Well, that won't be it, who'd want us on a postcard?'

'I recognise your white horse – I'm sure it was on the postcard. It has such a long body.'

'That's strange, eh?'

'Yeah, it was a postcard of the Kelly gang.'

Dan's face reacts as if he's just been shown something absurd or disgusting. 'The Kelly gang? Do we look like bushrangers to you, mate? They're dead.'

A long rumble of thunder intrudes from the distant storm. It rolls for ages.

'Could be mate. You give nothing away. You're both very secretive.'

'Give it a break, cobber,' Dan counters.

'Those Kellies were rabid dogs, and made life very hard for my family being impounded by the Association Laws and we didn't even know the bastards. Sent us broke. Imagine if ya were the family of the Police: a Kennedy? You'd feel even worse about them after they butchered ya kin. I would have dobbed them in, no worries, but my pa was against it, to keep us safe. Maybe you were associates of theirs? Bought their horse?'

'No mate, can't help ya. That grey horse is me pa's from over Sale way, and he bred it himself.'

The guy finally lets up, but I can see he isn't convinced. Truth is, we'd posed for a postcard when Ned was organising the revolution to show our supporters the traps hadn't intimidated us. Only later, when it was used to hunt us down, did he realise it was a stupid idea.

The shearer finishes his smoke, flicks the butt in a shower of sparks into the night and walks away, quite aware we aren't interested in speaking further.

'How did he find us? One of the sympathisers must have let the cat out of the bag,' I whisper.

Dan waits until the shearer is inside the sleeping quarters.

'Hard to believe... unless someone overheard... I'm gonna fix 'im up proper, like Joe fixed bloody Sherritt!

'We can't afford ta do that,' I say. 'He'd be a talker this one. Would have shared his suspicions with others, so too many would know we had it in fa the shite, if we killed him. Let's scarper, hope it all blows over.'

At that moment the wind gusts, swings the dancing carcasses to and fro, and the steel hooks they hang on groan forlornly in the darkness.

Dan, never one to take a backward step, sees merit in leaving, but won't do so without his wages. He fronts the shed boss, Kerry, who organises our wages, and promises to cover for us, if questioned. With money in our pocket, we pack and rat-out before daybreak.

We're solemn. We've ridden so far from the seat of our troubles only to find it's not far enough. Should we throw the towel in? Head back to Greta and face the music? It seems pointless to run if we can be discovered so easily. I check Dan and he doesn't appear concerned.

After a couple of hours and the sun high in the sky, we ride past a mulga patch where the deafening chorus of a large flock of birds fills the air. We ride in to investigate and find stunted trees swamped and swollen with colour, as if an artist has unloaded a paintbrush over their branches. I've never seen budgerigars in the wild and marvel at how tiny, delicate creatures survive in such harsh conditions. Afterwards, Dan hums a few Irish folk songs and I whistle parts I remember as we ride along.

We reach the Balonne River and St George after sundown, where we establish camp and secure the horses on the river bank, without entering the town, too tired to socialise.

We wake and walk to the pub to blow some of our wages on a grog or two. We need a plan. By our third gin, Henry Olsen appears, recognises us, and invites himself over.

'Did ya friend find ya?'

'No, which friend?… Where?'

'Oh, a chap arrived here a couple of days after you two. Says he was looking for a couple of young fellows from Victoria, who he thought might have headed up as far as here. Apparently he has news of a dead relative, and perhaps some inheritance.'

'What did he look like?'

'Tall, skinny fellow with big ears and tattoos. I mentioned you two but said you weren't from Victoria. Told him you'd gone to Bell Ridge.'

'Agh. Must of missed him,' I say, checking with Dan as I answer.

'I quizzed him about Ned Kelly, like I did you two, because he'd come from that area,' Henry adds. 'Says he's related to one of the murdered policemen. He thinks gang members have survived.'

'Is that so?'

'I showed him the picture in the paper. He says they're so burned it could be anybody. He's full of venom, that one.'

We buy Henry a rum and return to our camp to be free of him.

'Must be that lop-eared shearer,' says Dan, his breath disturbing the smoke from a roley hanging from his lips.

'Sounds like it. All right, what do we do now?'

'Agh, blessed if I know. I always had Ned to follow, so never needed a plan. We're on the run, so this could be our life, forever: someone recognises us, or might recognise us, we get spooked, dig up roots and move on, like hungry ghosts.'

'Well, we could continue shearing, or perhaps fossick for gold in North Queensland, where them shearers say people have struck it rich,' I offer.

'Yeah, fossicking,' he says. 'Anything to stay ahead of bastards like our shearer, wanting to claim the reward.'

18

THE shearers spoke of a new goldfield in the Cape near a place called Cooktown – 'gold sticking out of the river bank,' they said, and that appealed to us. But first, I wanted to visit the Gympie goldfield because my sister Jane and her husband live there.

We'd ridden for weeks, dodged large towns, or if we knew a trap was stationed there, even the small. At the Great Dividing Range we slipped into Toowoomba for supplies. We visited the Cramond and Stark drapery store, its red-brick with white timber façade and scalloped roof-line prominent amidst the rather droll buildings along Ruthven Street. We each bought a shirt more suitable for Queensland's warmer climes, though you would hardly believe it necessary, if chilled Toowoomba is any guide.

We meandered east along the range's fringed cliff-edge for a couple of days to enjoy the cooler weather and the wonderful views, then ambled over the edge and followed the track in the rough direction of Kingaroy.

We reach the settlement of Murgon. I breathe deep and twist in my saddle to take in the country.

'I could live here. The grass is so lush it reminds me a little of home, around Greta in a good season, only warmer.'

'The Wrights moved near here, from Greta,' Dan reminds me.

The Wrights are good friends of the Kellies. Even though Ned and Isiah 'Wild' Wright had staged a public fist fight to settle a grudge over a horse, Isiah was practically a member of the Kelly gang and supported us, and the Kelly women, until the final days. Dan knows he can call on the Wrights for help. We camp beside a lily-covered waterhole, and leave at sun-up.

We travel east from Murgon for a few days and make camp on the banks of a running creek near the settlement of Waluga. The sound of the water spilling over river rocks relaxes me. The water is so clear I can see the lung fish swim deep below. The campsite is a veritable paradise.

I undress and wade into the depths to bathe. I watch Dan do likewise and notice how much weight he's gained since the siege. He's now slightly larger than me, well proportioned, with fine muscles, which fairly ripple as he wades through the water. His cock and cods hang full, shiny. I glow to see him relaxed.

When closer, he extends his hand and I reach out, thinking he wants me to take it, but I'm mistaken. He's merely balanced to kick water my way and I watch it spray a silver mist into the fading sun's rays. It's a beautiful sight. I imagine it is how Mrs Gardiner's Greek poets would describe the Gods of the universe at play. He submerges beneath the clear water for a moment, as do I. We gaze silently at each other for some minutes, our eyes just above the water-line like two crocodiles. Dan raises his glistening head above the water.

'I've got a present for you.'

'For me?'

'Yes, you, nitwit, you. I got it in Toowoomba.'

I wonder what it can be? After only a few minutes submerged he makes for shore, while I remain to settle myself a little from the surprise of learning he cares enough to buy a gift. My body is alight from observing him. His shoulders and taut buttocks glisten with the sunlight reflecting from his moist skin and I see, again, the five large moles in the shape of the Southern Cross on his muscled back as he splashes ashore.

When I follow minutes later, he's already donned a singlet. He hands me a towel and while I'm drying he extracts a brown-paper parcel from his saddle bag and approaches.

'Here, put this on,' he says, unfurling a khaki-coloured dress from his outstretched hands.

I smile self-consciously, squirm my toes a little in the river sand, continue to dry my cods and between my legs.

'Here, take it. Don't put anything on beneath.'

I scrunch my face as if pondering a giant question. Then I lay the towel over a nearby flood-flattened softwood tree, take the dress and slide it over my head until it shimmers down my body. It clings a little to my hips and arse, then, with a shake, falls smooth. Like Dan, I'm clean shaven, perfect for when I dress as a woman. Teamed with a bonnet the picture could be complete.

'Jesus, me man, look at that,' he says, in genuine admiration. 'Oi tell you, mate, you look seriously good… Quite a girl.'

He loves me in a dress. Even in prison he made me wear a towel as if it were a little skirt. His father, Red, wore a red dress and explains his comfort now. At the time, in prison, I was surprised.

'Want to dance?' I say, as I raise my arms in dance mode and smile wide.

'No mate, just want to look at you.'

My shoulders slump and the magic of the moment is extinguished, but I wear the dress while we wait for the mutton to boil in the camp oven and, whenever I bend to attend to the cooking, Dan comments.

Gympie is busy as a bee-hive. We're concerned we'll bump into someone we know, so I don the dress and ride side-saddle to search for my sister, Jane, while Dan waits outside town on the Mary River.

I track Jane down via a postman who recognises the name. The chap isn't used to a man in a dress and appears uncomfortable as we talk. When I step into her hut, she is shocked to see me – stares as if I'm a ghost. The way she stands, wipes her pale hands on her thick apron, reminds me so much of Ma. She bursts into tears. I must be quite a sight in my new dress.

'Fa Christ's sake woman, stop yer blubbering,' I say, and move close to show I'm not a ghost.

'I'm alive and so is Dan.'

'I seen the photographs in the newspaper... Of you and Dan Kelly... All burnt... It was horrible!' She sobs; doesn't reach out. 'Dan's mum, poor Mrs Kelly, was still in gaol... you coulda sent a sign, something... anything, to let us know you were alive, ya bastard.'

She slaps my chest with both hands to express her fury.

'Ya did nothin'.'

I back up, so seriously is she beating me. It hurts.

'Unngh… jeeze, I thought it was better you believed we was dead and you could get on with ya lives and, maybe, the traps would leave you alone,' I say.

I hold her at arm's length. Her face is flushed and she breathes hard, as do I.

'But can't you see what it did to the families? Ma and Pa, burying their son. And poor Mrs Kelly in gaol and losin' two boys on top o' all what had happened to her. It could'a killed her.'

With that, her legs buckle. I rush to prop her up.

'The Byrnes never collected Joe, so ashamed they were,' she sobs.

I can't think of anything to say. My feet want to walk me out of there. 'Brother Dick took your body and we buried you, and Dan, in the same grave in a secret spot in Greta Cemetery to prevent the police from digging you up.'

'The traps want you to believe it's us, so there aren't so many innocent hostages reported dead; butchered by them at the massacre,' I argue.

Perhaps the boys who helped Dan from the Inn spirited our bodies away so the traps couldn't twig to the fact that it wasn't us?

'Don't be so bush ignorant. It was you, the Kelly Gang, who was blamed for the massacre, and we, family, became the brunt of that blame. You selfish bastards.'

Maybe I shouldn't have visited, but with time, and her husband's help, she calms enough for me to explain the situation. Within seconds she treats me with some kindness. I enjoy a brew, a quiet moment, and to learn of their lives in the northernmost colony.

I secure a room in a posh hotel and, later that night, I bring Dan in, through the mullock heaps and canvas lean-to campsites. We pass miners lying on their bunks, or playing cards beneath the light of a swinging kero-lamp; smell soap as we cross over a gully against a bath house; and hear a banjo plunking away in the clear air, against peals of laughter, from the various shanties selling cheap grog along the Mary's banks. The mutton smell of stews cooking in coal-covered camp-ovens is everywhere. It's a community, a new-born colony, bursting with life.

We spend three days relishing the luxury of the hotel, with bed-sheets and running bath water, while I visit with Jane.

My sister Ettie, being Ned's wife, shared secrets about their dreams, and the adventures she, and Ned, had enjoyed, even while the traps hunted us. Her tales bring back memories for Dan and I: memories we'd buried, in order to survive.

But she's family. I don't want to leave. I'm twenty-one and feeling this could be the last time I have contact with kin. So much has happened in the four years since borrowing the horse and my search for adventure. It's one thing to be alive, but it's another to be cast out into the big paddock without a bridle: a high price for liberty. It's like a life without a life – but Ned would probably say it's better than being a plaster-cast death mask. At least Dan and I are free, if you call this freedom.

I tell Jane we'll travel north. She can write to me at the Cairns Post Office and while I can't tell her when I'll get there, I promise I'll retrieve any mail within the twelve months.

'But you can't read, can you, Steve?'

'Not much. But I'll get someone I trust to read it. Address it to Fred Layton. That's me name now. Don't use the Hart, or Kelly, family name in the letter. You can use other family names or first names so I catch the gossip, or know you need me.'

We part on the understanding that I'll return in the morning to say farewell. I feel so much better in the presence of family.

It's dark by the time I return to our hotel and, as I climb the internal stairs to our room, I notice Dan at a table in the back bar, cheek-to-jowl with a blowsy, red-headed girl about our age. Her legs, bare to the thighs because her dress is rolled back, rest across his lap. My heart seizes. We're supposed to be lying low.

The moment I open the door to our room the sweet scent of perfume, mixed with the low-note odour of alcohol, rushes to meet me. Dan's bed is ruffled and lipstick smears are obvious on the pillow. Ginger pubic hairs lie upon the sheets, as solid evidence for love making as empty cartridge shells are of murder.

This is my first awareness that Dan lies with women. It's as if he has been torn from me as a child is torn from a mother's womb. The wrench is physical.

I storm downstairs.

'I want a w-w-word with you.'

'You'll have to wait.'

'I'm not waiting. If I have to wait one minute, I swear, I'll shoot you.'

The face of the redhead lying on his shoulder turns sallow.

'Settle down, cobber.'

'I'll give you s-s-settle down. I want you upstairs in one minute, and… and g-g-get rid of this h-h-harpy while you're at it.'

I storm upstairs. A few minutes later he walks through the door, smiling like a preacher.

'What the fuck are you doing, Danny? We're in this together. I'm dependent on you,' I start.

'No harm in a bit o buttered damper on the way.'

'You never told me you f-f-fucked women.'

'So what? You didn't really think I was visiting family, when I left with the boys, did ya?'

I cover my lips with my hand so he won't see them trembling with anger, or pain. I can't tell the difference. I'm as exposed as a hairless joey expelled from its mother's pouch. All I see is a vision of the two of them, naked and sweaty, thrashing away on the bed right here in this room. I can't stand to lose him, yet at the same time, I want to shoot him. Shoot him so he can't move like that again. Can't hold her. Can't give another so much pleasure.

That seals it for me. I want to run. Run from the red-haired bimbo, from the prospect of bumping into someone we know, someone from home, because people seem to swirl in and out of the place like the Mary in flood. I gather my hat.

'I'm outa here in the morning. Make up your mind if you're going to join me, or piss off.'

'Don't feel that way.'

'Don't you dare tell me what to feel, boyo.'

I slam the door and nearly tumble down the stairs. I find another pub to drown my sorrows. All I can think is, up in Cape York, on the Palmer, I'll be safe.

19

I wake the next morning to find Dan ready. I pack in silence, and without saying farewell to Jane, we ride out of town in single file.

We're both in low spirits. The horses have benefitted from the spell and have a spring in their step that isn't obvious in mine. In spite of Dan's presence, I find myself feeling a new level of aloneness, more painful than anything I've ever experienced. I've said goodbye to family, a significant rift has appeared in my relationship with Dan, and I'm heading further away from civilisation into the great unknown of Cape York, with no idea, whatsoever, of what lies in store for me.

We ride long arduous days, mostly in silence, aiming to avoid company for as long as we can, for fear someone has recognised us in Gympie. Without witnesses it will be more difficult for the traps, or the lop-eared shearer, to determine our direction.

The gold-magnet weaves its magic and the thought of riches draws us onward. I can't be angry with Dan for too long. I punish myself if I deprive him of my company.

Dan stands on his stirrups, hovers above his old cracked-leather saddle, as we ride.

'I think if I make it rich on the fields, I'm going to buy a softer saddle,' he says.

For some unknown reason I find it so funny and in spite of myself, laugh. We're mates again.

Maryborough, a thriving port near the mouth of the Mary River, already has the population of a city. We've ridden for weeks along the coastal side of the great Divide to get here. Sailing ships unload stores or collect produce for southern markets. A timber raft of giant logs slides down the river to the port for export. Immigrants in search of a better life in the new Colony, with its promises of agriculture and mining, are visible everywhere we turn. Like us, development follows the coastline north.

We decide to keep riding until Bundaberg, another booming town founded on cattle, and pass the odd cane-crop closer to the coast. We're a long way from anywhere.

Our need for a grog-up makes us "chance our hand" and visit Rockhampton. Ships sail thirty-five miles up the Fitzroy River as far as the natural rock ford, a barrier to further navigation but, also, a means of crossing the river on low tide. Fishermen land Barramundi from the rocks as we pass. The town, far smaller than Maryborough, is a very busy hub for commerce and access to the hinterland.

'Rocky has a great future,' the woman, where we rent a shower, says. 'The explorers assure us there's sweeping grass plains for cattle and sheep, that flow to the inland sea, and minerals, the likes of we've never seen.'

It sounds so wonderful, I'm tempted to change course and witness it myself.

We're impressed by the two and three-masted brigs that line the riverbank; the rows of wagons, loaded high with bales of wool from deep inland, headed south; and the splendour of the hotels and warehouses being built. A dockside pub beckons us and we sidle inside to be surprised by the number of languages spoken. What has happened to the Colony, our roots and our colonial way of life?

'Jesus, mate, have we been on Joe's opium and moved to a different world?' I say, gobsmacked by all before us.

I hear an English sea-shanty sung with gusto; a Scottish poem offered to the high ceiling; an argument between two white-haired sailors in a language full of hiss and gargle; and, over at the bar, an order for a beer, the words dripping in strange sounds. Our smiles say it all; it's so exciting. The sailors drink like the shearers or ringers do; as if the bar is the first they've seen for months and the last they may ever see. Drunk and loud, slatternly women, clothed in cotton and hemp, haunt the place, take advantage of their patron's drunkenness, to steal their money while failing to deliver on promises.

'Where's my Annie?'

A plaintive cry from a drunken sailor.

'She's gone home.'

'Home, but I paid her for the night.'

'Well, you'll have to take it up with her in the morning.'

'We sail at first light.'

'You better get going then, boyo.'

'Where's me change?'

'It's all in ya pocket, boyo.'

I'm pleased to see so many men walk as bow-legged as me. Life at sea seems to cause it.

'You'll never get me to sea,' I declare.

'Me neither,' says Dan. 'It's far, far, too strange. Oid kill meself first.'

We agree on that matter, at least. We don't chance our hand too long in Rockhampton. While I notice Dan's eyes swivel crab-like when a woman passes, he doesn't stray.

We plug north, past St. Lawrence, a customs house and little else, attempting to cross the dividing range that now edges the sea, where the coastline sweeps further west before heading north again. For coastal country it sure seems arid.

'Where are we, mate? The sun seems to have been in our faces all day. I'd be so rude as to say we is lost.'

'Yeah, Oi believe you're right.'

'About the sun or about being lost?'

'Both.'

'Hah. I think we better backtrack. Those steep ridges have thrown us off course.'

'The track has to be more obvious than the one we've been following.'

We circle about and by chance, pick up the trail north.

Five days later, on the crest of a sharp spur, we glimpse a view of the sea and rich scrubland of a wide river valley. We believe we are close to Mackay.

Two days later a farmer confirms the fact. We pass through miles of sugarcane fields, surprised to learn from a peddler there are thirty plantations and more than twenty sugar mills in this district alone. The plantation owners have built their homes along the Pioneer River, which snakes its way around the narrow delta and Mackay township, before sliding into the sea. They are sprawling mansions, often painted crisp white, surrounded by green lawns and lush gardens full of exotic plants and fruits, as befits the hot, wet tropics.

'That's what I'll have when me boat comes in,' I tell Dan. 'A bloody big house with gardens.'

We overnight at 'Palmyra', a plantation with three hundred and fifty acres under sugarcane, with its own mill to crush and refine the crop. This is considered small, compared to the large, foreign-owned mills with thousands of acres under sugar. We realise we have no idea about what is happening in this part of the world, or about sugar farming, if it comes to that. Most of the sugar pioneers, we learn, come from the Caribbean. We thought, wrongly, that slavery had stopped when the transportation of convicts ceased some fifteen years earlier. But we learn the plantation owners have imported a slavery of their own.

The plantation overseer walks us to our accommodation located in a line of huts behind the house. Our shirts are soaked with sweat – the humidity is so high it's difficult to breathe. A line of dark-skinned men crosses a road further out, each carries a hoe or a shovel, like a

Berrima gaol work gang.

'Who are the fellows in the blue work shirts?'

'Kanakas. Blacks, from the South Seas.'

'What, so many of them?'

'Yeah, there's a lot, eh? Fifty in all. They're the field workers. The blackbirders steal them from their islands and bring them in.'

Dan, like me, slaps at mosquitos and sand flies that attack our exposed flesh. The overseer appears not to notice those stuck to him like tiny tacks.

'Do the Kanakas live on site?'

'Yeah, their bunkhouses are those huts beyond the sheds. Six Kanakas in double bunkbeds, to a hut. Each hut has its own cooking fire inside and the smoke acts as a barrier against the mosquitoes. They don't discriminate, them bastards, eh? They feast equally on the blood of black or white.'

The smell, which leaks from each hut, makes me want to gag.

We wake to the crack of a stock-whip and witness the overseer whipping a Kanaka from horseback. We race to stop him. Dan is so angry he grabs at the overseer's leg.

'Huh, what?'

'If you use that whip again while we're around, it's the last whipping you'll ever do,' Dan says.

'You're threatening me.'

'No, mate — warning you! You don't know who you're dealing with. We've seen animals treated better than that.'

You'd have to be an ex-con to understand the passion that such actions as a flogging, stirs.

We walk to our hut and strap on our pistols. The overseer gets our meaning and backs off. It's criminal what they get away with in their treatment of the Islanders. We learn they starve and work thousands to death in the interest of prosperity. We are happy, later that day, to ride towards Townsville.

Ten hot, sticky days and we're outside Townsville without busting our horses. We skirt around it, to head west to Charters Towers, which is in the middle of a massive gold rush, mining ten large, gold reefs. Dan asks everyone he meets in Charters Towers:

'What happened to Jupiter?'

'Who you talking about mate?'

'Jupiter… Jupiter Mosman.'

'Never heard of him.'

'Is he rich? Is he now head of a large corporation?'

'Fecked if I know, digger,' they reply.

I'm sick of it. He's found a smart-arse point of niggle and wishes to rub it in.

'Why do you want to know, mate? Why have ya got a bee in ya bonnet about Jupiter?' I ask.

'Oi don't know. It's just some people have got it so unfair. Oi bet if it was a white surveyor, or a fat banker, who'd discovered the gold at Tower Hill, and not an Aborigine, everyone would know his name and at least he'd have the glory, if not the gold. As Ned used to say, "The real robbers aren't in the gaols."'

'Umm, well, that's just the way it is.'

'That's you to a "T" isn't it, Steve? Just go along with what you're given. Always the follower.'

'Better than walking around as if you've got a dingo nipping at ya arse, and a face like you've just drunk miner's arsenic when ya thought you was drinkin' whiskey. What are ya gonna do? Organise a revolution like ya brother?'

'Shut up Steve, before Oi knock you off your fookin' horse,' he says, and jogs ahead to the holding paddock where our horses rest.

Having binged for two days on the grog we choose not to fossick in the Towers.

With a hundred and thirty thousand residents it's the second largest city in Queensland, boasting its own Stock Exchange, housed in an arcade capped by an impressive stained-glass portal. The new rail-line to haul the mountains of gold to Townsville has just opened – the smell of paint still noticeable in the station building when I visit. The atmosphere reminds me of home. However, seeing the wealth the miners splash gives us itchy feet, impatient to reach the Palmer, and build our own fortune.

We collect stores and pieces of second-hand mining equipment, which may not be readily available on the Palmer – goods left behind by a disappointed or bankrupt miner, now that the river-of-gold has turned to a trickle. *That will never be us. We'll make our fortune.*

By sun-up next day we are two miles out of town destined for Cairns, a city we are told, perches by the ocean.

We unsaddle our horses on Cairns common. It takes an hour to light a fire in the damp tropical conditions. We can't believe our bushcraft fails us. We've barely lifted our head to consider stringing a fly to keep out imminent rain, when eight stockmen, their shirts wet with sweat, appear, followed by a drover's buggy and twenty spare horses.

Soon a very tall, dark-bearded, bullock-solid chap, slapping mossies from his neck, wanders over to introduce himself. He wipes his large hands on his baggy trousers before he reaches forward to shake.

'G'day fellas. I'm Harry Readford, drover. You from around these parts?'

I shake. He squeezes hard, rolls the bones of my hand. I try not to grimace.

'No, we're passin' through.'

'Where from?'

'Charters Towers, most recently,' I reply, not giving much away.

'Charters Towers, eh? What have you been doing for a crust, fossicking?'

'Cattle work.'

'Well, if you're in need of work, I'm looking for drovers.'

'Nope, we're not looking, sorry, Harry. We're actually on our way to the Palmer.'

I notice a mossie mining blood along my forearm. For a moment the drover looks confused, because we've just told him we weren't fossicking at Charters, yet, here we are, aiming to hit the Palmer. He recovers quickly. I slap the mossie.

'You too, eh? Well, forget the droving. How about helping us out mustering for a few weeks? We're getting a mob together to take to Dubbo, New South Wales.'

'Much obliged, Harry, but we're told we need to get to the Palmer as soon as we can, before the rains set in.'

I slap at another mossie on the back of my neck.

'Yeah, true, if you're serious about going further north it pays to leave in the *dry*. You wouldn't believe how wet it gets in the *wet*… Well, think about my offer, if you change your mind or it doesn't work out.'

'It'll work out, Harry. We've had experience down south, so this can't be too different.'

Next morning, it's pissing down rain but we ride into Cairns central, where I check the Post Office for mail from Jane.

'You wouldn't have mail for Fred Layton, would you?'

The clerk heads to a pigeon-hole at the end of his counter and flips through a pile of envelopes, selects one and returns.

'Here ya are. A traveller from Gympie?'

'Yep.'

'Sign here.'

I open the letter on the veranda, out of the rain, and between Dan and I, and the ever-present mossies, we make out its contents.

Dear S

It was lovely to see you and D, and assume you left safely and had reason not to say goodbye. About three weeks after you left, I had a visit from a bloke from down near home who says he was shearing with you at St George. I told him he must be mistaken because you are dead. He assures me I am wrong. He began to badger me and I got frightened. I started to cry so he backed off. Says he's heading north to Charters Towers in the hope of catching up with you both to renew the friendship. He's hunting Fred Layton and his mate.

I asked him what he wants them for? Says he has information. He's creepy. Believes the Gang were a pack of animals, and so too were those who ran with them. I guess we know who he means. I think he gets information from the Police. Might have a family member in the force?

May God be with you.
J xxx

The mongrel is not giving up.

Dan stands, impatient, as if he has an idea to act upon. 'I think our best bet is to keep heading north and hope he loses interest.'

I can't really argue that, so we continue north.

20

WE hit Palmerville, on the banks of the roaring Palmer River, in the wet of 1883, and we're not impressed. The town once boasted nine hotels and a population of seventeen thousand miners, but only two hotels and eighty Chinese miners remain. Maytown, further along, has some life with three banks, a hospital and several thousand miners. The "boom" is over and the pickings slim.

'I think we fooked up, Steve.'

'Why?'

'This place is dead – had it.'

Dan's face shines with sweat.

'We weren't to know, boyo.'

'Shoulda stayed at Charters Towers.'

'Maybe, but the shearer is on our tail, it's a big deal for him to travel further. We're safer here.'

'Yeah, but at least there was gold there.'

'There'll be gold here. We'll get a licence and have a look around. Our experience has to count for something.'

Even those lucky who find gold, pay through the nose for supplies: handing the money over to Chinese merchants. I've never seen so many Chinese. A barman informs me there were ten thousand at the height of the rush. Mistrust between the Macau and Cantonese miners from the Tong wars, five years earlier, is still very much alive. Both sides continue to accuse each other when gang members go missing. Rumours abound of discarded mine-shafts reeking with that unmistakable stench of decomposing human flesh.

'As if that isn't enough, the local Abo tribe, the Kuku Yanaji, eat them,' a miner tells us.

'Eat them?'

'Yes, eat them. When the Chinese walk along the oriental trail from Cooktown with their wheelbarrows, the local Abos grab a Chinese meal, leaving only the wheelbarrow. Abandoned wheelbarrows mark the spot where they disappeared.'

'Cripes.'

❖

Dan and I bust our guts to sink deep shafts, and sometimes it seems as if we're close to breaking into a gold seam.

'Dan, Dan, come below, I think we're onto something.'

'Coming... You could be right be-Christ. It could be a seam. Here, let me bust into it for you.'

But gold always eludes us.

It's been months of toil, and the strain shows. Dan, never one to be satisfied with anything for too long, is irritated. It's too hot. Too dry. Too wet. The locals too dumb.

'What are you doing now, Steve?'

'Tidying the tent.'

'Leave the bastard alone for a moment. Oi'm trying to rest.'

'We should be out there, prospecting.'

'Oi'm tired... crook.'

'If you'd stayed off the grog, you'd be fine.'

'Who the hell do you think you are, me ma?'

'No, mate, but we gotta wash some dirt, find some gold, or we'll starve.'

'If ya finished making that saddle, we wouldn't.'

'Maybe, but that's not why we came. We came to get rich.'

He stays out nights over at Maytown and creeps home awash with the odours of booze and women. He spends time and money on a big old whore named Chrissy. It pisses me off no end. Chrissy has a man-shaped body, with broad shoulders, small hips and thick thighs, and she carries extra weight in all the wrong places. Her beauty has faded and her habits of drink and drugs leave a lot to be desired. Most nights she makes no sense, she's so drunk, and Dan no better.

'I didn't travel to the end of the earth to throw in the towel,' I say. 'Where were you last night?'

'At the pub.'

'No ya weren't. I walked up to get ya, and they said you'd gone.'

'Went for a walk.'

'Bullshit! They said you'd taken Chrissy home. Here I was in the soggy tent on my own all night, and you're out dipping your wick.'

'Ya jealous, matey?'

I don't answer. I slap hard at a mozzie biting my sweaty neck.

'You could join me next time, mate. There's plenty to go around.'

He can be a heartless prick at times.

'I wouldn't know,' I say, with the sulkiest voice I can manage.

Evening rain drips onto the mildewed canvas in a pattern that mesmerises us. It's only days since our argument about Chrissy.

Dan fronts me.

'Steve, look at me, Oi'm soaked with sweat. The mossies have drawn every drop of me blood. I swear to ya, but for kangaroo stew and some weevil-spotted damper, I'd be starvin'. I'm not cut out for this. I'm a farmin' lad and I'm missin' family, me ma.'

I lick the salt sweat from my lips before I answer.

'Ah Jesus, Dan, we must strike it lucky soon?'

'I tell you mate, with or without you, Oi'm goin' home.'

I hear a horse pound up the path towards our tent. It's after dark and I wonder what is urgent enough for the rider to provoke the humidity that's hovering to drench every part of a moving body. The tent-flap is ripped aside and Chrissy appears. She shimmers with war-paint, sweat beads along her brow and her cherry lips shine in the lamp light.

'Fred, is James here?'

Dan uses the alias, James Ryan.

'No. Not yet. Why, is something wrong?'

Sweat drips off my nose onto my lap. *Damn it's hot.*

'It could be. I worked at Maytown today. One of the girls had a run-in with a very sick puppy. Said he was hunting two blokes, and that one rides a grey horse and may have put on a trick-riding show. Mentioned your name. Showed her a poster. She reckons it looked like James.'

'Jesus.'

'James told me you were both on the lam, from something or other.'

'Did he?'

The humidity has wet her dress below the breast-line; caused the fabric to turn a darker green.

'This bloke says you rode with Ned Kelly. Said he'll ask the Mines Office to see your prospecting licence, to find your claim.'

'How come she told you?'

'Well, he turns nasty. Calls her Ellen, and missus Kelly, nearly drives her head through the bed-board as they hump… and he… makes demands. You know – unseemly demands.'

She mimes out what she means, sweat flicks off her elbow as she moves.

'The girl screams. It saves her, luckily, because we all rush in.'

Ah, damn. I think the worst.

'Did he have big… f-f-funny… ears?'

'Could have. Another thing – she told the troopers he has *Ned* tattooed on his hand, the soft part of his thumb. He's out to get you.'

I pour her a whiskey to calm her. I can see she's concerned, but not as much as me. We wait for Dan, but after half an hour, she stands.

'I can't wait any longer, Fred. I have a business to run.'

'Alright.'

'Warn James if you see him.'

I remain in our tent as long as I can, then decide to hunt down Dan. I check his favourite pub and other haunts, with no luck. I return home by a different muddy route, through the edge of the Chinese miners' section. The rain falls vertical.

The smell of strange cooking odours pours from many tents. Chatter spills from two large tents in the centre of the block, and in the lamp light I see extended kitchens with rows of Chinese eating like praying mantis with chopsticks at long log tables. I pass a low-roofed hut and push through a haze of opium smoke as it wafts through the windows. On the step sit three silent, pock-faced Chinese, their foreheads encircled with sweaty bandanas, sharpening knives on long whet-stones. After I pass, I hear their chatter fire up. They don't get many like me here.

Eventually, unable to warn Dan, I slip exhausted into my bunk, but not without my pistol. I'm woken by my frightful dreams but realise it may not be a dream. I'm conscious of movement and rhythmical breathing in the room. I hear a clink against a tent peg outside. My eyes adjust to the dark and I see someone standing over Dan's bed. I relax. Dan has returned.

I'm about to tell him I'm awake, when I smell an odour common to Chinatown. I reach for my pistol as the human shape swings an object at Dan's bed. I hear the intruder's grunt at striking hessian, and not a person; the rip of cloth. I shoot through my blanket.

A scream and noisy stumble, a bump against the bed and the tin hand-basin. A shadow rushes out the tent-flap doorway. Another voice outside; an exchange in Cantonese. By this time, I'm at the doorway, gun ready, but shake like a newborn foal. *The shearer has put the Tong assassins onto us.* I hear footsteps run in the distance.

I can't sit in the dark and wait. I dress, strap my pistol on and jump at every shadow as I return to the pub. I wait there in the hope Dan avoids ambush until he finds me.

I wait until sun-up before I'm comfortable enough to go back and face the tent. I avoid Chinatown and as I spy our tent, I see Dan at the entrance. *Thank Christ.*

'Oi spent the night with Chrissy. She told me about the shearer.'

I nod.

'Oi saw me bed all slashed and blood everywhere. I was worried you might have been hurt, dead even. I was just about to look for you.'

My face is tense. I want to implore him.

'We need to run, mate. You didn't convince me to leave earlier, but I'm all yours now.'

'No, we need to shoot the fookin' shearer. Then run!'

'That'd be nice but I've managed to piss off a few thousand Chinese by shooting one, so odds are high we'll be dead before we even sight the shearer. Especially now they know we're worth a reward.'

A tick starts in his right eye, as if it's counting down the seconds while he thinks. He sees the sense in what I said. In minutes we pack enough stores to get us back to civilisation, but not enough to make it appear as if we're checking out. We fetch our horses and load them.

'We're heading up-river to do a bit of prospecting,' Dan informs the neighbour's wife as she returns from the latrine. 'We should be back by dark, unless we strike it lucky of course.'

He throws the famous Kelly smile her way, to dampen suspicion.

He insists we stop at Chrissy's to gift her our tent, cooking and mining gear she might like to sell. I'm against the delay but concede. I can see he's genuinely fond of her, even though it distresses me. He enters her building, while I hold the horses. Moments later, he's back, all agitated.

He rips the reins from me and Indian-mounts.

'The prick was here less than five minutes ago. I'll fix him for abusing my mother.' He turns the horse towards Palmerville.

'The shearer's heading for the Palace of Joy, up-town,' he shouts, as he spurs his horse in pursuit.

A swarm of mosquitos, nearly the shape of horse and rider, hangs in the air as stunned as me.

I follow within seconds, but I'm leading the pack horse with no hope of keeping up. I gallop the muddy streets and nearly upturn a hand-drawn vegetable cart when I misjudge its line of direction. Pedestrians curse when my horses spray street-muck over them. Horses' hooves clatter, the wind swirls against my hat. I lose sight of Dan.

I hear a gunshot and round the bend to see Dan, on foot, pistol in hand, enter a long, timber and canvas building. His horse skitters untethered on the street. More gunshots sound, and Dan backs out of the building at pace. I slide to a halt, grab his horse's reins, then spin in time to see dozens of Chinese pour from the building armed with chairs, woks and chopping instruments, all yabbering and shouting in pursuit.

'Dan, here… Indian mount!' I shout.

I canter between him and the hostiles. Some reel back and others throw implements at me. Dan realises what's on – trick riding – and holsters his pistol, grabs the pommel as I canter past, and executes a perfect bounce-mount. We scarper. The Chinese don't have horses, but the shearer and traps do.

21

DAN draws alongside as we gallop the partly-crowded streets.

'Oi hit him. He's wounded, at least. Hopefully, the bastard will bleed to death.'

I notice glee in his eyes and his voice – so different to Stringybark Creek.

'We'll head out Cooktown way, then double back,' I say.

He nods and spurs his horse to surge ahead. We drop off the main thoroughfare onto backstreets in case the shearer, or Chinese, follow. My arm aches from towing the packhorse as he struggles to keep pace. Ten minutes of this and we're at the edge of town, where we hit the oriental track heading east to Cooktown, and the coast. We gallop the track for five minutes, then each peel off at different places to avoid leaving an easy trail.

We pause on the ridge above the township for some minutes, before we let it pass out of sight. The newly risen sun taunts us by bathing the town in gold.

There's no sign of pursuing horses. Neither of us speaks but we swap looks as if to say, *well, that's another chapter in our life we've cocked up*.

Let's hope we can keep distance between ourselves and the ant nest we've just disturbed.

I hold resentments wedged like flesh between my teeth. We travelled fast the first day in silence but I can't contain myself any longer.

'We should have just snuck out. Like we planned.'

'What, leave with our tail between our legs?'

'No. But what have we gained apart from more enemies?'

'He might think twice about chasing us in future.'

'I doubt it… he's dingo-crazy.'

We stew on that for a period, and snipe at each other as the day evolves.

I want to clock him, the self-centred prick, but I'm pleased of one thing. We are free of Chrissy, an experiment of a more worrying kind. I realise I'm dispensable. Maybe I'm lame-brained but I didn't see this coming.

❖

After weeks of hard riding, we've struck Mareeba, on the Atherton Tablelands, thirty miles west of Cairns. Someone at the town's watering-trough informs us Harry Readford is in town. To check out if the work offer still stands, we ride to his camp-site where he's gathered a huge mob of cattle.

A young drover coils some rope beside a wagon. He looks our way as we ride in, so I ask him, 'Can you point us to Harry Readford?'

He points to Harry's tent – a lean-to canvas fly thrown over a cut sapling strapped between two trees. I couldn't make out his comment, obscured by the loud bellowing of the mob, but raise my finger in thanks.

Harry, seated on a bush chair, raises his eyes from what he's doing as we approach.

'Harry, remember me, Fred… and Dave?'

I point to Dan, beside me.

'Ah, Fred… yes, Cairns. Hello Dave.'

He stands as we swing off our horses, thrusts his huge hand forward as if he's going to grab me by the throat. I'd forgotten what a giant he is. He crushes my hand, painfully, in his welcoming grip. I curse that I didn't remember that grip, and protect my fingers.

He points that weapon of a hand at our saddle bags.

'Saddle bags full of gold?'

We laugh but anyone can tell it's tinged with pain.

'We don't even have hope in them bags no more,' says Dan.

'You wouldn't be the first to leave the diggings with less than you arrived, although… you do hear of the lucky ones.'

We nod. Let the comment pass.

'We wonder if that work offer is still open?' I ask.

His face turns glum; a vein pulses along his neck.

'Oh, sorry fellows.'

My hope throws itself upon a rock. He watches our mouths droop and our shoulders stoop. Then, his face lights up.

'Nah, just pulling your leg. When can you start? We're set to leave for the drive south in two days.'

He got us good and it takes a moment to recover, and see the funny side. I laugh.

'We'll camp here and be ready to start day after tomorrow, if that's alright? We need to get some clobber – clothes, new boots – in town. The tropics and mining wore ours out, as you can tell by lookin' at us.'

'Good, lads. Let your horses loose and eat with us – meet the others.'

We unsaddle, tether the horses and set up our swags before we join him.

His team is a motley lot, with five, middle-aged, leathery-faced fellows; two younger men, not much older than us; and three Aboriginal drovers from central Queensland, who have worked for Harry, on and off, since they were young boys. The cook is of indeterminate age and describes himself as an 'alco after dark'.

'As long as I do me work and have breakfast ready each morning, Harry don't seem to mind,' he explains, and Harry doesn't contradict him.

We dine on bacon-coated roast beef and vegetables. We pig-out, because it's the best meal we've had for ages and there's plenty. When the meal concludes, the cook, lean as a greyhound, stands at the end of the table, grubby cloth in hand.

'How was that, lads?'

'Good, cooky,' says Harry.

'Yeah, good cooky, good,' carol the others.

'Not as good as goanna,' the Aboriginal lads mumble.

'If ya want goanna, go and bloody catch one and go anna cook it yourself.'

'Yeah, maybe tomorrra, but then everyone will want us to cook for 'em, cooky, and you'll lose ya job,' the Aboriginal lad replies, with a grin wide across his face.

We all chuckle.

'This happens most nights,' Darryl, a white drover, explains. 'Cooky asks and one of us provides unhelpful feedback.'

We laugh. Grog is distributed because we're in town, but Harry explains that, apart from the cook, the crew aren't heavy drinkers and, essentially, it's a dry camp. A dry camp will be good for Dan who drinks far too much.

They aren't loud fellows and the meal is eaten in hushed tones. It's a bit different from the Kelly gang with our hooting and hollering and ribald jokes. I wonder if we will fit in, or cause problems, but believe we will be fine. I hope so, the scale of the trek to Dubbo means we'll be together for a long time.

I help one of the Aboriginal lads clean the dishes.

'What's ya name?' I ask.

'You,' he says.

I point at his chest.

'No. Ya name.'

'You.'

Louder this time.

'Is that your name?'

'Yes… You.'

'Tribal name?' I ask.

'No. White-fella name. Boss named me. He point at me all the time and say "Hey, You." So, that how I learnt me name.'

He is serious and I want to smile, but don't.

I think I'm going to like this team and head off to my swag pondering our good fortune.

After breakfast, Dan and I ride into town to shop. Mareeba is the centre of a thriving community with one general store. We've only, once, shopped together and it's fascinating now to note our different tastes. We try on trousers and, while I'm attracted to the jodhpur, Dan goes for the straight-leg pant.

We like coloured cowboy-cut check shirts with the fancy stitching, and prefer the high-heeled riding boot. The women's clothing is situated in the same area as the men's and, when the owner's back is turned, Dan grabs a skirt off the rack and holds it to his front and mimes that it would suit me. He places a blouse in his shopping, and then drops it on top of my pile, making me blush with embarrassment when I attempt to smuggle it back.

'You boys aren't from around here, are you?' says the owner at the check-out.

'No, we're not,' says Dan.

'Who ya with?'

'Drovin' with Harry Readford's outfit, near the saleyards.'

'Readford? He's Captain Starlight, the famous bushranger, isn't he? I read it in the paper the other day, just after he arrived.'

'Is he? Had no idea.'

'Yeah, horse and cattle thief, and accused of bailing up people for gold. Got off a charge of stealing a bull, but really a large mob of cattle out west, somewhere… Longreach, I think.'

I've never heard of Longreach, but the name suggests it's a long way out.

'My gosh, I hope he pays us.'

'I hope you'll pay me. That's a guinea, please,' he says, with a smile.

When I leave Mareeba, wearing my new clothes, I'll stand out like a freshly washed teenage ringer on his first visit to Melbourne, and Dan, very similar. On the shop veranda I catch his eye.

'Well, what have we got ourselves involved in, mate?'

'No idea. But it may work in our favour. Harry's not likely to lag us if we get found out, or make a slip… and we might stay one step ahead of the shearer.'

It makes sense. We blow the last of our cash and enjoy a big drink. Dan is as happy as a drunken parrot. The happiest he's been for many months, in fact. I can't quite grasp it. It's the old Dan, the happy-go-lucky, give-anything-a-go, Dan.

'What's with you, tonight?'

'I've got a good feeling about this,' he says.

Our swags are inches apart near the roaring fire. I watch the flames reflect off his blue eyes and his lush lips flash luminous in the fire light. I think he's referring to us. Inside, I flush with joy.

'Yes, we're heading home,' he says. 'Once at Dubbo, it's just a hop, skip and jump to Greta.'

'Oh, I hadn't thought of that,' I say, and pull the swag's groundsheet over my head to prevent him seeing my disappointment.

Not only do we have someone up our hammer hunting us for gain, Dan, now, wants us to put our heads back in the noose by returning to the scene of our woes. I can't believe him.

22

WE rise before sun-up and release the mob. The herd is so large it takes nearly an hour for the last beast to leave the holding paddock. By lunch I'm miles behind the main mob with a bunch of ornery weaners. They want to return to where they last saw their mothers and they're trying my patience. They keep swarming, heading for home – unafraid of man or beast. Not schooled in the usual rules of stop or go, they bend in stupid ways to the dog's bark and bite.

I'm at wit's end. I've done more swearing during this morning than I've done in a life-time. Dan often says he knows how the weaner feels – missing home and his ma – and would do anything to get back there.

Harry has trotted back to assist.

'This is more exciting than gold mining,' he shouts, as he gallops past to cut off a few weaners who have swirled past us, again.

I smile in spite of my frustration.

'It certainly is when you're not getting any sparkles in the pan!'

After an hour, we manage to return them to the herd.

Weeks later and I believe he's right. It is exciting. Similar to bushranging, droving has days of calm and routine until, without warning, all hell breaks loose. On the other hand, droving gives a man a lot of time to think. We're still young and, now, away from the pressure of lying traps chasing us day and night, we notice the benefits of fitting in with the mainstream mob. Having escaped the siege at Glenrowan, we dreamt and plotted revenge, but tailing cattle for a few weeks converts us, so we dream of a permanent job, of settling down.

I look around. The grass is yellow like standing hay. Waterholes are scarce and it's two days since the herd has watered. We've only been on the road for a couple of hours when we notice the cattle are restless and the old lead-bullock picks up pace, its bell jangles louder in response to its amble.

'Must have smelt water,' mutters Harry, in answer to my look and implied question. I think he's joking and smile back, half-convinced.

We crest a low rise to view, in the valley below, a vast expanse of marsh-land inhabited by thousands of black swans, clustered like a black eyelid across part of the lake. These coal-black creatures glisten in the morning sun as they glide across the surface of the wide billabong, like dancing girls: sometimes line-astern, sometimes line-abreast, their long necks and crimson beaks rising above and plunging below the surface of the silver water to the beat of divine music, available to them but not accessible to us.

Harry joins us where we sit, leg across the pummel, enjoying the moment.

'You know the British explorers wouldn't believe a black swan existed when they first saw them in the colony.'

'Why, what stopped them?'

'There were no black swans in Europe, only white, so the black swan became a symbol of the impossible. Something could not possibly happen, they'd argue. It would be like finding a black swan, when we all know such a swan doesn't exist. Kind of how they thought we couldn't sail over the horizon, because if we did we'd drop off the flat-earth.'

'Like believing someone is alive, despite many reports they've died,' offers Dan.

'Exactly. But here was a continent they didn't even know existed, which should undermine their surety. Yet, in spite of evidence to the contrary – drawings and specimens of black swans, brought back by Banks and other visitors to the colony – many retained their existing belief.'

Dan and I make faces, pick up on how the story relates to us, and the myth of our sorry death.

The cattle are thankful for the drink and push their way forward to stand at the water's edge with their necks bowed, submerging nostrils through water lilies, as if in homage to the wild birds whose home they've invaded. It's a sight that beggar's description. You informs us the local blackfellas call the place *Warruma*. We camp there for two days before we journey further.

The herd and drovers are as one as we sweep west, then south, like a brown fungus munching through open savannah and sweeping plains. We get to believe we are in control; that land and beast fall before us at our command. We get to know the animals at another level – both as individuals, and as part of the herd – and we fall in with that. We believe life is predictable, while understanding that it is not. We predict which individual will lead the mob, which will lag behind, which is fragile and which will complain. Out of the complexity we distil a simplicity to suit our purposes.

I wake early to muster the horses for the day. I look around, rub my eyes in disbelief. There's not a beast to be seen except the tethered night-horse. Insects and small frogs carry on with their pre-dawn symphony in the background, as do early magpies cheating on their mates. Usually, the cattle rest where we settle them the evening before, yet now, the landscape is vacant. I search the snoring drovers for someone awake to share in my bewilderment, but they're like chrysalis asleep in their swags.

I saddle the night-horse and head towards the horizon in the direction we've been travelling, imagining by dawn I'll find the mob grazing-out, just over the skyline. After a half-hour's riding, I crest the ridge-line only to be met by another horizon with barely a kangaroo in sight, let alone our stock. Where can they be? I've not followed their tracks in the dark – so confident was I that they would be in this vicinity. I ride in an easterly arc towards the camp, sure I'll cross their tracks if they've headed home to the coast.

I return to camp without finding a hoofmark. The men have finished their breakfast and are as surprised as I when I report that I've failed to find a single beast.

'I've got no idea where they are, Harry.'

'Well, they're not up my arse, Fred.'

I point off at an angle to our west.

'They must be in that region,' I say.

'What makes you say that?'

'Well, I didn't cross any tracks in the opposite direction.'

'Agh. Fred Layton, detective, has lost our mob, and is now hot on their trail,' he says.

'Do you think they've been duffed?'

'Duffed? From under our noses? Unlikely, lad. We're rooted without our horses, though, so we better hope they haven't been lifted.'

By this time the drovers have gathered.

'Here, one of you blackfellas… Lenny, go with our Fred and track the mob from the campsite, and jog along, alright?'

Len, the slimmest of the blackfellas, in his late thirties, jogs off barefooted in the direction of a low ridge, far to our right. I kick up the old night-horse and follow behind. We track the mob for about half an hour to a disturbance, a slight rise in the ground, a rock outcrop, on the close horizon.

Standing on one of the rocks ahead of me, Len points towards the ground. I ride up alongside and there, in a long channel below ground-level, the stock mill around a watercourse. The land around us is board-flat but down there, another world is exposed. The cavern looks as if the walls have been reamed out of stone and the entrance floor is littered with rock, as if the ceiling has collapsed.

'We'll go down and grab the horses,' I say.

Len shakes his head.

'No, Fred. I stay here.'

'What's up, mate, you puffed?'

'No!... Debbil in that place. Bad spirit. You whitefella, you go!'

I look at him, about to remark – perhaps ridicule his stance. But I see something in his eyes that tells me he's genuinely concerned, so think better of it. Perhaps it's something to do with Aboriginal spiritual life.

'Okay, I'll muster the horses, bring them up here, and you return them to camp.'

I push the old horse over the edge, where he picks his way through the fallen rocks to the floor below. We turn the horses towards the surface. I turn the hobble-rope I'd wrapped around the night-horse's neck into a makeshift halter for Len to use on his horse to herd the others.

I search for the lead bullocks, perhaps kilometres further along this exposed rock-tube. Within hours I'm joined by the rest of the drovers and, by lunch time, we've herded the mob to the surface.

From that point on, whenever I wonder aloud about something, Harry says, 'Detective Fred is on the hunt again.'

Occasionally, when we're sitting around the fire at night, Harry will say, 'I just want to know one thing, Fred?'

'What's that?'

'Where are you going to hide the mob tonight?'

Then, in a deep, dark rumble, from behind his bushy beard he'll piss himself laughing, as will the others. My reputation as a drover is made. How was I to know there's such a fascinating world around us? How was I to know?

Having pushed the mob from Mt Garnett to Conjuboy, then down behind the ranges, we're at Charters Towers, into country with which Dan and I are more familiar. Dan, the idiot, carries on again about Jupiter Mossman not getting recognition for discovering Charters Towers. He's a stirrer.

We have a big drink over a couple of days, the cook restocks the food wagon, then, just as we settle, Harry insists we leave the Towers and push the mob south, towards Emerald.

Emerald is nothing more than a store, shanty, post office, school, railway station and a few huts built to act as a base, while the central rail line was being built and now services local properties. We only overnight there. But, a few days west of Emerald, You shows Harry a dark rock, smeared with mud. Harry examines it.

'Yeah?'

"Im pretty, that rock,' says You.

'Ah, yeah? Don't look so pretty.'

The drover takes it from Harry, spits on it, rubs it for a while on his shirt, then holds it up to the sun. He returns it to Harry and encourages him to hold it against the sun. A few of us nudge our horses closer, while Harry holds the stone to the light.

'Well, I'll be damned. It is frickin' pretty.'

He passes me the stone and when I hold it to the light, its green insides blaze as if alight.

'What is that?'

'No idea but it must be a jewel of some kind. Keeps the blackfellas entertained.'

Nearly every day there is something to surprise and confound me about this wide land, and it's the surprise of it that captures me. A flat landscape and a hidden tunnel, a mud-covered rock and a prism of joy, a barren land and the most glorious morning-bird carolling.

We discover more stones and I put a range of different coloured ones in my saddle bags. The others merely look at the stones they've collected, then drop them. I want something to show as proof of some of the sights and events I've witnessed. But who will I share them with? Then I'm struck remembering that I lifted a watch, coins and gold at the risk of my life; where others, blackfellas, place no value upon them. I struggle to make sense of my desires.

We plod south-west towards Roma. It's a town well known to Harry, due to a famous but controversial court case, where a local jury found him not guilty of stealing nearly a thousand head of prime cattle and droving them two thousand miles to Moree. Unlike now, where he has a droving camp of twelve men plus a cook, he managed that trek with only two offsiders.

Local blackfellas tell our Aboriginal drovers of a water source in the cocoon of a mighty sandstone edifice, soon to appear in the purple distance during our trek south. Weeks later, a mountain range appears along the horizon to our right. The land around us is sunburnt and dry. The melon-holes, along the edges of the silvered maze of brigalow patches, hindering our progress, are bone dry. The vegetation and cactus push us west towards the range, and we pray the story of water is true.

Cactus has plagued parts of Queensland for thirty years but we are surprised by how far north and west it has spread. Harry explains that cactus was introduced to start a local cochineal industry, a dye used to colour the red-coats of the British Army, and with no local predators, it finds the local conditions to its liking.

'Farmers believed it was an inexpensive fence, spread it far and wide, until it got out of control... Slow going these past few weeks,' Harry moans, days later, around the camp fire. 'No water... easy for large mobs to get trapped.'

A mature cactus is as tall as a tree.

'Wouldn't have been too bad for the cockies if there'd been some profit from it, but by the time it was introduced, the red dye extracted from the cochineal bugs, meant to inhabit the cactus, had been replaced by a synthetic dye.'

'Bullshit,' says Dan.

'No, true.'

He chuckles.

'Need bloody tough cane-cutters to collect the fruit, with all them prickles.'

Having bumped against a plant, Dan digs a thorn from his thigh with his pocket knife. To avoid infection we have to remove thorns from ourselves and horses each evening. The blackfellas chew Wilga leaves into a poultice and place it on their infected sores, and within days the prickle is ejected and the wound cleaned. Infected thorns kill some horses before we realise. We lose bullocks.

'The bloody cactus is something I didn't count on,' Harry confesses. 'I'm not sure how long the cattle will last at this pace? If we don't find good water soon, we'll be like Leichardt and perish.'

We'd sighted trees blazed with Leichardt's initials only days earlier. At that moment You joins us, the wide flare of his jodhpur accentuating his fine features.

'What's up, You?' Harry asks.

I smile inside at the play his name makes.

'We can use fat tree to water some cattle.'

He points to a cluster of trees shaped like a fat bottle.

'Chop them and feed weakest, and poddy, till we reach water. Waterhole maybe soon.'

Next morning, as directed by You, we watch the poddies and weak cows chew the tree's pithy body with relish. I see Harry's stress subside by the minute.

In spite of being pushed further west by the impenetrable cactus, we force our way south until our path collides with the range's sandstone escarpment at its Southern tip. Harry has returned from a quick search to tell us he's found permanent water at the mouth of a narrow gorge, and steers the mob towards it.

The waterhole is a paradise of running spring water, from high in the gorge. We establish camp and settle the mob. Harry says that when he was in Roma, he'd heard of a range, similar to this, being noted by the explorers Leichardt and Mitchell, in the 1840's.

'I think they called it Carnarvon Range, but I'm not sure.'

We swim in the waterhole's crystal waters. Unlike Ned, Dan and I aren't great swimmers, but we're far better than Harry. There is no buoyancy in his large frame, so he dog-paddles with barely his nose above water. He sees us laugh.

'I don't need to swim, fellas. I'll let the horse drag me if I need to. I've done it before to cross flooded creeks,' he argues across the water.

'I suppose you're right, but I like the freedom of being able to swim, to float, to dive into the cold darkness,' I say.

'Each to his own.'

The three blackfellas dive from rocks lining the edge. How many thousands of years have humans frolicked in this paradise? Head-over-tail they go. The whites of their feet and the ebony of their teeth act like a spindle point of their flight. They laugh like young boys, yet are far older than Dan or I. When had I last laughed as freely as that? Very few times since entering gaol. Too few to recall. Next morning, we whitefellas explore the gorge but the Aboriginal drovers won't be enticed inside.

'They reckon it's a sacred place,' Harry explains.

We follow a running stream for miles into the enclosed gorge with three hundred foot walls. In places it settles in quiet mirror-pools, which reflect the sandstone cliffs and cloudless blue sky. I'm surprised by my own reflection, a gaunt, bearded stranger stares at me. I draw Dan's attention to it.

'I think I've aged a hundred years in the past few.'

'Yeah, can't believe Oi haven't noticed meself. Me beard's bushier than Ned's,' he whispers.

I smile as I reply.

'Not even Sergeant Steele would recognise me now.'

Further along, primitive vegetation and fragile ferns drape moss-laden caverns, where ancient water seeps through the sandstone walls. The area is moist and cool. We try to get a gunsight on the wood ducks that live on the ponds but they are too alert. All we hear is the whirr of their departing wings.

The protected walls of the sandstone escarpment are home to large galleries of rock art, scrapings and animal motifs, still vibrant from recent application of ochre and care. We scramble up for a better view. One large rock-painting shows a hand-stencil with the sign of the missing finger – a graphic explanation of recent deaths of many sick children. It details why the tribe quit the site.

'Bloody Measles. Bloody whitefellas,' Harry mutters, takes my arm above the elbow, shakes a wall of flies from my sleeve and steers me away from the place.

We notice bones stuck in holes along the sandstone cliff, and poking out of hollows in trees along the route. Dan scales one thinking that eagles may have dragged animal bones home. He peers in and nearly falls as he slides down at pace. His face pale as white ochre.

'Aw fook mate, they're human. A skull stared at me. Some bones have painted lines on 'em.'

'Aboriginal ancestors. Must be a burial ground.'

'Some look recent.'

'Look, babies wrapped in bark.'

Dan goes quiet. I guess he's thinking about Ned or, like me, thinking of his own death. Will we die in the wilderness in some lonely grave? We think of the lop-eared shearer. Has he worked out where we are and closes-in, due to our slow progress?

I believe it is time to move on because we are unsure how far the gorge continues. I step out. A long wooden spear hits the ground at my feet and vibrates from the shock. I freeze. Another lands three yards before Dan. He springs to his feet and slaps for his pistol. A roar like the loud bellow of a beast fills the cavity, followed by others equally loud. I sight three warriors on a ledge, high on the gorge wall, twirling objects on a rope above their head. The noise is terrifying.

A startled wallaby bounds for safety across the track barely three horse lengths in front of us only to be impaled mid-flight by a long spear, this time from the opposite wall. Harry swipes Dan's pistol arm aside.

'Don't shoot. They're warning us to stay clear.'

'No, they're not. They're out to kill us. They're no match for our pistols.'

Dan wrestles the gun from Harry, wants to shoot the spear throwers. Harry locks him up in a bear hug.

'If they wanted to kill us, we'd be dead now. The wallaby is a demonstration of their accuracy.'

Voices from various places around us, shout and scream like crazy fruit bats. We're ambushed.

Harry holds his nerve.

'Back out, boys, now. Don't turn your backs.'

Pistols pointed, we retreat towards the entrance, then turn and run. When convinced we are not followed, we slow to a walk and suck in the hot air. It's a sober trek to camp with much to ponder. I can't help but feel the similarity of the events in this gorge with the events in our region. The squatters, the rich settlers, the flooding of our culture caused by the gold rush. Our harsh treatment at the hands of the traps, our dramatic yet futile resistance, our unrespected leaders. It was all there. Makes me feel akin to, but even worse for, the blackfellas.

Our cattle have regained some vigour so, when we reach camp, Harry decrees it is time to leave. No point in provoking the locals. We tie a bullock to a tree and leave it for the warriors. We should make Roma in good time, where Harry plans to rest a week on the common.

Locals are keen to shake the hand of someone who, for all the wrong reasons, has put their town on the map. Harry's duffing charges were acquitted by a trial held in Roma. If he returns to camp, he's invariably drunk, brags that he hasn't spent a ha'penny on booze. He's one happy fellow. The nights he doesn't return he makes us envious next morning with stories of making passionate love with a young matron he knows. I can't believe how these stories excite Dan, making Harry appear a manly and romantic chap.

The police, obviously, don't share the town's enthusiasm for the cattle thief and ride through our mob. They ride one side of the herd, Dan and I ride the other, which works fine. They find nothing. Two days later they arrive at dinner-time, and catch us unaware by the fire. The Sergeant looks down on us from upon his horse.

'Where you blokes from?'

'Palmerville.'

'What were you doing there?'

'Mining.'

'And before that?'

'Charters Towers.'

'Is that what you do? Prospect?'

'Mostly, but we do a bit of cattle work to make wages when it doesn't pan out in mining.'

'Known Readford long?'

'No, first met him as we passed through and he offered us a job.'

'Where abouts?'

'Mareeba.'

'Nice horse, the Grey. Got papers for her?'

'No. Didn't buy her. Family bred her.'

'Where's family?'

'Gympie.'

'Any of these cattle yours?'

'Nah.'

'Got a brand?'

'Nah, no need for one.'

'Harry got one?'

'I suppose so. I haven't asked.'

The scrutiny unnerves us, because they question us about our background, a story which we haven't rehearsed, and may expose us. It takes us a while to appreciate that it's Harry they're after.

He's reluctant to leave Roma but we hear it's rained down south, so head for St George, then will chase the green pick to fatten the cattle down to Dubbo.

❖

Free of Roma and suspicious eyes, and closing in on St George, I wonder what it would be like to be guilt free, with no dark corners, and nothing to hide. I realise that had the Roma traps caught us with cattle that we couldn't account for, the consequences would be deadly.

I'd barely put the thought to bed when Harry pointed to a mob of cattle on a ridge.

'Hey, fellas! Go and check that mob for any cleanskins. We need to make up the numbers for those we lost in the cactus country.'

Dan springs to life, swings his horse towards the ridge. I hesitate. That's the difference. He doesn't.

'Come on Steve. Oi can't cull them by myself.'

'I mightn't want to.'

'No time to be precious, now. Harry's the boss… we all benefit.'

We'd never spoken about going straight.

'Alright, but we need to talk about this, soon, or at least make a definite decision. Our luck can't last forever.'

I join him and we career across the plain at a gallop to demonstrate our worth and skill. We manage to extract ten Mickey bulls and work the horses hard to keep the ring-ins from returning to their mates on the hill. They settle when they join our herd.

Late that afternoon I ride beside Dan.

'I don't like it, I tell ya. If we continue to lift things, there's only one future for us.'

'Riches.'

'Capture and death.'

Dan looks at me, rides in silence for a moment or two.

'Perhaps you're right. But we'll never be invited to high tea in any squatter's castle, or invited to marry his daughter, no matter what we do. Our future is fleeced, mate. We may as well cause murder, rape and mayhem, and enjoy ourselves, while we have breath in us.'

I ignore his comment, raise my tone.

'While we make wages and keep our identity hidden, we can have a fair life without lifting.'

Dan shakes his head, turns his horse to ride away.

'Ya dreamin'. It ain't gonna happen.'

'I'm just saying, is all.'

Over many months we've helped Harry push a mob fifteen hundred miles through the length of Queensland, and half-way through New South Wales, here to Dubbo. It's a history-making feat.

Dubbo is as close as I ever want to get to our past, or old friends, but Dan is quite affected by its proximity to home.

'It can't be all that far to Greta from here.'

'Four hundred miles at least. We're halfway up New South Wales.'

'A lot closer than when we were at Cairns.'

I can't argue that.

'I can smell home,' he says.

'I can smell traps, a hangman's noose.'

I can't stand the thought of losing him, even though he treats me rough. I would be lost without him. My sanity is connected to his existence. First, for reassurance that I wasn't exterminated at Glenrowan: a public witness to the horror and bastardry of that day. Second, because I fear I will not know how to survive without him, having bonded to him like a baby duckling to a puppy. I'm stranded in 'no man's land', unable to thrive in either, but happy on the edges of both.

I sleep a restless sleep, not knowing if I will follow him into danger or turn tail and head back with the drovers.

NEXT morning, we seek out Harry.

'I'm sad to see you lads leave.'

'Yeah, need a break. Maybe catch up with some family who've moved down south.'

'You know you've left me in a tough spot. I've accepted a job with Goldsborough Mort, back in Queensland.'

'Sorry, Harry. Oi didn't know that,' Dan says.

I shake my head to back up Dan's words.

'Well, the point is, I only agreed because I thought I had you lads as back-up.'

'Aw shit, sorry. We've made plans.'

'I was going to bring you in as partners, you know, share the profit.'

'Ah. That's generous. Look, we'll have a think over a drink, tonight, and let you know.'

Sanity prevails and we join the drovers north.

Harry's fame as a drover grows, following the Dubbo trip. He's now a major celebrity and considered an explorer of a different kind. The famous explorers, Leichardt and Burke, whose paths we'd crossed, merely dashed over inhospitable territory in their race to reach a place of their dreams – an inland sea, Eldorado, a distant shore. We drovers, however, forced to a snail's pace because of our herd, have to live off the country to survive. Harry will probably never be short of work, given his fame. Nor, therefore, will we: being happy to be on the move, and hidden from traps, or bounty hunters like the lop-eared shearer.

Harry is the sort of guy you'd follow anywhere. He's a strapping, handsome fellow, a thinker, excellent horseman and marksman. He's taught me, someone who viewed Aborigines as primitive, to respect their knowledge and science, which he uses to our advantage.

Unlike Ned, and other mug lair crims, bushranger-Readford acts the part of a respectable citizen. He seldom draws attention to himself, ensuring that it takes ages for the traps to wise up to him. Of course, we all share in the proceeds of a swelling herd and that ensures our silence.

This latest contract involves moving three thousand head of cattle for McDonald Smith and Company. We'll travel north-west, from the Barcoo River in western Queensland (where Burke and Wills perished), across far-western Queensland to the Barkly, in order to stock the newly-acquired Brunette Downs Station.

True to his word Harry signs us as partners. We will lead the drovers out to the Barcoo to muster the cattle while Harry travels via Roma, to sort out some finances and make applications for ballot blocks, stripped from the larger holdings in Queensland and the Northern Territory.

We'll steer the droving team back through St George because we are familiar with part of the route.

In the pub at St George, I notice Henry Olsen approach, rubbing his chin as if stroking a beard.

'Jesus, fellas, I wouldn't have recognised you. Looks like you haven't sighted a shearer in ten years.'

'Yeah, something like that, Henry. We don't hit town often.'

'There's a barber here now. Progress.'

'Yeah, yeah, we should get a shave.'

'Talking of shaves. Did that shearer from Bell Ridge ever catch up with you?'

'No, managed to miss him.'

'He came through just after you, and I said I thought you were going to the gold fields.'

'That's helpful, thanks, Henry.'

So that's how the bastard knew where we were travelling.

'He's very keen to catch up with you. I get the idea he's not really your friend though.'

'Why's that?'

'Well, if he was your friend, you would have told him your movements.'

'You're right Henry, he's not. We owe him money from cards.'

'Shit, serious stuff.'

'Yeah, lead him astray if you see him again. Get him off our backs.'

'Sure, fellas, thanks for the skinny.'

I buy him a rum, then we take a bottle of gin back to camp. As we walk Dan goes berserk.

'Who is this bastard? I should'a finished him when Oi had the chance.'

'Hopefully, he never recovered from the wounding you gave him at the Palmer. Surely, by now, we've given him the slip… How could he know we joined Starlight?'

The shearer, like Missus Gardiner's prediction, is always on my mind. Since the siege I wait for the next boot to drop. *When will someone appear to finger me? What will they do — shoot me? Why have I survived and others haven't?*

Tomorrow, we'll depart, head out through bright-red Windorah sand dunes, skirt the edge of the gibber plains until, weeks later, we reach the Barcoo.

The Barcoo is part of a desert river network. Debris hangs on the trees along the bank to suggest the rivers flow not to the sea, but inland. There must be a sea there.

The monsoons in the north have pushed floodwater down into the channel country, ensuring the bare floodplains are now lush with green pick. It's partly why there's an abundance of strong cattle to move north.

An extra bit of luck. Harry had believed we had to muster the cattle for shipping, but the stock and station agents had ordered the cattle owner to muster, so the mix-up meant we only had a couple of weeks work to be ready to travel.

Confident we had the correct tally and the right stock to undertake the journey, we wait until Harry joins us from Roma.

He arrives and we ride through the mob. He's pleased with our selection and we agree to depart in the morning, because the stock are hungry from being yarded without rations.

'I need to have a word,' he says, 'before we return to camp.'

He points ahead and tells You, 'Ride ahead, you mob.'

Dan and I share a questioning look. Harry's face is serious. I tense inside.

'The Roma Police took me in for questioning. They told me they're looking for you two.'

'Why? What for?'

'Said you're accused of being members of the Kelly gang.'

We both laugh on cue, as is our standard response to questions of this nature.

'They're serious… Dan Kelly and Steve Hart.'

We pull, *you-can't-be-serious*, faces.

'Why now?'

'Some fellow is stirring up a big hunt… They gave me this.'

He pulls a folded sheet from his pocket, flicks it open and flashes it in front. It's the poster displaying our faces.

'I suspected you were on the lam, but this? Is it true? Did you survive the fire?'

We could lie and say the guy is crazy, but I decide to trust Harry.

'Yeah, it's true, sorry.'

'Don't be sorry. I understand. But this is serious bushranging.'

'What'd you say to the traps?'

'Look, they remember you from Roma. I said I had no idea… told them I'd paid you out when the drive ended at Dubbo and that you headed south… best I could do to throw them off your scent.'

'Jesus. Thanks. Hopefully, they'll not want to ride all this way to check.'

'No, but they reckon the chap who claims you're both alive is not beyond doing it.'

We spend a few hours explaining what occurred at Glenrowan and what followed. I believed it went into a bank-safe in Harry's head and he discarded the key.

I've not slept well. We release the cattle for our journey north and not too soon, as far as Dan and I are concerned. The threat from traps, or the shearer, seems even more real in the light of day. We aim at a spot in the featureless horizon and push the cattle mile after mile across the glistening burnished gibbers, locate another landmark and do it again. The heat and dry withers my tongue, cracks my lips, dries any sweat in moments.

A week later the desert presents its other face to us, with a spectacular array of wild flowers along the base of sand dunes. Earlier storms have crossed the region and sparked the transformation.

The dunes are covered in herbage and alight with a delicate plant that Harry says is the Hairy Desert Pea, with its pink to purple, heart-shaped petals. It is the queen of the desert flowers, I decide. Sprinkled through this garden is a plant with a poached-egg flower. Another woody plant has pink, white or purple flowers. I feel like a vandal as I watch the plants churned underfoot by the herd but, from up high, realise how insignificant this damage is in the scale of the endless desert vista. A sea of colour. It makes Melbourne's Gardens, I once thought impressive, a child's playpen. There's something *spiritual*, to borrow a word from Harry, in understanding that this display is witnessed by so few, perhaps presented for non-human reasons.

'It's like a Tibetan monk's mandala,' Harry says. 'Offered not for personal gain, not for posterity, but for the sacred space and moment.'

'I'll take your word for it,' I say. 'It's simply bloody wonderful.'

We plod past.

❖

Weeks into the drive the sweet pick withers under the relentless sun. We are back into the dry zone and the cattle need water. Dan and I ride far ahead of the dusty mob in search of it. In the desert you swear you see vast, shimmering lakes of water, sometimes nearby and, sometimes, way out along the horizon, only to find they dissolve into a mirage – a trick of light, or your parched imagination.

If we take the mob on these pointless excursions, they'll perish of thirst before reaching the next water. That's why we scout ahead. In better country the task is given to the camp cook, but in tough times, key men scout ahead on more mobile arrangements.

We spot, when we crest a low ridge after hours of riding, a tree-covered depression in the stark landscape. I roll my tongue around my dry mouth to moisten it enough to speak.

'Do you think she's real, or another mirage?'

'Could be the real thing: a billabong.'

'Let's have a look.'

I lick my cracked lips, kick the weary horse in the ribs, raise dust from its coat.

We've been up a few dry gullies the past two days, where we ride for hours only to prove it's a mirage, yet now, ride with hopes high. But, as we draw closer and are assured it is real, an eerie moan echoes from the Coolabah stand. I'd heard of the Bunyip, the mythical creature spoken of by the Aboriginal drovers, and always dismissed it. But there is nothing in my experience that can explain this weird noise: something akin to listening to the eerie breathing of a giant creature. I check with Dan.

'What in God's name is that noise?'

'Dunno.'

I squint my dry eyes towards the oasis.

'A Bunyip?… It's coming from over there, in the trees.'

'Sober up, Steve.'

'Might be a blackfella ceremony. I don't want to be the main meal. I've seen the results of being fried. I'm out of here.'

'Won't hurt to have a Captain Cook.'

'You don't know that!'

'We'll sneak in, but piss off at the first sign of trouble,' Dan argues.

I want to give it a miss, turn around, but Dan, always the explorer, insists we continue.

'Fine, but if you get me in the shit again, I'll be back to haunt you.'

We draw our rifles from their holsters, wipe bull-dust from the sights, nudge our dusty horses through the timber-line, into the wall of sound, expecting the worst.

What we witness defies description. It isn't a bunyip, but a shallow billabong about two football fields in size, surrounded by coolabah trees, completely covered by Brolgas, large grey birds with extended necks. Thousands of them dance as a waving grey mass, chattering on like a Country Women's Association morning tea. At different times the grey wave rolls bright-pink as they raise their wings to expose the beautiful under-surface, while dancing a most delicate dance on their spidery legs. We sit there, Dan and I, careful not to disturb them while we soak up this wonderful spectacle. For once, Dan's daring-do has led to an uplifting, enjoyable outcome.

His smile is as wide as a Wangaratta pie, and when he looks at me, I'm sure he recognises my delight. There's no need to speak at moments like this; we communicate clearly, the way our horses do. It's one of the joys of being mates.

When the horses move closer to drink it doesn't faze the birds. They don't fear us because they've had little, to no, contact with horses, to know if they're dangerous. We agree we should avoid using their sanctuary for a cattle camp – to prevent our massive herd destroying it. After an hour in the cool shade, we leave with full water bags to search the shimmering desert. I'm not confident we'll locate other water but we'll try. I turn to Dan.

'That's a type of paradise, mate.'

He nods his head for a moment or two.

'Exactly. Oh, to be so secluded, safe and innocent, as those beauties.'

He summed it up. We need to search for our equivalent of a life like this. I wonder if it's outside our reach.

We break, a day later, in the shade of a giant sand dune. It's been a few weeks since we arrived in the Barcoo, or Cooper's Creek. I examine a sore on my shin, one of many across my body, and scratch the dead flesh away from its oozing core, when I see movement: something way out on the glaring horizon. I point.

'What's that, mate… a mirage?'

'Must be, because I've got no idea what else it could be.'

'Might be another mob, being herded from the south.'

We fall silent and stare at the spot.

'No, Oi think it's horses… It's not a mirage.'

'Don't be bloody stupid. Brumbies out here? You're going desert-loopy.'

'Maybe.'

The objects move towards us across the vast landscape.

'Jesus, there's a bloke sitting on one of them or I'm a possum's uncle.'

'On the lead one? All wavery?'

'Yeah.'

I squint my eyes and stare hard until it dawns on me.

'They're camels. That's what them blighters are: camels.'

Our horses agitate, snort and twitch their ears, as the train approaches. They've never struck camels before, nor have we.

The rider is dark-skinned, covered in a shapeless light robe, with a type of turban on his head. When he smiles, his white teeth reflect the sun and beam stark against his dark complexion. I assume he's an Aborigine but I've never seen one in costume before. I stand and push scarce sticks on the fire in case he wants a brew.

When he reaches us, I tilt my head back to talk to him astride his tall camel, hoping he understands English.

'G'day.'

'Hello sirs,' he replies. He sounds posh, the same as the sentencing Magistrate at Wangaratta. 'To where are you travelling?'

'We're droving a mob of cattle, held about a day's ride over in that direction,' Dan replies, points at an angle to the direction from which our visitor has arrived. 'We're heading up past the Curry, and through Camooweal.'

'Ah, a long way. I've been to the Curry but no further. I'm due in Bedourie within the week with these supplies.'

He gestures to the camel train and their load. Dan moves into the shadow of his tall mount and screws his nose up at its smell.

'Rest your bones and have a brew. We've just boiled up.'

'I'll use your fire but make my own brew, if you don't mind.'

He pokes his riding crop into his mount's shoulder. Mutters some commands in a strange language. The camel appears to buckle at the front into a kneeling position, then, swaying like a water-bag in the wind, eases itself with an almighty groan, and a shower of dust, into a squat on the hot sand before us. The twenty camels in the procession follow.

The rider steps off, then hangs a shoulder bag and his riding crop over the animal's hump. He rattles around in a long, dusty, cloth-covered saddle-bag, fringed with tassels, and extracts a carpet, a colourful pillow, a silver pot and a small sachet of brown powder. He lays the narrow carpet on the fiery sand and sits upon the pillow. He tips the powder into the silver pot, pours water into the base then nestles the pot into the fire.

Dan and I sit open-mouthed, as if we're watching a magician at the Beechworth Show. We live so rough in comparison.

The chap, elegantly taller than Dan or I, sits cross-legged beside us and explains that he's from Afghanistan, delivers supplies to large British holdings scattered across isolated Australia. The deal is, he gets to haul their wool to the coastal markets on the return trip. He speaks perfect English, having been educated in a British school in Afghanistan.

'I was to take an administrative post until I was struck with the travel bug. I'd listened to fellow students' stories about the strange and wonderful places they had witnessed, and took my leave.'

It isn't long before the silver pot burps and gurgles, sends glorious aromas to spark my senses.

'What is that?' I ask, having been too polite to ask earlier.

'Coffee,' he says, as he pours vile-coloured liquid into a small silver cup. 'Would you like some?'

'Yeah, why not? It smells great.'

I hand him the cap of my quart pot, because he's prepared such a small quantity. He pours.

'That's enough, just a taste, thanks.'

He offers some to Dan, who shakes his head vigorously. I take a sip and my face twists, and my stomach squirms, while the liquid is only halfway down my throat. I've tasted strychnine, dog poison an old dingo-trapper talked me into sharing with him one night, and the Afghan's potion tastes far worse.

A polite smile sneaks across our visitor's face.

'An acquired taste, apparently.'

'Jesus, it doesn't taste a bit like it smells.'

'Ah, yes, I do recall as a child living in the Hindu Kush, wondering why someone in their right mind might drink it… Tell me, why aren't you with your herd?'

'Lookin' for water. We're getting desperate.'

'Ah, I see. There is an excellent water hole, about a day's ride north of here, so you're not far off.'

'Great. That's a relief.'

We chat about his customers' properties, and how many trips he has done, and argue camels versus horses, Australian deserts versus Afghan, and wish he would camp for the night, but he insists on moving on.

'Allah willing, I will make that waterhole before morning and rest there.'

He squares-up and looks us in the eye.

'By the way,' he says. 'The police stopped me at Oodnadatta and told me to be on the lookout for two dangerous criminals. Apparently, they're reported dead but rumoured to be alive in the desert. It's a national hunt. Keep your eyes open.'

He hands me a folded piece of paper.

The sun hovers on the horizon and he excuses himself, rolls out a red prayer mat, washes his hands and face, then prostrates himself on the mat for many minutes. We sit in silence, not wishing to stare. It's very different from our Catholic experience.

He finishes his prayers, packs and mounts his camel, and at a single-word command, twenty camels rise. He flashes a smile, waves his riding crop and rides into the sun. Our eyes follow him through the gloom, until the creeping darkness swallows him on the far horizon.

'Cripes, mate. What a lonely life.'

'Yeah, what a fella.'

'He's a real pioneer, that one.'

'Yeah, takes all types, eh?'

'What did he say he was? Oi didn't get it.'

'An Afghan.'

'No, not that... his religion?'

'Err... a Muslim.'

'Muslim, eh? Amazing how he practices it out here, where no one would ever know if he did or he didn't.'

'Yeah. Be strange if you saw one of us Micks kneeling in the sand.'

'True. You'd think the Mick has dropped tuppence, and won't leave until it's found.'

The whole incident is a surprise, a bit like meeting a prophet in the desert, but the prophet doesn't preach, he just *is*. He's comfortable in his own skin, and very brave to face the desert alone. I could learn something – how to be alone. We all could.

I unravel the paper he handed me. Note a police banner on the top. There are photos of Dan and me as youngsters.

'When are these bastards going to stop?'

'That bloody shearer. He must have a lot of influence to re-open a manhunt.'

'We could be out here for a long, long time.'

Dan stands, takes his pistol from his saddle bag.

'Yeah, too long. But I guess we have to do something. Can't hang around.'

'What, shoot the Afghan?'

'No one would find him.'

'Jesus, he's not going to lam on us.'

'Why not?'

'Put yourself in his position. Would you have shown us the poster? Placed yourself in danger, two against one?'

Dan stares back, non-committal. I continue.

'No?... So, he's helping us. He trusts us enough to give us a warning, if he did recognise us.'

We let the camel driver continue unharmed, discuss his visit well into the night.

'You know, Steve, Oi always wanted to travel.'

'You did not. You've never mentioned it.'

'No, Oi did. Listening, as a kid, to the strangers passing through

Ma's shanty made me curious.'

'Where would you go?'

'Anywhere but bloody Ireland.'

'Europe?'

'Aye, Europe. Oi'd really like to go to America. To California. Apparently, it's God's country.'

'I reckon here is God's country.'

'Oi think so too, but we've got 'here', already. We really should think about it. We'd be free of them traps and always lookin' behind.'

'Yeah, that'd be nice.'

'We could go and meet Jesse James and Sitting Bull. We should think about it.'

It isn't something I've ever desired. I feel like I'm being unfaithful to Australia, even thinking about it. But what has Australia ever given us? Nothing.

24

FOLLOWING the Afghan's visit, we're not as surprised when, a day later, a large flock of Pelicans, too many to count, fly overhead, using their large wingspan to ride the thermal currents to the heavens. They're like dinosaurs. It's as if they've visited these sandy shores since before the oceans rolled out, and they're merely repeating what, for millions of years, they've always done. They circle like a drover-less white herd against the blue sky, to check us out, then wheel to head south-east, perhaps to the inland sea. This is in the opposite direction to our route.

Further along the dune-line we locate the Afghan's billabong. It's suitable for a cattle camp and allows us to keep the Brolga's hideout secret. We head back to rejoin Harry and the herd. Perhaps we need to get used to this nomadic lifestyle.

For weeks we've dawdled north through the featureless landscape, across vast heated gibber plains, and along the edge of sand dunes, following green pick or new saltbush. We've moved out of the desert country and spinifex, onto vast Mitchell and Flinders' grass plains, ever closer to civilisation.

Harry makes us aware that we will be moving through the land of the Kalkadoon, a legendary Aboriginal warrior tribe. A pair of our Aboriginal drovers disappeared at Cunnamulla.

'Where have them other fellas gone, You?' Harry asked.

'Back to country, boss.'

'Why?… Sorry business?'

'No boss, don't want to get eaten by Kalkadoons.'

Before this they had, happily, travelled across numerous tribal lands on their way to Dubbo. We take this as an indication of the ferocity and the truth behind the legend.

Station owners tell us that since the Battle Mountain massacre, north-west of Cloncurry, where settlers, police and native troopers armed with muskets killed two hundred spear-carrying warriors, the tribes had retired from hostility. I, for one, breathed more easily for my safety after that news.

On the outskirts of Boulia two of our drovers, whitefellas, pick up Aboriginal women from their riverbank camp.

I thought Harry would have been concerned about this development but he explains to us that many a drover has an Aboriginal woman as a companion.

'They'll drop 'em off at the next town or the women will run away before long.'

'Oh.'

'Some of them make excellent drovers, and pay for their keep that way.'

My weeping sores multiply and annoy me. No matter what I try, I cannot cure myself.

During lunch, despite the sticky flies, I sit nearly naked in the oven-like heat, hoping the sun will heal them, or at least dry the puss and muck, which covers them. The women appear by my side, jabber amongst themselves, point at my red, swollen flesh, then walk into the sand dunes to return with green herbs, plus a few small, yellow bottle-shaped fruit. They make a goo by grinding the herbs with water on a flat rock, and make signs I should put the goo on my sores.

I hesitate, look across at Dan.

'What ya got to lose, mate? Probably ya leg, if ya don't do something.'

That evening, after dinner, they boil the spinach-like herbs in water, indicating I should eat the mash with my corned meat. They hand around some fruit and, again, demonstrate it is something we all should eat. We learn it has a pleasant citrus taste. In two days, my sores begin to dry, and the constipation we all complain of also eases. My affection for the women rises from that day.

'Remember Burke and Wills died from malnutrition out here,' Harry says, '… while these people thrived. They left food for the explorers, who died because they were picky.'

Two days later the women disappear.

❖

'No need ta get your moleskins in a knot, Harry,' says Dan. 'Just give me a reason. We can ride in one night and out next day, from what Oi can tell.'

'Remember Roma? The court-case?'

'Yeah.'

'Well, it was here, outside Longreach, that I duffed the mob, along with the 'white bull' I got charged for stealing, when they caught up with me in South Australia.'

'Yeah, but you was cleared for that.'

'True, but not in the minds of people in this town. I also left a girlfriend on bad terms here,' he says, quietly, a look washing across his face reminiscent of a soppy-eyed puppy chastising itself for stealing corn-beef off the table.

'Ah!… Well, she would have forgotten you by now, surely?'

'Umm, if she has, then her husband hasn't.'

Harry looks sheepish. It makes the rest of us smirk at the thought of the great Harry Readford, bold bushranger, being run out of town by an irate husband.

'How come it all blew up?'

'The woman was married to a prominent member of the Longreach Club, discovered I was two-timing her with the young wife of another member. She kicked up a ruckus at the club and all hell broke loose. Women and hard grog don't mix, I tell ya.'

He removes his Stetson and wipes the pickling sweat from his brow with the back of his huge hand. The flies, disturbed, don't know where to land.

Dan slips me a wink.

'Ah, Oi see.'

'On top of that, stealing the cattle, and being cleared of any wrongdoing, was too much for the town. I… I won't go back.'

There is a saying on the isolated stations, whenever a bitch has inexplicably coloured or mixed-breed puppies, that it 'must have been the drover's dog'. Sometimes, the drover gets blamed for a host of other maladies; lost tools, open gates, fences down, and unplanned children included. As a consequence of Harry's reputation, and in accordance with his wishes, we steer a wide berth of Longreach and, coincidently, the chance for a piss-up to slake the almighty thirst we've developed after months in the desert.

Harry sends one of the senior drovers and the cook into the mining township of Cloncurry for supplies. The drover is to ensure the cook stays off the grog.

That afternoon, as we wait for their return, we witness the power of the great almighty. Storm clouds gather on the horizon to hover menacingly above the rust-red ridges where whispy, white gums add ghostly contrast to the darkening sky. I point to direct Dan's attention.

'Them gums look like they're alive.'

As the clouds move, the trees appear to dance, to shimmer and wave their white arms festooned with ceremonial lettuce-green wreaths, to the storm's beat. Dan nods.

'I see what you mean.'

I look across and both You and Len are cantering to the cook's wagon.

'What's up with them?'

Lightning tears across the heavens in a white and yellow sheet, strikes a giant bolt into the copper-laden hills. Its thunder boom wipes out my answer. The acrid sulphur smell fills my nostrils. I see

Len and You beneath the wagon.

The wind roars, blows spinifex everywhere. I turn my face to shield it from the biting dust. The lightning and cloud pass in minutes. It's dramatic theatre, produces barely a shower, yet the relief from the heat, the cool of the raindrops against my dust-filled skin, the drama of the event, are worth every inconvenience.

The boys emerge from beneath the wagon and gallop away. What's up? The herd has spooked and roars along the narrow valley between the ruptured landscape. Dan and I spur our horses and take pursuit along the ridge above. We realise Harry and his dogs are on the opposite ridge, about to turn the herd. It swings up our ridge; ominous danger of stampede. But the dogs have its measure, and slow it enough for us to get ahead and, with whips cracking, we turn it in upon itself.

Harry joins us, quite pale.

'They spooked like Len and You,' he says, through heavy breaths, '… they'll get used to it.'

We roll a smoke to settle our nerves while we watch the swirling herd sort itself ready for the track.

The cattle do get used to the storms. Len and You however, remain obviously uncomfortable.

'Debil in them clouds,' they explain.

Nothing we say convinces them otherwise.

The rest of us look forward to the cool relief of the afternoons as we move our sluggish herd like a muddy-flood through that country. We have to remain on our guard most afternoons during the rainy season, but it adds adventure.

25

WE reach Camooweal, on the Georgina River, pleased to learn that we're outside the storm zone. Harry is advised by the station owner to take two of the local Aboriginal women with us, to act as guides. The owner believes they are more reliable than some of the men, and their presence on his station causes conflicts among the young men, so he's happy to offload them.

'Getting the gins out of the way for a while will help settle things,' he argues.

The women arrive dressed in men's gear and, from a distance, and even up close, under their broad-brimmed Stetsons, are indistinguishable from other drovers.

'I suppose we'll be doing twice the work, now,' Dan complains.

'Maybe, but Harry and the station owner know their business,' I reply. 'Perhaps they can cook and give us a break from Cooky's muck.'

I say it quietly, because the last thing I want to do is to get the cook offside and starve.

The recruits prove invaluable in locating waterholes in the inhospitable country, and tracking wayward stock over rocky terrain. They are competent riders and bushies. We pass them off as "boys" to avoid comment from visitors or observers. I'm told it's a tradition widespread among drovers. The power of clothes to deceive.

For weeks we wander vast plains with barely a tree to break the hot monotony. We've not sighted another human being, or even a reminder of their presence. We round a gully to confront a lone, elderly Aboriginal man in the dust beneath a stunted wisp of a tree. He's just skin and bones, with a white line painted down the centre

172

of his body. Flies swarm his shoulders. Harry calls the "boys" to his side, and the rest of us gather, curious.

'Chances are the old man is loco, on pituri, or dying from a whitefella's disease,' Harry says.

'It could be a trap. He might be a stalking horse, to divert our attention to trigger an ambush?' suggests Darcy Ingham, a whitefella.

Our minds work overtime, fuelled by earlier campfire discussions about the Aboriginal warrior's ability to "shift change", or camouflage themselves to ambush their enemy, or to mesmerise their victims so they fail to sense the warriors until they feel a spear force its way past their ribs. Our hands hover above our pistols and I search about nervously, in spite of believing that it's ridiculous because there is absolutely nowhere for anyone to hide.

Harry rides closer to the "boys".

'Should we go over to the old fella?'

'No boss.'

'Should you go over?'

'No boss. Leave 'im alone.'

'He might need help.'

'No boss. Best leave 'im, that one.'

'Why? He seems harmless enough.'

'Him Kadaicha.'

'Kadaicha?'

'Yeah. Sorcerer. Spirit man.'

'Danger?'

'Can be boss.'

'What's he do?'

'He can heal sick, has medicine; and he can punish. Even sing 'em bad person to death. Point bone.'

'Ah,' Harry says, as if he understands.

'We leave him alone, then?'

'Yeah, it best, boss.'

'All right then.'

'He probably hunting someone.'

'A person?'

'Yeah, someone who broke the law. He never give up, that fella.'

We lift our reins, nudge our horse's ribs to join the mob, leave the frail silver-haired man naked and alone on the barren ridge. Dan rides on the point closest to him and, as he passes, the Kadaicha raises his thin arm to point a long bony finger at him and continues to do so, even as he disappears from view.

That night I can't scratch the old man from my mind. At times, I too, feel as if life has left me behind, left me to wander in the wilderness like a wandering spirit; neither at home in my body or in the company of man.

'It seems so cruel to leave that man alone,' I say to the boys, over a brew.

'He always alone, that Kadaicha fella.'

'That's even sadder, still. A wandering soul,' I say.

'His job is to be alone.'

'No family?'

'Not his own… He widow-man.'

'Ah, widowed? Lost his wife?'

'No, when man in tribe lose his wife, husband not allowed to go to any other woman for a long time, until ceremony to make it good. That wife's spirit goes to Kadaicha and he can comfort husband.'

In some ways it's a revelation that this culture has lore, perhaps sacred ways, of dealing with human desire. I have so many questions to ask I'm nearly beside myself, but I know these women either will not have, or will not provide, the answers, so hold my silence.

Harry changes the subject by recounting a tale about how he was forced to make the decision to kill, or leave, a faithful, but ill, horse, on his well-known Adelaide drive.

'I aimed my rifle at this poor horse and although I could see it was wasting away, I couldn't bring myself to shoot it. How was I to know what, or when, the end would be?' he says. 'I left it for the fates to decide. For all I know the horse is still out there with the wild herds.'

The conversation centres around lame, ill, dangerous horses until we hit the swags. By morning I've practically forgotten the Kadaicha, but Dan hasn't.

'He pointed at me as if he'd singled me out, knew me,' he says, across his horse's back as we saddle up.

'He's just a crazy old man.'

'No, I tell you. He's a hunter. He knows we're on the lam.'

Flies swarmed around his cracked lips.

'Well, he's gone now.'

'The lop-eared shearer may have hired him?'

'Oh bullshit Dan. The shearer's sniffing up his own tail over on the coast.'

I sound confident but I'm not. That sense of being hunted returns in a cloying flash. A man on the lam doesn't need a real hunter to feel threatened, tormented or stalked. Many puppeteers pull those inner-strings to make the puppet dance to a sick, sick tune.

I don't know when it dawns on the boys that our large herd destroys the Aboriginal watering sites, making it impossible for local tribes to survive. I twig to it when I watch their faces writhe with concern as the cattle trample a beautiful sand-soak into oblivion.

Further north-west we pass over an escarpment of exposed rock for many, many days. The cattle are footsore from the hard ground, but also desperately thirsty. My lips are cracked and sore from dehydration and sunburn.

Harry argues with the boys, uses his hands to remonstrate.

'There must be water nearby.'

'No water, boss. All gone.'

'There must be – all the kangaroos are fat and happy.'

'Long way that one,' they argue with downturned eyes.

Ellin draws an arc in the dust with the toe of her boot, scrapes a short line across it at the end.

'If we don't find water in the next twenty-four hours many of the herd will die. Longer, and we'll lose most of them.'

Already, the herd has split because the weak find it more difficult to keep up. We are paid by the head delivered, so it affects us all. 'If I learn you're lying about water, I'll shoot you, right?' Harry shouts, his voice husky from thirst. He turns his horse and rides after the mob, doesn't look back.

We are as shocked as the boys at his anger. We pull some faces to let them know we noticed, before we, too, plod after the herd, our horses unresponsive because of thirst. I don't even brush the flies from my lips.

First, one bullock, then another, buckles and refuses to rise. We leave a trail of dying behind us stretching for miles. We see the crows hover ready to pluck out their eyes before they die.

Near dusk, Cynthia, the other boy, rides back to Harry with a change of direction.

'Why change course?'

'Signs tell us dry water that way, 'arry.'

'What do you mean, signs?'

'Messages left by the old people.'

'What do you mean by dry water?'

'In big dry, waterhole might still be there.'

'You're not sure?'

Cynthia shakes her head, dislodges flies from her hat.

We wheel the mob and just as the sun sets, the bullocks at the front of the herd walk faster, break into a jog, raise dust as we crest a ridge, then flow at a jog into a long waterhole saddled in the rock-gully below.

We join the cattle; take long swigs of water from the folded brim of our hats. Dan's so excited he flounders in, immerses himself in the deep. It seems silly not to join him. We splash and frolic like ghostly brolgas beside the mud-coloured herd; for a moment, happy.

The boys direct us only to large waterholes, and even then, reluctantly. There are times when the herd goes without water but is sustained by local runoff from the occasional storm.

Harry returns from scouting at lunch-time, to find us beneath a small, shrubby tree, eating Cooky's stew. He ties his horse to the cart and fronts the boys.

'I just come back from east of here.'

He points off at a right-angle to the herd's direction.

'There's a small waterhole barely half a mile away.'

The boys keep their heads down, look at a space between their crossed legs.

'What do ya think I am. An idiot?' His voice rises.

The boys remain rock-still and silent.

'Well, do ya?… Think I'm an idiot?'

Harry swipes Cynthia's dusty hat from her head with his open hand. Flies rise like an angry swarm.

'Talk, boy!'

I'm on my feet before I realise it. The child in me responds as if I'm hit.

'Steady, Harry.'

'They're gammin us.'

'Bigger water ahead,' Cynthia murmurs, barely audible.

'What did she say?'

'There's better, more water ahead.'

He points east again.

'What's wrong with that water?'

'That one sacred,' she says, just as quietly, and doesn't lift her head.

He looks at her, looks at Ellin. Puts his hands on his hips, shakes his head, then walks with a stiffened gait across to Cooky's cart to dish himself lunch.

I can't blame them for protecting their country and society, for which I have growing admiration, having witnessed the challenge of living in this arid hot-box.

❖

I lie on my back in the darkness, on a large flat rock, well beyond the fire-light where Dan and the rest of the team play cards. For months the boys have guided us by the stars across featureless country and I stare into the sparkling skyscape attempting to make sense of it; mesmerised by the sheer scale. The stars swirl, appear so much closer in the clear desert air, their light nearly extinguishing the dark backdrop they dance upon. Cynthia glides over and sits beside me to bum a rollie. I smell the tobacco smoke as she exhales.

'You see the old emu?'

I sit up and search around. *What? Is another of her uncanny powers an ability to see in the pitch dark?*

She chuckles quietly. Points.

'No… up in the sky… the stars. See?'

I follow her outstretched finger. I look but cannot see.

'See… her pointed head, the long neck, the fat body… the bent legs,' she says, as her finger traces a form across the sky.

'Agh, not quite.'

I roll closer to her so I can sight along her arm. She repeats the description.

'Oh, yes! I see it. Amazing.'

'Over there… kangaroo?'

'My God, yes.'

'And, there, yellow belly.'

She makes the shape of the fish.

At this point she lies back and points out a few more. I'm struck by how small we are and how each of us is confined to the same canoe, to float along this highway of darkness and speckled light. I reach across and take her free hand and hold it in the space between us. It's warm and soft, and I think I should never let it go. I hear the swirling mass of stars hum in the night sky in rhythm to my heart.

Seeing my interest, the boys, each night, try to teach me the stars and constellations, using local objects, which are a perfect description of our sky. As hard as I try, I can't remember their words for them. They chuckle at my attempts to pronounce the words in language, reassure me they don't take umbrage.

Unlike the words, though, the local images stick. Far better than the double-Dutch of Greek signs. Knowing these new icons, I never look at a rock-art gallery in the same way. I see the sky captured on those ceilings, like a nun might leave an atlas of the world on the blackboard to promote learning.

Each morning the boys give Harry a bearing on the horizon, a landmark to guide him, before they steer the herd in that direction. It's uncanny. Better navigators than Cook, Harry reckons.

I think about my direction. Can I afford to have plans, a future, to think of where I've been? We seem to have shaken the drover. For the first time in ages, I begin to hope.

I feel a sense of relief upon sighting Brunette Creek.

Day after day, and mile after agonisingly slow mile, we've plodded our dusty way west, behind the herd, in hot and in cold weather and, occasionally, through thunderstorms, but mostly under a relentless sun, to reach Brunette Downs.

I'm excited to see the bones of a new homestead stand proud on a low fractured-rock ridge above the flood-line of the glistening creek. Stunted trees nearby have debris perched high in their branches, to remind us of the wild monsoon floods, which must pour past here; in places, kilometres wide. I imagine a garden and lawns, sweeping down to the river from the house, making it even more habitable.

The homestead's galvanised-iron roof reflects the sunlight but, as yet, has no walls. A metal tank on the roof adds an otherworldly effect. In a deep saw-pit, men sweat to cut the wall-timbers, with cross-cut saws, to clothe its frame. I hear their noisy conversations while they work. Another workgroup toils to erect a stone fireplace with chimney, for the station kitchen. It will be a grand homestead and a permanent reminder of civilisation in this untamed landscape.

We build a temporary holding paddock. Then, after a head-count done in our presence, because we are paid by the beast, Harry pays us out.

We organise a big drink under a brush lean-to. I'm sad to see our team bust-up. We've crossed a lot of dry and wet gullies together. Young or old, black or white, man or woman, animal or human, they're my friends.

Harry drags Dan and me aside to discuss something before the grog smashes us.

'What are your plans, boys?'

'Thought we might head back to New South Wales and go shearing,' Dan replies.

'Well, if you've a mind to hang around, I'd like you to stay on and help us build this place. I've been offered the Manager's job, and I'd appreciate having you two as back-up.'

'Ah. Okay… as ringers?'

'Overseers. We'll build you a hut when the homestead is finished. Think about it. You're out of the way here. Away from the long reach of the law.'

The next day, after the alcohol clears, we let him know that we'll stay. I enjoy Harry's temperament compared to Ned's. He's forceful when he needs to be but, generally, is of good cheer, and inclusive. I have learned a lot under his tutelage and become more comfortable in my own skin, feel less need to promote myself and to operate at breakneck pace. Even Dan appears to have calmed.

Our overseer's hut stands pristine beside a rock outcrop. It has taken a couple of months but, at last, a reality. A ringers' hut sits further away from the homestead, and out of sight. Dan and I have settled in to station life. Harry has kept Ellin and Cynthia on the payroll and they've become capable domestics under the guidance of a station cook. Their quarters are attached to the homestead.

It is the most settled I've ever felt – safe and secure – whereas, while droving I felt safe, but not necessarily secure, due to our nomadic existence.

I do most of the household duties, because I'm desperate for order. While we eat most meals over at the big house, I enjoy, at times, to cook for us, alone. I love to carve a roast, or a juicy piece of corned beef, fresh from the camp oven. The best I get in appreciation is, 'Any more left?' from Dan, but I can live with that.

Some nights I wear my special clothes and, while I haven't come out about my strange need, I suspect that others in our community are aware of my habit. The two women, Ellin and Cynthia, especially, because they spend most of their spare time outdoors in the shade, or in the cool air of the evening, and don't miss a trick. But no one comments. I wash those clothes in secret. When I wear my costume another person hovers. I call her Mona, but only have glimpses as to the part she plays in my life. We live in a cocoon and we all have our demons, and understand the prospect of their existence in others.

Dan and I seldom argue. It's as if we've matured. There are some days we hardly speak, so well do we know each other, and so comfortable are we in the company of the other. If he dallies with the Aboriginal women, I haven't noticed. But he does say he misses women's company and, often, shouts out loud that he 'needs a root', as he puts it. I bite my tongue. As I say: we are safe and it is more than we can expect.

I look across at the women half-hidden beneath the vines that traipse along the homestead veranda. I see the red glow of Ellin's fag wax and wane in the darkness as she draws upon it. I watch her flick the butt across the dusty house yard and return inside, extinguish her lamp-light.

Dan has long been asleep and it is as if I have the world to myself. I recall standing for a while, after, but have no memory of sliding into my bunk.

I'm choking. Someone is astride my chest with hands around my throat and is squeezing. I squirm, thrash about. They're naked. I feel their bare arse brush my bare thighs as I attempt to dislodge them. I open my eyes and it's Ellin, her wonderful face and long hair obvious in the moonlight. I can't buck her off and she has me tight by the throat, so I can't breathe. She should release me – immediately. I'm terrified, yet, I feel such desire. Please, Ellin, release me!

It's not Ellin. It's the Kadaicha man with face painted white, who points the long bony finger of his free hand directly into my eyes. I can't breathe: hard as I try. I don't want to die. It's not a finger… it's a pointed bone-knife and now the Kadaicha inserts it below my ribs, his hand follows to remove my liver. Blood spills, steals my desire. My desire for life.

I scream but no sound emerges. I shake my head and spy the lop-eared drover leer over the Kadaicha's shoulder, laugh with revenge as I take my last breath.

'Steve, Steve.'

'What do ya want ya prick. How'd ya find me?'

'Steve. Wake. You're having a dream.'

Dan's face hovers above me. I'm a lather of sweat; my sheet is twirled around my legs.

'Shit. The shearer had me. It's a bad sign.'

'Just another dream, mate.'

Perhaps it's a sign to move on. I don't ever want a nightmare like that again. Truth is I've had a few.

Harry informs us he's leaving Brunette Downs to move east towards the gulf. He's purchased a property called Corella Downs.

'I want you two fellows with me. We've worked together all these years and I count on you now.'

'It'll be hard to give up this place.'

'Yeah, but I've a chance to make my own way.'

'I guess that's a big pull for you, alright.'

'We'll set her up similar to here,' he says.

Dan and I talk it over and agree to join him in his latest venture.

We've helped Harry develop his property from scratch, like we did at Brunette Downs, and drawn great satisfaction from doing it.

Harry has read in the southern newspapers, which we get twice a year, that the colonies have attempted to join together, to end tariffs that strangle the nation. Key politicians in 1989 rattled the drum, concerned to unite the colonies to repel prospective invasion by hostile European nations and to support a referendum, to decide the form of any Federation. There's a stoush in South Africa, wherever that is. None of it appears relevant to us up here.

Harry lies the paper flat. Shakes his head, oozes cynicism.

'Some fat capitalist will have their hand out, somewhere, if they're looking for the Colonies to change.'

He has to explain to me what a capitalist is. I can't see the difference between that and what the squatters, and Harry himself, practice.

Harry's herd has grown and I've watched him, like his herd, grow fatter and richer. He's built a stylish homestead, and a hut for us, nearby. The "boys" have joined us from Brunette Downs. One morning they just appeared at the homestead. We were pleased to see them and they set about putting order into the household.

One piece of information they passed on troubled us. Gracie handed me a piece of paper.

'A tall fella arrived at the Downs lookin' for you boys. He say you bushrangers – both of you.'

I open the sheet of paper and it's the poster.

'Yeah, we were in trouble when we was youngsters, but we've changed… What happened?'

'Says the police huntin' ya and we had to tell him where you went.'

'Did you?'

'No. The boss was out on camp, so we played Myall, pretended to have only little bit English. He got cranky and Jimmy, the old trapper… you remember him? He stepped in with his rifle.'

'Sorry, Gracie.'

'Fella said he'd be back but we never see him. He looked pretty crook. Barcoo rot I bet. Jimmy followed him for couple of days. He was heading to coast, but I reckon he be lucky to get there, he so crook.'

I let Dan know but we didn't panic. We settled into familiar patterns.

By now, though, nearing the turn of the century, Dan and I suffer itchy feet and are tired of this isolated lifestyle. If truth be told, Dan has itchy feet and this unsettles me. Perhaps my thinking has changed regarding a merry life, and, now, I seek a safe one.

So, eighteen years after our death at Glenrowan and no longer boys, we discuss parting ways with Starlight. The shearer might return, and Dan's worried about his old ma being without menfolk and wants to drop some money off to her at Greta, and assure her he's still alive.

He goes on and on about it, I'm ready to cut out his voice-box. He reckons we can try to find the saddlebags of jewellery and gold Ned stashed, and give that to our families, or set ourselves up somewhere safe.

'Do you know where to look?'

'Oi've got an idea.'

'Did ya actually see him put them there?'

'No. You remember when he did it.'

'Is it in a building?'

'No, in a paddock.'

'Then it'd be like finding a needle in a haystack.'

I am of two minds. First, will a visit stir up old memories and cause a shock to his old ma? And, second, can we trust that tongues will not wag? I'm against it but Dan is determined.

Why don't I have these feelings for home, for family? It worries me, my self-containment.

Dan's ma, Ellen Kelly, is a force to be reckoned with, and was 'front and centre' in the boy's life. There was no father to guide him, so Ellen was it. But Ellen is needy and, sometimes, the poddy has to parent the cow. The boys, Ned and Dan, glued to her a bit unnatural. With Ned gone she plays on Dan's mind in a way my folks, who are much older and distant, don't play on mine. Besides, I have him. He's my family and it cuts me something fierce that he doesn't feel the same way. What are we to do? Do as Dan desires?

26

'YOU'RE not really leaving, are you fellas?'

'Yeah, Harry, for real this time. Oi told Fred I have to catch up with me ma.'

'Understood! You know I'll miss you, and there's always a spot here, if you get bored down there.'

'We know, Harry. There's a lot of us remains here. Old 'Music' is buried beside the creek; we've sweat beside every post in those cattle yards. We helped select most of the cattle,' I add.

'True.'

'You're established and can manage without us. So, a good time to leave, Oi believe.'

'We'll survive,' Harry says, so quietly I can barely hear him.

He looks away for a long moment before he continues

'Sorry, fellas… there's been a lot unspoken between us, and I guess I always thought we'd have more time to say it. But you've been like sons to me, and I really mean it when I say you're going to be missed. I know what has happened in your previous life. It's a bastard but, take it from me, it's forged your characters into steel, which will stand you in good stead wherever you find yourselves. Now get on ya horse and piss off, before I blubber.'

We shake his hand then mount-up.

'Our pay is held in accounts with the Bank of New South Wales, you say?'

'Yep, just give 'em that number I wrote down for you last night.'

'All good, then. Bye.'

I look around. The two "boys" are on the veranda and I give them a heartfelt wave as we ride away. Harry stands in the yard for a long time; watches us disappear.

We are at Armidale, New South Wales. It's my birthday and we locate a hotel to celebrate. A date, carved into the capstone above the door, shows the pub was built thirty-six years ago, in 1863, four years after I was born. A sandstone building, two-stories high, walls and gutters in need of paint, made me think it was older. Like me, it's had a hard life.

Tobacco smoke fills our nostrils and the warmth from two roaring brick fireplaces wraps around our exposed faces as, hat in hand, we cross the stoop. The pub is packed with drinkers. The noise deafens us, so unused are we to socialising. But the commotion ceases the moment we enter. We hear an old man tell someone at the rear of the room that he should leave, because his 'missus will have his dinner ready'.

Baulked at the entrance, we stick-out like warts on the end of a nose. A roomful of khaki-uniformed men stare at us. Convinced we've walked into a den of traps or troopers, my knees buckle slightly. I nudge Dan forward and we edge to the bar. The conversations around us resume. Whew!

I front a gnarled string-bean serving behind the counter.

'Two beers please, mate.'

He pours two beers, leans his head at the angle of the tap's lever as he concentrates on pouring, straightens it whenever he releases the handle to manage the foam, only to lean again as the liquid spouts.

'Is it a policeman's party?' I ask, using my head to point at the tables of uniforms, not wishing to be noticed.

'No, not police… volunteers, for military service.'

'Oh.'

He returns his head to the vertical, which indicates - beers poured. I pay and follow Dan to a seat at the rear, where we drink in the scene. We may have passed the odd comment about what we witness – many loud, very drunk young men, playing pranks, dealing cards – we may have smiled too broadly at the wrong time: I'm not sure.

Whatever we did, or did not do, something encourages a uniformed bloke, full of piss and wind, to bowl up to me before I've even finished me beer, and with his jaw extended, ask in a challenging tone, to the merriment of his military mates.

'What are you poofters looking at?'

'Nothing cobber, just havin' a quiet drink with me mate,' I say, holding his eye and trying a friendly smile.

I hear the challenge in his tone. I hate his accusation but I don't want a fight. He isn't much taller than me, although the uniform makes him look bigger.

'This ain't a ladies' bar,' he wisecracks.

Dan rises to his feet before I can answer.

'Well, how'd you get in here then, squirt?'

'Don't call me squirt,' says the uniform, and pushes at Dan's chest. Dan lashes out with a crisp right, and drops him.

Dan faces the mob.

'Who's next?'

I stand, and push back my chair, half-stumble in the process.

Another youngster singles me out but, even by the way he shapes-up, I can tell he'll only win by a lucky punch. I drop my chin low into my shoulder to protect my pretty face and step towards him as he swings a haymaker, which glances off my skull. Pain registers across his face. Probably broke his hand. Despite the buzz in my head, I hit him with a straight one-two before he's realised it. He, too, drops to the ground. These guys are nothing compared to a spar with Ned.

A pair of khaki-clad giants, brothers, judging by their size and prominent teeth, push through the crowd; shape-up. We're in for a hiding, unless a miracle happens, because even if we flatten these two, others will keep coming. Here I am, again, in too deep, out of control and in danger, because bloody Dan can't think further ahead than his temper. I back up and we collide, stand back-to-back. This hiding is going to hurt.

Just then a shot rings out and a booming voice, shouts, 'Ten-shun,' at a volume that shakes the cobwebs in the hotel ceiling.

The uniforms jump to their feet, as if a brown snake has been thrown on the floor beneath them, and snap to attention. The largest man I have ever seen storms across the room, and fronts the frozen ranks. Three white stripes on his jacket sleeves stand out against the khaki and his angry, red face. A slim officer wearing a peaked, brightly-badged cap and sporting a row of shining brass pips on each uniformed shoulder, follows close behind.

'You men are a disgrace,' the giant starts, as if hailing through a megaphone. 'Leave your fighting until we get to Africa or you'll have me to answer to… Get those two out of here,' he orders, pointing to the chaps lying on the floor.

Two men, a single stripe on their sleeves, step forward and drag the wounded soldiers outside. Dan and I remain shaped to fight, in case we've misread the situation.

The smaller officer approaches.

'Sorry about that, chaps.' The thin moustache above his top lip barely moves while he speaks. It's as if he strains each word through his teeth for fear of being too exuberant. 'They're feeling their oats. They've been training to fight the Boer, and have had no outlet.'

We don't react, except, perhaps, alter our stance, lower our hands slightly.

'Can I buy you men a drink?'

Now, there's fighting words.

'Sure, fella,' I say, deliberately not wanting to acknowledge his rank or social order. I know Dan can't speak because his dander is riled, and it will take a while to hose him down.

'I'm Colonel Townsend and I'm in charge of this Brigade. We're off to Africa to help the Brits, tidy-up this war.'

'What war? I haven't heard about a war,' I say.

'Where have you roosters been? There's a war alright and we need all the good men we can get. It would be grand to have mature blokes, such as yourselves, along to provide leadership for the youngsters. That's if you're interested?'

'Thanks Colonel, we'll think it over.'

I certainly don't intend to.

We return to our table. Dan breasts the bar for the promised round. The string-bean barman has his back turned reading a poster on the wall.

He turns, catches Dan peering over his shoulder.

'Oh, there you are. I've sent someone to fetch the police. They should be here soon to see if you two want to press charges.'

Dan nods, points to the poster.

'Looks like a wanted poster.'

'Yeah, it is. Reward for information on two fellas from the Kelly gang.'

'Is it, b'jeesus?'

'Yeah. Some Victorian keeps riding through stirring the police up, warning them that the Kellies will pass through. Must have some influence.'

Dan squeezes through the crowd to our table.

'Our wanted poster is on the wall.'

'Jeesus.'

'My thoughts exactly. The traps are on their way so let's get outa here.'

We down our beer like a croc swallows a water-hen, and crack out through the back door. Our decision is made for us. We're off to Africa.

It may not be all bad. It could even be a bit of a lark, fighting for crown and country, that is if it isn't over before we get there.

Another beauty is, you get to take your own horse, and sail to Cape Town. I am game for adventure and, when Dan is shown how to mail money to his ma, so is he – we sign up.

We've travelled with the Brigade to Victoria Barracks in Paddington, Sydney. We bivouacked a couple of times on the way to learn the basics of army life, such as horse drills to ensure we can march straight, march as a column, line abreast or wheel as one. We learnt to shoot from a moving horse, and make a full charge, that type of stuff.

It may have been important for soldiering, but we travelled too slow if the police are onto us; if the barman did recognise us and wanted a share of the reward. I didn't sleep at night. Dan was cranky. I, honestly, thought we'd been out of circulation so long, we'd dropped off the traps' memory, so seeing the poster was a shock.

'Oi wish I'd shot the bastard, back at Bell Ridge,'

'Yeah, I wake up with the sweats most nights, since Armidale.'

'Me too. I'd forgotten what it's like.'

'I didn't realise we'd have to shave our beards to serve. We look more like the poster photos now,' I say, as I stare into barrack bathroom mirrors.

We parade down George Street all spit and polish.

I must say I like the attention. Folks worshipped Ned, and I got a kick out of that, but after years as a fugitive, it feels wonderful to contribute to society. As we parade, the office girls cheer from the pavement and the children wave and stretch-out to pat the horses. I can't stop grinning in spite of trying to act tough and aloof. It's like a big party and we don't see anything solemn in the occasion.

Following the farewell parade, we're granted two day's leave. Dan wants to hang with other troopers, so we sweep like a small band of brown, ground pigeons through the city proper, on our way to the racetrack. We have a choice of race meetings but settle on Randwick. We ride the new electric trams, impressed with its lighter carriage and fresher smell, than the heavy, smoke-engulfed Melbourne steam trams we'd, previously, ridden.

Dan bets and wins and, with a few too many beers under our belt, conversations turn to adventure, possible death, lack of having lived life, dying a virgin. The group decide it's a life-or-death necessity to get a 'root' down at the Rocks, or up at King's Cross. So, a root it is.

We aren't the first to be concerned about our mortality. There's a long line of our lads outside a two-story knockin' shop and, inside, it's packed to the smoke-filled rafters with noisy, randy troopers. All enjoy the sly grog and the SP bookmaking service, while they wait their turn. Some lads joke about a concerted bayonet attack, such is their anticipation.

If we want a particular girl, perhaps the most beautiful, we are advised it could take hours. Eager puppies ahead of us have booked 'seconds', which adds to the jam. It's decided we aren't fussy and order 'one off the rack', as one of our chaps from a drapery business jokes. One of the veterinarians, sent to check the girls for diseases, is surrounded by chaps for advice as to 'clean' choices. Various 'girls' parade through the room at different times in flimsy lingerie, call the name of the next candidate.

'Bluey Coote!'

'Tom Raggsdale. Oh, there you are Tom? My, you're a handsome one.'

When my name is called, I stand, to be fronted by a pleasant looking woman about my own age.

'You Fred?'

'Yep.'

She takes my limp hand.

'Follow me, sweetheart.'

We push through the throng. She leads. I sweat and the lack of saliva makes my tongue stick to the roof of my mouth. I pant, silent, tip of my tongue protruding like my sister's cat pants on a scorching day, as I mount the stairs.

'Here we are, me lovely.'

She leads me into a small stable-style room with air vents: narrow windows along the top of each wall. I hear a drunken laugh, a bed squeak, flesh slap against flesh in the next room. I smell perfume and sweat, notice an unmade bed. I'm so anxious I stand rigid as a soldier on guard. The woman moves closer, begins to undo my webbing. This is moving too fast.

'C-c-c-can we have a m-m-minute?'

'Sure, sweetie, but you only have fifteen.'

'I… I… thought we'd warm up.'

'That's what I was doing, sweetie, warming you up.'

'D-d-d-d-don't you hug and stuff?'

'I don't kiss, if that's what you mean? Here… maybe if you inspect the goods, that will help.'

She loosens her robe, exposes her lingerie, places a hand beneath each breast and lifts as she sways her hips. I sit on the unmade bed, its sheets covered with numerous moist spots, and watch her, or more particularly, her sensuous underclothes.

'Why don't you kiss?' I ask.

My eyes remain rooted to the white frill, hedging the edges of her red-silk panties. I'm mesmerised. She weighs up whether to answer.

'I stay faithful to my husband. He's the only one I kiss, that way… On the mouth… lips apart.'

I raise my eyes. Perhaps the surprise shows in my face.

'I've had, probably, thirty of you fellows today. Imagine if I'd kissed all of you. It's too close... kissing. It would mess me head up.'

She removes her bra and is about to throw it on a stool, perched over two small ceramic bowls, containing fluids.

'Don't,' I say. 'Pass it here... the bra. Thanks.'

I press it against my cheek, while she removes her panties, which I also gather and hold to my face. It's a glorious moment.

She stands before me fluffing the hair on her female part. I'm interested to learn that it lies between her legs and not half-way up her stomach, as I've imagined.

'You're a strange one, aren't you?' she says, as she leans in and draws my head towards her breasts.

The erection I'd noticed emerging as I'd fingered the underwear, subsides. She tugs at her panties as if to remove them from my grasp.

'I've never seen clothes… so… so fine,' I say.

'Umm… very strange, indeed,' she says, while she rubs her breasts against my face.

'It may be all over for some fellows by now. A little tug and they're gone, before they even get inside me,' she offers, moving her hands up and down in a polishing gesture. 'That's desire.'

'Mm maybe I am strange,' I say. 'It's not how I imagined it.'

'What?'

'The set up.'

I rake my eyes about the room, the bowls, her body, the bed. She watches me with head tilted and lips pursed, as if to say 'loopy'.

'Perhaps next time,' I murmur.

'Okay my lovely. Time's up,' she says, then kisses me on the top of my head, making a disappointed face, suggesting she has failed as a professional in the same way I, perhaps, have failed as a man.

She reaches out to reclaim her panties. I tug them away then hand them over. In the waiting room I realise I should have offered to purchase them. *Next time*, I muse, to comfort myself. *Next time I might give it a go with a woman. It can't be that difficult?*

As we recount the day's adventures, I lie. The more embellished the trooper's stories the more hopeless I feel. I lie awake, and wonder what adventures lie ahead. How will we deal with weeks at sea and the bloody war, which seems to favour the enemy, if one is to read between the lines of despatches from the front? Will I, also, fail as a soldier? Not be up to it?

27

SHOWERS blown in from sea greet us as we fall into line for reveille and roll-call. It's 18 March, 1890. We're off to Africa.

We pass inspection and deliver our horses at the dock for loading, then assemble in the departure lounge for clearance to board. Dan notices two waist-coated civvies behind the counter with papers in hand, arguing like two spiv bookie's clerks at the races. At times, they stare at us beneath concerned brows.

'What do you think those jokers are on about?' Dan mutters.

'No friggin' idea.'

At the embarkation gate the Immigration Officer orders us to a side room. Moments later the colonel joins the clerks. All three stare at the paperwork, argue.

'We're stuffed, mate,' I say. 'They've made some link to our past, to our criminal record… perhaps the poster. We're trapped worse in this sheep pen than at Glenrowan.'

I look at the many uniforms and layers of authority devoted to our capture. We are a floor above dock-level and unarmed, with only one way out.

Dan grabs me at the point of my shoulder.

'First chance we get, run for it.'

'Yeah, run. But they've got our horses. We'll be running, all right, but on foot.'

'Ya neck, or your horse, which would you prefer?' he hisses.

'Neck, ya prick, but how?'

'Let's leave now! We hit the rifle-rack on our way, grab our rifle and then keep shooting until we find broad daylight, right?' He's so close to my face, spit ricochets off my cheeks as he speaks.

We stand as one and push through the door, rush towards the rifle rack, which is ready to be hoisted on board. At that moment we bump into the colonel. We're sunk. I can tell. We pretend we're on our feet for a stretch.

'Good morning, Colonel.'

Our salutes are as sharp as glass. He doesn't respond.

'There's a little problem with your release,' he says. 'They have no record of your birth.'

'What, how come? Oi know Oi was born.'

'You may well have been but there's no record.'

'What did you tell them?'

'I told them you were birthed and raised in a hut, in far-west Queensland and, therefore, have no record. I said you can't read or write so don't understand the forms.'

'You're right about the last part,' I say.

Why did he lie for us?

'I've told them to prepare a Birth Certificate because I can vouch for you.'

'Can they do that?'

'Yep. That's what they're doing now. There're numerous chaps in the brigade in the same predicament. They lived so far out bush their parents never registered them. Be patient.'

After an hour wait, we are handed our embarkation papers, as well as a Birth Certificate showing I'm now two years older. Lady luck has smiled on us. We are legitimate – real persons again.

Two hours later, along with the rest of our troop, we're gathered on the dock-side of the ship to watch it cast-off. A small black-and-white-painted steam-tug stands to seaward, to weave us through the harbour obstacles and numerous small boats. Some families are present to wish their menfolk a loving farewell. Military police tear soldiers from the arms of their loved ones, and escort them up the gangway. Men in suits with smart felt hats, baggy trousers and shiny shoes, are left to comfort teary women in white sundresses and bonnets. Most wave, or shake tiny handkerchiefs, at a sea of anonymous khaki jackets lined along the ship's deck above them.

My breathing stops as if I've been punched and winded. On the dock, stands the lop-eared shearer with two policemen. I can't believe it. *How does he keep on us like this?* He argues with an officer at the gangway, waves a wad of paper; attempts to push past. The officer shakes his head, holds his ground.

I search for Dan. We might have to jump ship. The shearer rages at the boarding officer. I imagine I hear his voice over the crowd.

Where's Dan? We've got to move. I'm convinced the boat is stuck to the dock, it's so slow. I see Dan light a fag near one of the smoke-stacks, mid-deck, and rush to him.

'Look, on the dock.'

I point. He turns to the dock.

'The shearer,' I hiss.

'Oh shit. No! We were so close to getting away.'

'Yes. What'll we do?'

Time ticks. The gangway rattles. Does it mean it's lifting, or settling to allow the traps on board?

'We need to run, jump into the sea before the prick finds us.'

Dan grabs me by the shoulder, points at the gangway rising behind the arguing couple. Will the shearer jump across the space onboard? It's now two foot off the dock… four feet… six… sailors stow it onboard. The ship remains fast; doesn't move.

Bells ring. Whistles blow. The deck lurches. The tug takes up the tow-rope slack, and we're wrenched towards the headlands, so that my neck jolts sideways and my pulse resumes. The shearer watches the *SS Armenian* get under way.

'I'll be here when you get back, Kelly. You mark my words,' we hear him scream to the winds.

The wharf recedes; the tug slips free. Under our own steam we breach Sydney heads, join the open ocean. Colonel Townsend approaches and hands me a sheet of paper he's pulled from the clip-board he carries under his arm.

'Here, Layton, get rid of this.'

'Sir?'

It's the shearer's poster. I look at the colonel as if I have a question to ask.

'You're the Army's now. We look after our own,' he says, then about-turns and walks away.

'He seems a decent chap,' I say.

'Oi wouldn't trust him,' Dan replies.

28

DAY five of a predicted twenty-day voyage. I've managed to drag myself on deck as I've been sick from the moment we boarded. We continue to train for war and the topic of the day is marksmanship.

The *Armenian* is a British vessel, built four years before the war then converted to take horses and a few hundred troops – us 'Bushies' – to war. It has a smoke-stack midships, a mast, both fore and aft, and is considered quite fast. After years in open spaces, the one hundred and fifty by twenty yards of ship life is crushing. I feel like a rat trapped in a bucket of water. The noise and stench of "down below" is unbearable.

We live like fruit bats in cramped hammocks. We eat and toilet within feet of each other. We joke we don't know which area smells worse, the head or the mess. It's like gaol to me. I can't speak with Dan in private no more and I resent that.

Marksmanship entails practice at shooting from the stern at targets towed at the end of a long rope. One section lines up and discharges a volley. Colonel Townsend has a telescope but even we can tell that very few, if any, hit the target.

'You sorry lot,' he shouts above the roar of the ocean. 'Not one of you hit the target.'

Dan looks at me and laughs. The colonel strides towards him and bellows, 'What do you find so funny, James Ryan? Can you do better?'

'Oi reckon,' Dan says, all smug.

'Okay, soldier, grab an Enfield and show us.'

Dan loads, aims as best he can on the heaving deck, and fires. A small splash rises a foot from the target.

'Jesus Christ, is there nobody who can shoot in this man's army?' the colonel rages.

I raise my hand.

'I c-c-can.'

'Better than your mate, I hope.'

'I hope so t-t-t-too, sir.'

'Very well, show them how it's done.'

I load, aim, and when the boat lifts with the swell to have me shooting in line with the target, snap off a shot. I hear the smack of the bullet hit the buoy.

'That's better, at least one of us can shoot, we won't have to rely on frightening the Boer to death,' he says.

'OK, Layton, you're in charge of target practice, along with Lieutenant Withers, and I want every soldier a marksman by the time we reach Cape Town. Understood?'

'Yes, Sir.'

Very few have fired a rifle, let alone killed anything. In a stoush, we'll be in trouble if it doesn't improve.

'The Boer have been at war a long time,' Colonel Townsend reminds us as he paces back and forth. 'Although they're amateurs they've had some serious success against a professional British army.'

Dan and I hope we put on a better show than the Brits.

I didn't realise that Dan would take my marksmanship personally: that I hit the target, he missed, as some personal slight. Reality is, he's never been an expert shot, and whilst he trained with his thirty-two Henkler and Co. pistol at Bullock Creek when we were preparing for the rebellion, I practiced with the rifle. Ned chose me to accompany him to Glenrowan because I was a better shot. If we'd got into a fair fight – Ned and I, both good shots – were a formidable pair.

Dan dodges me. Doesn't sit with me at meals. It continues too long to be coincidence. I bump into him on the mess deck.

'Is there something wrong, Dan?'

'No, nothing.'

'You appear pissed off.'

'No. Oi just don't like it when you show off.'

'When did I show off?'

'Shooting. You made a real jackass out of me.'

'Well, you put yourself forward. I felt we should show them 'Proddy' Queenslanders that we Greta lads can shoot. It had nothing to do with topping you.'

'Well, ya did.'

I realise he sees our relationship as a competition, whereas I only want what's good for him, the bloody cock-of-the-walk. Although in trouble with the law since age five, he remains horribly naive.

On his first day as a fifteen-year-old in gaol, he was nearly crying he was so lost. He wouldn't have cried, our Dan, but he sure wanted to. I was two years older than him. From that day I was hooked to care for him and I get joy out of his success. But it isn't like that for him. He just gives me enough to keep our friendship spluttering and me under his control. I'm useful like a tool is useful.

Something has woken me.

'Land. I see frickin' land!' some trooper hollers.

I peer through my porthole to find, towering over the shore-line, a flat-topped mountain.

Table Mountain, the captain assures us, flanks Cape Town, our destination. Our arrival hasn't come soon enough. While three-quarters of the lads can now hit the moving target, many like me, are sparrow-thin from sea sickness and lack of rations. Half our horses are starved and scoured, and many could not last more than another week at sea. We are a sorry fighting force.

We swarm below to groom our horses and clean our kit until, just on dusk, we're allowed ashore. It is only that the weather has turned clear, allowing us to sleep in the open, inside the British barracks, that we are allowed to disembark. Anxiety is high because we believe we are stepping directly into a war zone.

❖

Dry land. What a wonderful place. Welcome to South Africa. After last night ashore, we're assembled on the parade ground to be informed the battle is hundreds of miles away. The Pommie General, Kitchener, inspects us.

'Gentlemen,' he shouts, from atop his majestic pitch-black stallion. 'On behalf of the Queen and her government, let me welcome you to South Africa. It is very timely that the Colonies join us to show these disloyal Boers that Queen and country remain important bulwarks against disunity and lawlessness. The tide is turning against the Boer due to Britain's superior troop numbers, and our heroism, but there's still a lot to do. What!'

'You … colonial chappies, would do well to learn soldiering from my troops, and the glorious British tradition. Otherwise, you could well find yourself at the Boer's mercy.'

A murmur ripples through the ranks, the occasional chuckle.

'I'll be briefing your officers in the mess, regarding the situation and how I intend to use your unit. You'll operate under our leadership and rules of engagement, so we expect a level of discipline… what… a level you may not be used to. Apart from that, I wish you every success.'

He salutes us, as we present arms, then rides off. He cuts a stylish figure in khaki jacket, shiny leather webbing, silver sword, rows of medals and has a tidy seat on a mount.

I impersonate the General with a horse's body-brush under my nose representing his moustache, a scraggy stick for a baton, while walking like I've a case of the rickets.

'What's this Ponsonby? You've cracked your tea set? You have? Well… send for mummy to bring you another, what! That's a good chap.'

'Where is Oar...stralia, Jeeves? Do you think they've showered?'

I get a few laughs, and only have to wriggle my eyebrows during the afternoon briefings to draw a laugh from some in the room.

During dinner that evening there is an announcement: 'Attention Queenslanders. I'm pleased to announce that the General has agreed to two-day's leave, commencing 0800 hours, tomorrow. Gather your leave pass and pay packet from the staff sergeant in A Block before you depart.'

'Hip hip hooray,' someone shouts and the Queenslanders all respond 'and so say all of us.'

You'd swear we've been given the keys to the city, so much do we whoop and holler.

'First thing I'm going to do when I hit town is buy a woman for an hour and get myself a "root",' Bluey Cooch shouts out across the barrack room.

'What you gonna say for the remaining fifty-nine minutes?' replies Corporal Rawlings.

'Swahili,' jokes Bluey.

'Good, at least you've got the language down pat,' replies the Corporal.

'What's the first thing you're going to do, Layton?' Bluey asks.

'Hire a room and have a hot shower,' I say, then notice all in the room turn in my direction. Dan keeps polishing his shoes. 'Then, I won't be far behind you,' I add in my best blokey voice.

29

AN African hangover feels similar to an Australian. We've come to fight a war but the sea voyage has robbed us of our vigour and the horses are so feeble, we are forced to spend weeks in Cape Town. We do parade-ground drills and route marches, like scum foot soldiers, to allow us and our horses to recuperate. Many complain, but I'm not one of them. Listening to the Poms' account of the war, I believe there'll be plenty of time for action and killing, and it will be no picnic. I'm in no rush. I know the reality of being shot at.

I've never ridden in a train. That soon changes when we and our mounts are herded onto one to head north, towards the city of Kimberly. I like the roll of the carriages as they tear through the countryside, and the repetitive clack of rails as the steel wheels cross over a join in the track, creating a song in my head.

There you go; there you go
There you go again
Sometimes it's nine times.
Others it is ten.

I hang my head out the window to cool down and yikes, my eyes feel like tiny hornets have attacked them. It's the soot in the smoke. I pull my head in and don't attempt it again.

Kimberley is where the Boers discovered diamonds, which probably triggered the war. The Brits want to control the new Boer territories, once thought worthless, to get their hands on the mountains of diamonds and are in the process of capturing the major cities in the Boer's Republic of Transvaal and the Orange Free state. We will end our journey south of the city.

'This is the life,' says Bluey, rocking to the train's rhythm.

'Why?'

'Mate, compared to the ship this is heaven. It's clean, we get to stretch our legs.'

It's taken us a few weeks of patrolling to reach Kimberley only to learn the British troops have sacked it, so no glory for us here.

Mick White, the biggest whinger and troop bookie, wanders around with his hat out in the begging position. 'I told you it would all be over by the time we got here. Pay up please.'

He's been taking bets since Tamworth that we'd miss the action. He has an exaggerated accountant's stoop and is as blind as a bat. How he ever passed medical is beyond me.

'They'd heard you were coming, Mick, and didn't want to put up with your whingeing,' says Corporal Reid, his section's NCO.

We're disappointed that the set-piece battle is over, given we've travelled so far to enter the fray. Many, but not me, long to see how we will fare in a stoush and look forward to seeing how effective we can be in laying down fire as a unit, or attacking in a full-gallop charge.

We join the British contingent already garrisoned here and, within hours, run security pickets to relieve the battle-weary Brits. Like other foreign detachments, we are under their command.

We face our second major disappointment when out troop is split into teams and assigned different roles for the immediate future.

Dan and I are ordered to ride with 'Breaker' Morant. He has a reputation for adventure, is handsome as a vaudeville star, fit as a Mallee bull, brave, a hit with the ladies at the local dance hall: a great soldier.

I'm showing off a bit of fancy riding and shooting.

'You… the man on the bay,' he says.

'Me?'

'Yes, you… Fancy yourself as a rider, do you?'

'No, sir… was just keeping me hand in. We don't get to do too much demanding riding and I don't want to lose me skills.'

'Don't apologise, man. Report to Sergeant Tait at the horse wranglers. We might have a job for you getting more horses up to speed for the Bushies. They lost too many on the trip over.'

He's a freak at calming a young'un to take the bit. Any skills I pick up from 'the breaker', will stand me in good stead.

Our strategy in Africa is to travel in small cavalry troops, deep behind enemy lines, disrupt Boer livelihood and hit him where he lives and works. We have the cities and now need to strangle the land owners. The whole campaign is like mustering wild cattle on the Barkly – find where they hide, cut their water off and run them into the open Veldt, or run them down, then yard 'em.

On our first raid we approach a basic, Boer farmhouse: low-set, stonewalled, thatched roof. Lieutenant Morant points to our group.

'Listen up! You men go with Corporal Stephens around the back. The rest of us will approach the farmhouse from the front. We're told this farmer's the head of a local commando, and they're the ones who torched the Church of England last week.'

'Will do, sir,' says the Corporal.

'Any shooting… shoot to kill. Remember, the Boer don't take prisoners.'

We are reduced to tit-for-tat, with each army wearing the other down, until one group hasn't a tit left to tat with.

On a signal from the lieutenant, we spur our horses towards the house in order to surprise its inhabitants. I sweep to the rear, dismount on the run, swing my carbine from my shoulder and form a line with others, to target windows and doors.

A firefight erupts at the front and the moment the backdoor opens, thinking we are under threat, or terrorists escaping, we pull the trigger. It's us or them, as we are taught.

Two women and two little girls tumble out like dolls from a music box. Lie motionless. My gut twists with the realisation.

'What the heck, Corporal? Children?'

'Hold the line, men.'

'Why weren't we told they were talking about a family?'

'Don't blame others. You shouldn't have reacted so quick. Select your targets when you have the benefit of surprise,' rages the Corporal.

How come such a prospect never crossed my mind? These are family homes not bloody military forts. Of course, there'd be women and children. Welcome to the war, Steve!

I've seen innocents slaughtered at the hands of police at Glenrowan, but it's so much worse when it's you that has pulled the trigger. The shocked look on those little girls' faces, the prisoner's devastating wail, as we lead him away from his burning house to be interrogated, I'll carry with me forever, like a worm in my belly.

We were told to take no prisoners, if the Boer resist. I'm told the Brits finish many Boers off while they lie wounded, or even after they surrender, unhurt. It's amazing what the two sides of our brain can juggle. In peace, one set of standards, in war, another. I wonder if Ned would have been hanged if our revolution were a declared war?

I am on orderly duties at the Officers' Mess, the tidiest I've been in months.

'Poor bloody Morant,' says Major Turnbridge. 'No written orders. I heard Kitchener say, directly, "take no prisoners", and not just khaki wearers.'

The major is referring to the Breaker's court-martial by the Brits for war crimes.

'I heard Captain Taylor hand out the instruction to Morant with me own ears, Sir,' says Lieutenant Kirk.

'Did you indeed? Pass me the cauliflower would you, my man.'

That answered questions I had about an incident I was part of, some months before.

'What have we here, Lieutenant Morant?'

'Boer prisoners, sir.'

'Did I ask for prisoners or for information?'

'Information, Captain, but I've managed to bring you both.'

For months Morant takes prisoners in defiance of his orders, until his friend Lieutenant Hunt is killed by the Boer. It is then he seems to snap.

We, of the Irish, are a wake-up to the treacherous ways of the English, but the cornstalks remain naive in the ways of King and Crown. I relate it to Dan.

'How do you think Ned would have liked the war?' he asks.

'Umm... dunno. In some ways Ned would have enjoyed it: the adventure, the horse dash, the shooting, living under the stars, the mateship – he'd have made a good soldier.'

'Yeah, maybe, but overall, I think 'e would have hated it because the boot's on the other foot here. We're the traps. Find some poor Boer farmhouse and drag families out of bed, act all tough, loud and arrogant like Sergeant Fitzpatrick did against we poor Irish settlers.'

'Tell you one thing, though, mate, how easy is it to take a personal dislike to some idjit, you know... some Boer farmer... just because he's outwitted us?'

'Poor joke, though, when we say, "Mate, you're as lucky as Ned Kelly," before we persecute the poor jabbering bastard until he cracks, and then lock him up.'

'Ha, yeah, no one gets it… like he really wasn't lucky – the Boer, or Ned for that matter.'

I think about this regularly – the fine line between human and animal. Were the traps, animals?

Next night we've surrounded a house. Men and youths exit with arms high. Surrendered without a fight.

'Fred. Do a sweep inside the house.'

I dismount and enter the front door, careful, carbine at the ready. All clear in the living area. I enter a short hall and push the door to my right and sight an unmade bed. I sense movement, feel a brush of clothing, then a thud on my head, fierce pain. Porcelain shards spill around me. My legs buckle as I turn, grab someone's arm, fall on my back, bring them on top of me. I'm dizzy, can barely see, feel an arm move above me, grab it, feel something slice my hand. I buck my hips to dislodge my assailant, but am unable. They're holding a knife and I resolve not to release my grip.

I smell lavender. I bring my head up from the floor to crack the face of the person above and feel their nose crush, hear a sharp cry of pain. Twist them over, while they are surprised, hear the knife rattle away on the floor. Lie between their legs while I grasp them by the throat, squeeze. See it's a woman, dark hair splayed about, one breast exposed from a light night-dress. See fear in her eyes, sense her vulnerability. Feel an instant erection, witness an urgent desire to bury myself inside her flesh, stab with my flesh, take her silently and ruthlessly.

I push myself away as if I've witnessed horror, sit upright leaning on one arm, the other searching for the carbine, shame and revulsion smeared across my face.

'Ji wil my naai, verkragter moet, ji nie!' she screams in Afrikaans.

'You tried to kill me, bitch... There's someone in here, lieutenant!' I shout.

Others arrive, drag her away. I find a well to wash the blood from my head wound. I look at the woman being trussed with the male prisoners, wonder what made her so desirable. Think, when the chips were down, I desired a woman, perhaps for the wrong reasons, but telling, nonetheless. Something in my core comforts me, signals a change.

The house alight, we ride away through the smoke. It stings my eyes, makes them water.

30

WE ride with another Brigade in a new century.

If we *are* winning the war, it's only because we have more troops, starve the guerrillas, and terrorise the population. We are not a superior species, nor better, or more courageous warriors but, merely, have superior resources.

Three hundred of us Aussies, as we now know ourselves after the recent Federation referendum, are protecting a supply dump on the Elans River, hundreds of miles from the front. We are lightly armed, as fits our role of The Queensland Citizens Bushmen Unit. The ridge is stony; we have no trenching tools, so we're not dug in; and sleep under the stars in open rows.

I wake. Dan and I completed a night sentry-picket, so I'm surprised I stir before sunrise. Dan peers around.

'Jesus, what's that?'

There's no need for an answer. Artillery shells whistle overhead and explode around us, and men to the left and right of us, already out of their swags, fall or stagger to a bloodied stop, raked by machine guns.

'Stay low, mate.' Dan shouts.

We crawl, drag our rifles, towards a stone building a cricket pitch away, while smoke and dust swirl. Fire rages in the nearby mess hut, and the smell of cordite from the explosives makes me want to vomit. I hear horses squealing in panic and pain, between explosions, whose concussion pumps into my chest, removes my breath. I can't see how we'll survive such a heavy ambush, but crawl regardless.

We reach the stone building; take a moment to recce. We determine that the enemy machine gun fire is concentrated in selected areas, and rifle fire is not yet in great force. Those of us in the building direct fire at the machine guns in an effort to close them down. I concentrate, over many hours, on eliminating snipers exposed by the smoke issuing from their gun barrels.

'Good work you men along this approach,' says Colonel Townsend who crawls to our position. 'You've managed to suppress the sniper fire in this quadrant. I want two teams of two men to move along that dead ground with grenades and, when the rest lay covering fire, I'd like you to close on that machine-gun's flanks and take it out.'

He looks at our eyes to see if we understand; to test our resolve.

'When it's knocked out, I need this squad to push forward to regain our in-depth defence.'

'Yes sir,' says Lieutenant Kirk.

'From what we can ascertain, the Boers are supported by five or six regular cannons and three, automatic 'pom pom' cannons. So far, we've only met snipers, but there's around three thousand Boer massing further away, to attack us once the barrage is over.'

'Jesus.'

'Yes, that's why we need depth in our defence to slow their attack and make us less vulnerable to artillery. We suffered severe bombardment today. We need to spread out, without losing our ability to concentrate our force, when required.'

Two teams, myself included, depart to knock out the machine guns. The others have a clear indication of the snipers' positions and, when we are ready to engage, they lay down fire. Not a shot is returned. The machine gun chatters, forcing the Aussies' heads down.

Minutes later and close enough, we hurl grenades and the chatter stops.

'Hooray,' from various trenches.

The human loss from bombardment is light, given our poor

preparation, but the cost to supplies and to our livestock is horrendous.

In the morning I'm charged with sniping so leave Dan in the shallow trench we managed to scrape out during the darkness of evening. For the first time the Boer meet bushmen similar to them, comfortable in the outdoors and able to conceal, move and out-snipe the sniper. Mid-afternoon we've eliminated most of them.

Dan isn't far from my mind because I overlook his position from my vantage point. Whenever I think a shell is headed in his direction, I check on him. Somehow, I've convinced myself I can will a shell off-course.

For most of the day the barrages have fallen elsewhere but, I see a creeping-barrage move across his position. It's as if I am under the barrage, so intensely do I feel the trauma of hell and fury passing through, then over, his trench. I'm sure he's been killed because, when the dust has settled, our trench is rubble. I break orders and rush to the site. The makeshift roof is demolished and churned into the soil that now fills the trench. There's no sign of Dan.

'Dan, Dan.'

I drop to my knees and dig with my bare hands.

'Dan.'

I dig and dig, until I feel hair in my fingers; clear a space, until I feel a face. I remove rubble from his nose and mouth, both of which, along with his ears, stream blood. The percussion has pummelled him. I clear away more debris to free his shoulders. The overhang we created has prevented soil from covering his legs, so I haul him to the surface, slap his face to revive him. All the time the barrage continues.

Oh God, not a breath. I pump his chest, and pump his chest, then miracle of miracles, a moment later he takes a breath. I pour the contents of my water bottle over his soft and bloodied face, and into his swollen lips. He stares at me, barely focussed.

'You're crying, mate,' he says.

His first words.

'Don't be stupid mate, it's the smoke and dust from the shells. I've been like this all day.'

'Thought I was a gonna, didn't you?… Who'd look after you if I carked?'

Does he care more than he lets on?

It's nightfall on the second day and, having endured another eight-hundred shell barrage, the wranglers report fifteen-hundred horses, mules and bullocks, have been killed. But now we're dug-in, even created a field hospital, all while repelling a number of serious Boer raids. We feel less exposed and ready for the fight.

We'd heard that the reason the traps didn't rush us at Glenrowan was that Superintendent Hare was awaiting the delivery of a cannon from Melbourne.

'I've never seen so much destruction,' Dan says, a day or two after the shelling. 'I can't imagine what would have happened at Glenrowan if they had that blasted cannon.'

I shake my head.

'I've never been so angry. Not even when the police swamped us at Glenrowan, did I feel like this. I can't believe how the Boer could target all those innocent horses.'

I've loved horses from my first contact with them. The sight of a thousand bloated horses lying with body-parts spread everywhere, affects us. Dan, especially, is taking it hard. I think being buried alive has unhinged him a little. He threatens to charge their line in revenge.

'Yeah, heartless bastards. Oi'm not sure how much of this I can take.'

I remember him sobbing his heart out at Stringybark Creek after we'd ambushed the police. Ned gave him a big serve, told him to act like a man.

'Let me get my hands on one of them bastards and I'll make

them pay,' I snarl, thinking I'm reacting as Ned would have, to inspire his baby brother.

The Boer appear to have woken to the fact that killing the livestock and demolishing the storerooms and wagons, destroys what they'd hoped to capture. They limit the shelling. When the battle rhythm slows, I reflect.

I wonder, amidst the mayhem of the siege, why, except for the moment he was buried, I'm not as upset about Dan as I am about the horses. Am I maturing, or have I realised I have no hold over him? I'm barely concerned about my own life, which is equally as worrying. We've endured so much, I swing between believing we are invincible to believing we have turned to slate: numb to all usual, human feelings.

For a moment after stringybark I valued the power of being able to kill, to protect my rights, to project myself onto the landscape, but killing abhors me at this point. Even Dan doesn't take to it like Ned, or even Joe. He's more sensitive, to reflect his delicate frame, until he has his dander up.

Being the elder I feel a responsibility to protect him, to comfort him, but it's obvious he's unable to return that affection. He's becoming a burden, and where I, once, would have taken a bullet for him and probably have – for it is during this battle I am twice wounded with shrapnel – I'm beginning to resent his apathy.

❖

We've kept our heads down and responded where, and when, we can. Sometimes we defend the parapets or our arc of fire and other times join probing raids to check if the enemy remains in force or, merely, pins us down in order to attack elsewhere.

I'm on security picket to our pommy officer when the Boer general visits under white flags, to offer us the opportunity to surrender.

'We need those supplies, Colonel,' the Boer interpreter tells the pom. 'We'll go to any lengths to secure them… You're hopelessly

214

outnumbered. Surrender, and your troops will be safe… You have the General's word.'

The pom's concern is written across his face.

'I can't surrender. I'm in charge of Australian troops and they'd cut my throat if I surrendered.'

The General leaves and I walk beside the Colonel back to our lines.

'What has happened to our reinforcements, Colonel?'

'Not sure… I sent a squad out on the first day to slip through Boer lines and get help. They've either been killed, captured or lost.'

'Perhaps I could give it a s-s-shot?'

The Colonel looks at me a little startled.

'Go on.'

'I think I could ride through… at night. My horse and I are used to operating quietly in the dark when moonlighting wild cattle. If we do get through, it wouldn't take us long to reach help.'

'We're surrounded by thousands of Boer.'

'I know Sir, but when sniping I've noticed a gully runs parallel to the river for a while and might provide cover to enable me to slip through without attracting too much attention.'

The Colonel walks in silence as we cross the bridge to return to our position on the ridge.

'Would you be able to locate the HQ about twenty miles from here?'

'Yes, Sir, I'm like a homing pigeon. Once I've been somewhere in the bush, I never forget.'

'It might be worth the risk, Layton. As you heard, the Boer aren't going to go away by themselves.'

'Indeed, Sir… I have one request. Can you issue me with a revolver instead of my rifle?'

I retrieve my horse and bridle him. After dark I take two jackets off our dead, cut them into pieces and bind my horse's hooves with the cloth to deaden any sound. When most in our respective armies are sleeping, I set off bareback.

At the perimeter I alert the nearest sentry that I'm leaving and ask him to remember the password I'll use if, and when, I return.

'I'll use the words *Ned Kelly* when challenged. Most Boer wouldn't have heard of him, yet most Aussies would have.'

'Good one. Best of luck, mate. I've seen someone light a cigarette over on that point, occasionally, so avoid exposing yourself there, if you can.'

I step the horse into no man's land. I'm counting on the fact that many animals wander free since the artillery and I will not cause too much alarm until I'm quite close to any observer. I lie along my horse so I don't offer an obvious profile. We pick our way along the gully and don't encounter a soul. At the creek bank we enter the water carefully. I remove the horses binding and swim him across the river. We scramble up the opposite bank and a voice calls out, very close.

'Stop wie gaan daarheen?'

The challenger stands and I shoot him between the eyes, spur the horse and gallop away without another shot fired.

I ride at pace and locate HQ where I report; hand them the Colonel's penned message. The duty officer reads it, and says;

'We wondered why we weren't getting supplies. The person we sent to check hasn't returned. Tell your Colonel to hold fast. That it will take a few days to assemble help and get them there, but we will get there. I'll write the orders.'

'Will do, Sir. Can I have a fresh mount?'

I ensure my weary horse is fed and watered before I canter back to the river on the new mount, not as responsive as my own. At the river, when I peer through the morning fog, I see Boer further along the bank cooking and some down at the water's edge, washing. I urge the horse into the river but he panics, starts to flounder, and I have to urge him forward. We are making quite a ruckus compared to my earlier traverse. He reaches shallow water on the far side and I hear voices from those Boers at the water's edge. They've spotted us. I duck into the gully and jog towards our sentry. I hear an enemy shot but don't hear the buzz or ricochet of the bullet, which I think bites into the bank above me. I spur the horse to gallop towards our line. More bullets track me and hit the bank above. I see a bushie's hat ahead. Bullets spit everywhere.

'Ned Kelly, Ned Kelly,' I yell at the hat.

A wall of sound and smoke explodes to my front and I think the sentry must have not alerted others to my return, or password, and my companions have targeted me. But no bullets arrive. The boys are laying-down covering fire to keep Boer heads down. I gallop to our lines with hornets buzzing in increasing numbers as I ride. I jump across a barricade, roll off the horse, exhausted but, also, desperate to find cover. The Colonel crawls to me while the return fire thuds around us. Perhaps he's worried I'll be shot before I pass on the news.

'How'd you go?'

'Good, Sir. Here's a letter from HQ. They said to hold on, regardless.'

'Well done, Layton. You may have saved our bacon.'

What a turnaround, hated criminal to 'saving bacon'. But who will ever know? Dan's close shave with death highlights the transitory nature of life and memory. If he is not around there will be no record that I lived, that I contributed.

I survive to see reinforcements arrive, and the Boer surrender. I've retrieved my horse. We've relied heavily on the horse during the campaign. The Boer cavalry flogged us early due to their mobility and speed. We relied on cavalry to compete.

Like the lonely drover, we soldiers share loneliness with our mount but, more importantly, we share our fear. Often our courage is bolstered by our horse's bravery and skill in the heat of battle. We share a bond.

The Australian Units are gathered to re-form the Battalion, and parade on the ploughed paddock beside the base. The colonel addresses us from atop his mount.

'Battalion! At ease!'

'The war is officially over and tomorrow, at 0700 hours, we will embark by train to the port of Durban. From there we will depart for home.

'You have performed admirably during this campaign and Queen Victoria, Lord Kitchener, and the Australian Prime Minister, along with his government, wish to congratulate you, and thank you for your unselfish service to Queen and country.

'We have lost many comrades-in-arms who we will not forget. There will be a service to commemorate them at 1800 hours this evening.

'I, also, have received advice from the Australian War Office that, in line with British Commonwealth policy, the Army will not transport your horse home. You are to hand your saddlery kit in to the quartermaster's shed by 1500 hours today, and let your mount loose into the green holding yard. There will be no exceptions.'

A general murmur rattles along the ranks. I can't believe the inhumanity of the order.

'What will happen to them?' shouts some insubordinate.

'The Army will decide, but most likely they'll be sold to the locals.'

'Will we get compensated?'

'That is to be decided.'

'Apart from that, gentlemen, I wish you well on the journey home. Dismissed.'

I'm one of the lucky ones whose horse has survived both the journey to Africa, and the ravages of the campaign, while more than four hundred and fifty thousand horses were killed, or maimed. I'm devastated to think I'll lose my mate, but feel better knowing that he may go to a good home.

I remove his bridle; wrap my arms around his neck.

'See you, old fellow.'

It's like he knows what lies ahead because he's slow to pull away. The tears roll and I'm not on me Pat Malone. Many men, including Dan, stand there until darkness washes the vision of their abandoned horse from their sight, and don't attend the church ceremony for lost comrades.

If I suffered travelling to the war then I'm suffering far worse on the journey home, being, now, confined to my bed with illness.

We departed on 10 July, 1902 on the *SS Drayton Grange*, a 6200-ton ship rented from the Brits to transport fifteen hundred troops home. In reality, there are nineteen hundred-and-eighty ordinary ranks, and forty-two officers on board. The ship, only a year old, but designed to transport frozen meat, is not up to the task. Nor are our two leaders, Lt Colonel Lyster, or Medical Officer, Captain Shields.

Having endured the hardships of the Boer campaign and survived, when thousands haven't, plus returning to an uncertain future, I'm not in a responsible mood. I don't want to party; I just want to lose control. I want to rebel against authority, especially the nonsensical. I play pranks and, used to scavenging off the land while I hunted the Boer, I'm not averse to stealing rations or grog from the ship's store, or from members of another unit. I feel so 'dirty' for some of the atrocious things I've done and seen; I let my discipline and personal hygiene, also slide.

I presume many others on board are in the same boat. At a bunk, further along, someone calls.

'Has anyone seen my green bag?'

'No, why would we?'

'Well, you said you'd be here to watch it.'

'Yes, but not for a frickin' hour.'

'You thieving bastard.'

'It's not me, mate. We're all losing stuff.'

Dan appears beside my bunk, stands close to talk.

'You hangin' in, mate?'

'Battling,' I say. 'Can't hold anything down with the sea sickness.'

'You're not missing anything. We're on half-rations and even that food is 'off'. Makes ya want to throw up.'

'Why half-rations?'

'Overcrowding. They don't have enough stores.'

'That's woeful.'

Overcrowding reduces the quality of sleep and creates conditions ripe for disease and vermin. The rough weather prevents exercise and our clothes are always damp, leading to coughs and lung conditions. Having suffered hunger, cold and heat on the long patrols in South Africa, many of us have boarded with a low tolerance to disease.

'Here I am, forced to look after those grubby Boer in their concentration camps and I pick up their typhoid and other germs,' remarked one very ill Corporal, a day or two earlier.

'I could have infected half the ship, myself, according to Doc.'

'Ah shit. Now ya tell me. Stay well away.'

Many of us have been infected by our ship-mates, since departure and lack of medicines allows disease to run rampant. Will we survive for a hero's march?

Two lonely painters-and-dockers secure the ship to the Sydney wharf in the morning mist. There's no band, beautiful women or innocent children, to welcome us, the avenging warriors. I imagine me mum, or perhaps, my sisters, or Dan's family, standing and cheering us, crying at being so happy to learn we're alive. But there's no one.

The officers disembark first, then mill around, while all is readied for our turn. But we have to wait… and wait. A number of hospital wagons appear through the mist from the landward end of the wharf; their horses' hooves rattle its wooden decking. Numerous men are stretchered off and packed into wagons, then we're relieved to see the first line of soldiers file down the gangplank, loaded to the gunnels with their kit.

There's no swagger in their stride. Emaciated, their uniforms flutter over them like ripples on a calm sea. Their heads fail to swivel, seek others for jest, as they did when we departed for war. What waits for us? Will Australia care? By this time, news has been released of our return. I search the wharf for the lop-eared shearer; pray he is not here.

31

DAN and I are convinced we can make a life for ourselves farming. We had our heroes' march. Our mighty cavalry of horse reduced to marching like mere foot soldiers. How pathetic? *Light attendance*, the paper reports.

I am honourably discharged and invited to make my home in Queensland, where the regiment demobs. I have papers to prove it; dated 1902. I've made friends in the regiment, and decide to settle with Dan around Allora, on the Darling Downs, where many live.

We arrange to sharecrop, three miles north-west of the township. Even with money saved from our service, and years of wages unspent at the Barkly, we still can't afford to buy and develop land that the Government releases. We might do so if we jag bumper crops, sell them at decent prices and bank the profits. As sharecroppers we rent the land to cultivate but we keep the crop, or any profit.

We've built a bush timber and galvanised-iron roofed house, and cleared an acre of the rich black-earth river-flat, with axe, grubber and fire. We purchased a plough but borrowed the draught horse to pull it. I looked at the plough when we first unloaded it, and recalled how we'd fashioned suits of armour from one similar. I think of Ned and Joe, and how their blood had spilled across the blades. Ants run down my spine, a shiver. Here we are, now – soldier's swords swapped for ploughshares.

I click the horse and the mouldboards turn the aromatic earth so it curls and falls back in furrows, like rich chocolate waves to worship the sun. We intend to grow corn and vegetables on our acre, and the thought of it makes me right proud.

It's an ideal life and I'm sure all our troubles are over, so we can, at last, have a quiet life. But one cloud wants to rain on my parade. Dan spends a lot of time drunk since Africa, and has comforted up with Tessa, a local lass, so I seldom see him, much to my disappointment. We've been friends since teenagers, and it's because of him I signed up for a "short but merry life" of bushranging. I'm not used to living long periods without him, but her father talks about setting the couple up with land and bullocks to draw a plough. Them bullocks signal to me that Dan and I are being torn apart. I have never imagined a future without him.

I attend the Dalby horse races in search of a ride, determined to overcome the fear of losing Dan, and keep my nightmares at bay. Someone points me in the direction of a large ex-army tent, with numerous horses tethered. Nervous, I move closer to a group of men seated inside.

'Hi, I'm F-f-fred Layton. I'm looking for the boss.'

A stout fellow in grey work trousers and checked shirt lifts his eyes.

'That's me. What can I do for you?'

'I've j-j-just returned from the African war. I trained as a jockey when I was younger and I'm looking for a ride. I want to pick up me old life, if possible. S-s-s-someone pointed me in your direction.'

'Ah, sorry, but I've hired a hoop for this meet.'

He didn't smile but I caught a glimpse of missing teeth.

'All good. Perhaps you'll keep me in mind. I have a farm in Allora. I'm also a farrier, s-s-s-so you get two for the price of one.'

'Yeah, will do, Fred. That's good to know.'

I shake his hand and leave.

'Oh Fred,' he calls.

'Yeah?'

I turn.

'Bill Hislop might be looking for a hoop. His son usually rides but had a fall during the week and is unable.'

'Thanks, I'll do that.'

I track down Hislop, a wizened man with a bad hip, which makes his leg swing as he walks. I offer to ride for nothing to prove my worth.

I ride the winner on my first ride. Hislop's over the moon. Locals look at me with some respect. See, I remind myself, life is fine after all.

A photographer has posed the owners holding the trophy in front of me on the horse.

'Would you mind if I had one of those photographs as a record?' I ask the photographer. '… the one you took of me on the horse.'

'No trouble, Fred. It's on us,' says a jubilant, and thus generous, Hislop, who hears me ask.

I'm concerned that I have no pictorial record of the real me, or of my exploits. I've dodged all photographs in fear of being found out, identified as a Kelly member.

I want something to remind myself, if not others, that this skin and flesh has contributed, has lived, has ridden race horses. There's been no family to hold these memories because I've slipped myself free of that knot, and my mate is about to slip himself free of my reins. He'll no longer vouch for the life I have lived. I'm stranded.

I'll frame the photo and have the framer write in pencil *Jockey, Fred Layton, Dalby, 1902*. I want it to say Steve Hart, so I don't become a mere shadow to the Kellies. You know, an afterthought.

'Oh, and then there was Steve Hart.'

Late afternoon the sun is flat on the horizon and the trees' shadows have stretched out of shape. I watch a horse gallop across the grass-flat towards our humpy. The snake, ever-present in my gut, curls tight at the sight. I duck inside and grab my pistol in case the visitor is hostile. In my mind, a galloping horse means trouble from trap or

Boer. As the rider closes, I recognise Dan's horse, then his delicate face under the leather hat I'd made. I've always thought the brim too small for his face and have meant to make a better one, but haven't.

'Steve, Steve you're in danger,' he says, as soon as he reins in, ahead of a cloud of dust, at our doorstep.

'Wooah, settle down, boyo. Settle down. What's the matter?'

'Tessa's brother was in the bottom shanty and overheard some fellas talking. It turns out they're Stock Squad, and they're looking for you, Fred Layton, for poddy and horse stealing. Her brother scooted home to tell me, and he says someone has already given them directions to our hut.'

'I haven't stolen no poddies or horses!'

'Oi know, but ya can't stand and argue now. They're on their way. Take my horse and get the crap outa here. Quick! Meet me at the Six Mile after dark, tonight.'

'What about you?'

'Oi'll be right. It's you they want. I'll make up a story. Christ, there they are now... two of 'em about a half-mile away.'

The snake strikes. My heart shudders, shoulders droop. He's right. Two horsemen jog in our direction.

'Piss off out the back; quick. I'll think a somethin' ta slow em down.'

I mount and canter into the scrub behind the hut. Dan takes up the axe, splits fence rails as if he's been working there all day. Thank heavens he warned me or I'd be done. It's such a blow to up-and-leave again, just when I was settled. I can't take a trick.

Come late afternoon I make my way to the six-mile creek crossing on the Dalrymple, and light a campfire. I have only the clothes I stand in and my pistol – a real desperado.

Dark storms rumble in the afternoon heat and build columns of steam along the horizon. Rain appears imminent. Soon after last-light Dan appears. He has my bedding, some trinkets, and documents from the war, along with a few days' food.

'The traps say they are hunting fellows who rode with Starlight, and Fred Layton's name came up in the newspaper, winning a horse race at Dalby. Starlight is accused of cattle duffing and lifting horses. The fooking shearer has told them you worked for Starlight. They told me, he – Starlight – is dead: drowned swimming Corella Creek in flood – so the government has to nail someone for the crime, and you're the best break they've had.'

'Oh Jesus, what a bastard… so unfair.'

I can barely talk. My tongue has gone all lorikeet with disgust. I'd thought all this was behind me.

'Oi said I don't stay at the hut much. Hadn't seen you for a coupla days: that you sometimes gets on the drink. They say they'll call again in a few days. Come first light, I bet they're back on the doorstep, for I'm certain they didn't believe me.'

'Me photograph… on the ledge in the bedroom?'

'Photograph? What? Where?'

'Me, at the Dalby races.'

'Ah shit. Oi didn't remember that one.'

'What else have ya forgotten? Have you any idea how important that thing is to me? Have you?'

Then, I realise he's not packed his own belongings. My heart wallows around without a beat.

'You didn't bring your stuff? Ya not bailin' out on me?'

'Yeah mate, me and Tessa talked it over and I want to stay. My name is not on the police list, I don't use that one anymore. You need to blow through, though... but maybe, you can come back and join me, when the heat dies down? Ya can get your photograph.'

'Ah, forget the bastard.'

It's then, in spite of numerous other attempts by the fates to have me killed, I die.

I look at him. A brief thought passes my mind that he may have dobbed me in so he can live with Tessa. He would gain the proceeds from the crop and the pay packets I've poured into the place. But I disregard it. I want to beg him to leave with me but can't bring myself to do it. I wrap my arms around him, draw him in close, but I feel his reserve. A vacuum sucks me all so dry, creates a hole, where part of me has been. That part of me has been him.

'Bye Dan. You've been family to me, and family wouldn't hold you back,' I whisper. 'They'd want you to be happy.'

What about me? I think, as I say it. *What about me?*

I hold him by the shoulders at arms' length to look into his eyes, for what could be, the final time. I remember holding him in prison, holding him after the Stringybark massacre, and being in his arms after Glenrowan, and again, during the siege at Elans River. I wonder how I can ever survive without holding him again.

'Bye Steve, Oi wish you well.'

He's unable to keep my eye contact. I want to be generous.

'You too, mate. I'm going to miss you. I really am.'

Dan unsaddles my horse, which he's just ridden in on, swaps the saddle to the horse he'd lent me, mounts and rides into the night.

I have no idea what will become of him, but the life we have led and the chemistry of his make up, I think, will have left him, like me, very much alone but for different reasons.

I'M in Landsborough's Mellum Club Hotel, gin in hand, to silence a raging thirst.

I had dribbled about the Darling Downs for a few days in a funk, then decided to visit my sister, Jane, in Gympie. I overhear a conversation.

'Lingard doesn't want anything to do with the road going through his property.'

'Can he stop it?'

'Not legally, but he may be able to persuade the logging company to divert around the mountain. Reckons he didn't come all the way from St George for peace and quiet only to be pushed onto a public thoroughfare.'

'St George?'

'Yeah, he managed a Station there for years, before he bought here.'

I squirm off my wooden stool.

'Sorry, but I overheard you mention a chap, Lingard. That wouldn't be Kerry Lingard, would it?'

'That's right.'

'He lives here... local, you say?'

'Yeah, off the Maleny Road. Why? Do you know him?'

'I might do. I sheared for a guy of the same name, a few years ago.'

'Sounds like him, eh? If you have time, perhaps drop in on him.'

I hope to camp the night on his block. I turn off where I was advised and ride into a dense-green softwood pocket, surrounded by a horseshoe of high ridges. A neat sawn-timber house backs into the scrub at the end of the track.

'Is anybody home?' I call, from my horse. 'Is anybody home?'

Silence. I ride around the side of the house to where a small-framed woman hangs washing on a wire clothesline, the wooden props lowered to enable her to reach. The copper bubbles furiously, so she may not have heard me. Older, and now with baby in a basket beside her, I recognize her from Bell Ridge.

'Hello,' I say, quietly.

The woman jumps high enough to land in the baby's basket, but doesn't.

'Sorry. Didn't mean to frighten you… Is Kerry around?'

'No, he's not. Sorry, I was away with the fairies. We seldom get visitors.'

'I sang out a few times, smelled cooking… knew you weren't too far away. Ah, will he be gone long?'

'Why, who are you?'

'Fred Layton, I used to work on Bell Ridge.'

'Ah, Fred… He won't be back until the weekend.'

'That's a shame… I was wondering if I could camp up the back somewhere? I wouldn't bother you… like to catch up with him.'

'No, sure! There's a nice spot further up the creek.'

I camp there beneath a canvas-fly and, to entertain myself, prospect for gold. Late Friday afternoon Kerry appears through the gloom.

'Do you remember me?' I ask.

'No. But I recognise the voice.'

'Benalla? Bell Ridge.'

'Ah, yes, Steve. I wondered what had happened to ya.'

We yarn for a few hours over a cuppa, while I update him on our doings, and quiz him for gossip from Victoria. He's been home since we'd last met and has news, albeit a few years old, of the Greta mob.

'I heard your brother Dick is fencing out Albury-Wodonga way.'

'Oh, good. He's stayed out of gaol?'

'Yeah, appears so. I'm unsure about the rest of your family, though. Ellen Kelly is still alive. She re-married, then moved on. I think she lives with one of her daughters.'

'I wondered what had happened to her, the girls and young Jim.'

'Yeah, I don't think it's Kate Kelly she lives with. She joined Skuthorpe's Wild West Show, trick ridin' and shootin' and living larger than life.'

'Right, not Kate.'

'Joe's parents are alive, but the story goes that Missus Byrne feels bitter towards the Kellies, and runs Ellen down at any opportunity.'

'Umm, not sure they was ever close.'

'Which reminds me. The Glenrowan Hotel was rebuilt, but burnt down again. I can't remember the full story. Of course, not sure if you knew that Annie Jones had gone to gaol for aiding and abetting the Kelly Gang during the siege? Young Jane died from her wounds a couple of years after the siege, and Annie lost all hope, and sold up.'

'I'm surprised young Jane lived so long, it were a horrible wound.'

'Yeah, each year another rumour starts that the hotel is to be rebuilt. Not sure if anyone would invest. Some say the place is jinxed.'

'What about that lop-eared shearer from Bell Ridge?'

'Martin?'

'Is that his name?'

'Yeah, he had it in for you two. He had two bullets with your names carved into them.'

'Did he, the prick?'

'He took-off a couple of days after you did. I was worried he might bushwhack you.'

'No, he never caught up… until the Palmer.'

'He's a bit sick, I think. Unnatural.'

'You're not kidding.'

'He's out ta kill ya, Steve.'

I tell him Dan remained in Africa after the war. If he's ever questioned, at least Dan will be safe. Night closes in and he excuses himself. I tell him I'll be gone in the morning. It is good to have reconnected.

❖

Jane is pleased to see me.

'My gosh Steve let me have a look at you… you're no longer a boy.'

'I guess I'm moving on. You haven't changed, though,' I lie.

Her hips have spread and her belly rolls about when she walks or laughs. She's punched out a few kids. She holds her head back and thrusts her hands forward, as if she's pushing me to stand out from the crowd.

'You're looking more like Father.'

I don't argue. When I had occasion to look in the mirror, I was surprised to find Pa looking at me. I don't like the comparison, but it's true. The ravages of events such as the sieges at Glenrowan and Elans River, plus the weather on long, tortured treks across the deserts of Australia, and the open veldts of Africa, have taken their toll. When I look in her mirror, I see grey hair and deep gullies etched across my tanned face. If truth be told, given the cowboy-stoop I now have from years astride a horse, I look far older than my years.

Jane has not been home to Wangaratta, so can't add much to what Kerry told me a week earlier. One thing she has learned, is that Pa and Ma are dead.

'Dead?'

'Yep, six years ago.'

'The farm?'

'Dick's running it. He returned from Albury-Wodonga after

Dad's death. Mum died a year later.'

'He's always with me, you know? Pa… Even though I haven't laid sight on the bastard in all this time, his voice is in me head.'

'Yeah, me too. He was pretty large in our lives.'

'He were a prick that's what he were.'

While my parents' death is a sobering aspect of the visit, it's wonderful to share a home-cooked meal in the company of family – women, children. Jane's children are at an age that a strange uncle Fred only has to make a face and they're like a bag of cats. They giggle, squirm in their seats, and earn their mother's wrath for misbehaviour. It's nice to be me, Steve, with my sister, but we decide it would be better that the kids don't know quite who I am, in case they, in their innocence, reveal my identity. Can I ever be the true me in the company of others? The answer, I grow to understand, is no, never. I'll need to peel back many layers of self and then, even I may not recognise the real me.

'Thanks for your letter and the warning about the shearer. We may have dropped our guard without that.'

'Something strange happened, which I couldn't warn you about because I heard of it too late.'

'Oh, what was that?'

'Jane Mawson lives two tents up. The night after the shearer visited, she was threatened in her tent. He kept hissing that Steve deserved it. Things could have got far worse except the neighbour in the tent next door asked if she was alright. It was horrible. She reported his tattoo, with the word *Ned* near his thumb. Saw it as he covered her mouth. I think he mistook that Jane… for me,' Jane says, softly.

A shiver slides like a knife along my spine.

'I'm so sorry, Jane.'

I stay two days longer than I intended. To be captured, after such a long run of freedom, would be too much to take.

'What's your plan?' she asks.

'I have no idea.'

Then, like floodwaters spread across the parched channel country, an image of Murgon rolls out in my mind, as if I hover above it, like an eagle.

'I'll probably go further north and lay low for a while.'

She knows not to ask for details.

'You need to settle.'

'I know that. Life has a habit of getting in the way, though. Each time I'm feeling settled, something or someone seems determined to root me out of my security.'

'You need to make better decisions.'

'They seem to be made for me… the fates.'

'Fates be damned. You let others lead you too easily.'

'Not true.'

I know it is.

'I just want you to be safe.'

On that impulse I head to Murgon. I realise I need to change my name and, in a pub in neighbouring Nanango, I notice bottles of fancy mead on the bar shelf. That's it. I change my name to Billy Meade. It gives me comfort that I belong somewhere. It's like I was born in the district. Ha.

33

THE low silver-leaf Ironbark ridge with the lush grasses, I remember from years earlier, is now sliced apart by a rail-line, to service new settlers.

I ride up to the new siding and rub my hands over "MURGON: 1903" chiselled into its wooden sign. Settlers have taken up land made available by the same Queensland Government Act, which split the large holdings in Allora. A few houses have sprung up around the site, but softwood scrub to the north and west of the town still pushes up against Boatshed Mountain further to the west. It appeals to me.

Following a rinse in the lilied waterhole, I track down the Wright's sawn-timber house on a creek-block on the township's outer rim. Dan said they're from back home. I knock on the front door, but there's no answer. Maybe I have the wrong house? I turn to leave, when I hear the door creak. I spin in time to see a young girl peer at me through the crack of the part-open door. She's cute, no taller than the door handle. I attempt a Kelly smile to appear friendly.

'Is Mummy or Daddy at home?'

'They're out the back.'

A pudgy little hand, to match the sweet voice, points through the opening.

'Go around the side.'

I tip my hat to her, then enter through the picket gate and make my way beneath a lush Moreton Bay Fig to the back yard. I'm noticed by a woman seated upon a bush timber chair, opposite a man in shirt and braces with his back to me. Her face registers both

234

surprise and fear, just as Sergeant Kennedy's had at Stringybark when we appeared.

'Billy,' she whispers, desperate to get the attention of the male seated opposite her, without embarrassing or provoking me, her intruder. 'Billy, there's someone here… Behind you.'

I take this as a cue to speak.

'A young lady at the front door directed me. I'm from Benalla, and I'm looking for the Wrights.'

The man turns with a broad smile, which fades upon sighting me.

'D…d… do I know you?'

'N-n-no, we've never met, but my friends, the Kellies, s-s-said if ever I were up this way and needed help, I should make myself known to you… I'm S-s-steve Hart.'

He jumps out of his chair; extends his hand.

'Of course, you are… Billy Wright!… My wife, Sophie. Sit down… Like a cuppa?… Is Dan with you?'

It's as if he's expecting me and knows we couldn't have perished in the fire. Their welcome is the most promising of starts to, perhaps, a new future.

The second Christmas in Murgon I'm invited to join the Wrights and the Roberts' families at a picnic by the creek.

The nation was only two years old when I'd arrived. There's a sense of hope and a desire to look forward, especially after the African war, and its controversies. No one worries about a little event in Glenrowan twenty-three years earlier, and any outrage over the exploits of Captain Starlight has died.

I'd lived with the Wrights for weeks and, after I was sure no one had followed me from Allora, I left them and lived in a tent out bush, near Redgate, until I built my slab-hut. I settled in, worked for neighbours and sold leatherwork to put food on the table.

I'm comfortable with the Wrights and Roberts, but there's

another family, also present at the picnic. It's stinking hot.

Bill Wright removes his shoes and declares to the crowd.

'That water looks so good. I'm going to jump in; have a swim.'

The children cheer, then undress in a rush to join him. Some run ahead to the sandbank.

Mrs Roberts tidies their clothes, face concerned.

'Careful children, stay in the shallows near the sand.'

The other adults, also, prepare for the swim. Mrs Roberts cocks her head in my direction, squints her eyes.

'You coming in, Billy?'

'No, I don't swim.'

'Never mind that.' She swats my objection away with her hand as she would a fly. 'Stay in the shallows with us ladies.'

'Ugh, I don't know. I'm not really dressed for swimming.'

'You'll be fine. Wear your undershorts. Billy's wearing his.'

No matter what I raise as an excuse, they counter it, so I comply. I remove my riding boots along with my oversized peaked Stetson, then shuffle around the bend of the creek to remove my shirt and jodhpurs in private. I enter the creek from there, conscious of my bandy legs, dainty underclothes and many scars. I return to the others half-submerged, only my head visible. I don't want to explain myself to people I barely know.

I hear Mrs Wright inform the other ladies how she has 'never seen me in a short-sleeved shirt, or working singlet.' She's unaware how easily sound travels across water.

'Even on the hottest of days he keeps his collar and sleeves buttoned down.'

The swim is fine, as is the occasion, but the risk immense and I hope never to put myself in this position again.

I live secluded, a hermit, as much a matter of self-preservation as anything. I never allow myself to get too close to anyone for fear of my past catching up with me, like it did to my family, destroying folks that I cared about. I'll probably regret it later; having no loved ones, but what can I do?

As a consequence of military service and a need for order, I keep my hut tidy. Locals regard that behaviour as acting like an "old woman". I sweep the path from my fence to the doorstep and rake the rolled ant-bed arrival area, where the track from the road and the shed merge, because I'm often away on business and it helps me see, by the tracks they leave, who has visited. I also can hear anyone cross the ant-bed, by its distinctive crunch.

Being the local farrier, I'm often able to identify who's visited by the tracks they leave. I surprise them later by enquiring why they'd visited.

'I see you were at the hut the other day, Dave. What did you want?' I ask the local transport operator.

'I came out to see if you had any horses for sale, Billy.'

I panic those times I don't recognise the tracks, think it may be the traps, or the lop-eared bounty hunter, chasing the massive reward still on my head. A man on the lam is never free. He always looks over his shoulder in dread of what he might find. In my forced solitude I imagine and dream the worst possible outcomes. For a long time, I suspect I'm crazy.

34

I wake. Sit bolt upright. Drenched in sweat. Every part of me shakes and my heart races. I've had the worst dream. I was trapped in the bar at Glenrowan encircled by flames, my ankles on fire. Dan was melting. The hot shrapnel from Eylands River coursed through my body. Ann Jones clawed at my arms. I apologised to the girls shot in Africa, to the Boer woman I assaulted. Ned galloped away. I called and called but he didn't hear. I panicked, screamed, tore at my flesh.

Hey you!

Who?

You.

You mean me?

Yes! Get a grip… Okay, control my breathing try and switch off. It was just a dream. But it's still with me. Night is no sanctuary, nor is daylight. My head is alive with thoughts; crickets chirp at each other, crash and collide within my brain.

Once, it was an occasional dream, the odd nightmare, but they have grown in number and intensity. Once, it needed something external to trigger them: a sound like gunshot, a contorted face, horses galloping unseen. Now it needs no invitation. I'm not sure I can continue. I feel as if my plait unravels, I'm shredding.

I'm not interested in relationships, except perhaps with my horse, and I'm damned sick of the desert, which is inside me. Anger consumes me.

I'm afraid to go back to sleep. Drag myself out of bed. Feel my fine underclothes for small comfort. Put on my boots. Stalk about outside in the dark, in my underpants. Check behind trees, jump at shadows. Speak to Mona who inhabits part of my body. Beg her to piss off. Leave me.

I tramp inside. *Who am I?* I check the mirror. Only one face stares at me. Loathsome face. Loathsome me.

I bend down and open the box in the corner where my pistol hides. I take her out, convinced this time I'm going to use her, finish it once and for all. The world, myself included, will be better free of me.

I weigh her in my hand, point her up, then down, like a pigeon's tail wagging. I make a deal with the devil. I dress in my finest lace-underwear, powder my face, and tease my hair high.

'Devil, let's play a game,' I say aloud. 'I'll put two bullets in the cylinder, place the barrel to my mouth and pull the trigger. If I'm shot, dressed like this, all will know that as a person I'm a tragic lie and the truth of my double-life will be out, but my pain will cease as I go to my grave. If it doesn't fire, then you win, and I'll live to suffer for the rest of my life, perhaps for eternity.'

I can't remove the Catholic from my thinking.

I place the pistol in my mouth, spin the magazine and close my lips around the cold steel. I think of my mother, I think of young Jane Jones, I think of my sisters, and I think of Dan. I want comfort – perhaps Mother Mary.

My hand trembles. Sweat broils along my brow. What am I waiting for? What?... G-g-gutless me. A clock in my brain ticks. Tick... tick.

I pull the trigger.

The click in my ears is as loud as a rifle's discharge, but it's just a click. I suck in breath as if the air has disappeared. Convulse. Settle.

I lift the barrel to my mouth but tremble so violently I'm not sure I can insert it. I use two hands to control the shake. The bush outside the hut is darker than Hades, quieter than the grave.

I squeeze my eyes tight and ready myself to accept the bullet as it penetrates me... pull again.

Click.

I'm still alive.

The odds of my Russian roulette are shorter than the usual one-in-six chance, but still, they choose to favour me. The devil must not want me. I'm alive. Perhaps there's a bigger plan for me?

Perhaps I've been handed a bush redemption? I hang the pistol limply between my legs and breathe. I do this for many minutes. Exhausted, I return the gun to its oil-cloth and hide her again, as if she's a sacred object, and retire to my cot, knowing that blessed sleep is barely a breath away.

I wake and it's as if there is a crack in my mind through which sunlight wants to peek. I search for small things to celebrate – sunrise, bird songs, the smell of my piss on the eucalypt leaves, or the monotonous rhythm of the horse's movement, rocking me like a babe in the womb as I ride about my business. Regular things I can count upon to give me peace.

Old regimental mate, George Green, who's moved east of Crow's Nest, near Toowoomba, acts pleased to see me. Shakes my hand inside both his. Claps my shoulder as I walk past. It's only days since I've rolled the rock aside from the suicide attempt, and I'm hoping a change of scenery might improve my sanity.

He leads me inside and, after introducing me to his wife, the two of us move outdoors to a log in the warm sunlight. He's packed on the weight. Married life obviously suits him, and the smell of prosperity hangs about him like a comforting perfume, an image helped by his polished boots, soft hands and glossy cheeks.

'Believe it or not, I've been looking for ya, Fred. No one knows where the hell ya got to. Ya just disappeared.'

'I had to go bush, mate. The police was after me for "poddy dodging" before the war. I'd worked for this drover who did some lifting, and he drowned before they could nail him, so they went after people who worked for him. I was set-up to take the blame, for someone else's doings.'

'That doesn't sound fair.'

His fat bottom lip continues to flutter.

'No, it's not fair, but I didn't want to sit around and argue the toss, so shot through. Changed me name to Billy Meade.'

'Oh, Billy, is it?'

'Yeah, is now. What was you looking for me for, George?'

'Major Houghton, remember him… from Africa?'

'Yes, I do.'

'Well, he's become the new Australian Army Quartermaster, and with the rumblings in the air about a war in Europe, the army needs cavalry horses. We're talking about thousands.'

His bottom lip flutters again, as if he has more to say.

'What's this about a war?'

'Some spat between the royal families in Europe. The army believes it might lead to a stoush. The Major, specifically, mentioned your name.'

'Why me?'

'He remembers you as one of the wranglers in Africa and hoped you were still in the horse business. Says you'd know what type of horse flesh they're looking for… there'd be a lot of money in it,' he notes, then pauses for effect. 'If I have you involved, I feel sure I can score one of the supply contracts.'

'I haven't been on my game, recently,' I confess. 'A bit crook to tell the truth. May not be up to it, but… I'll give it some thought.'

I want to talk to him about the crickets. See if he, too, has problems with his brain, with sleeping, with anger, with mixing with others, but on the surface he appears fine, so I hold back.

'If you think you're interested, then let me know,' he says. 'It would be good to be able to guarantee a few hundred horses in advance. I think it would turn the contract our way. We have a month to put something together.'

I thought I may have been able to partner-up with a couple of brothers from Blackbutt, who run brumbies from the D'Aguilars.

They could take over the contract if I can't cope. So, on my way home, I swing down to visit them.

Blackbutt boasts a few timber-cutters' huts, a pub, post office, store, school and a nearby railway station. It thrives, having prospered from a brief gold find late in the previous century, and ongoing access to great forests. It's perched on the edge of the D'Aguilar Range and, although the large grazing stations have been cut up for smaller pastoral leases, the scrub still contains large herds of wild horses and cattle.

I've tracked the two brothers down to a large shack on the edge of town. Its slab walls and shingled roof are cut from the local Blackbutt eucalyptus, after which the town is named, and though humble, is solid. I knock on their door.

Within seconds the door scratches open as it drags on its leather hinges. A squat broad-shouldered man with a ginger beard and ruddy nose stands beside his double in the entrance.

'Hi, I'm Billy Meade. I'm looking for the Noble brothers.'

'That's us!'

I stick my hand out and they shake it in turn, out of politeness, both unsure what the hell I'm on about.

'What can we do for you, Billy?'

'I have a contact in the Australian Army, who has the task of adding thousands of horses to their Cavalry stock, and I hear you chaps might be able to raise big mobs of them.'

'Nah, not that many. Perhaps hundreds… Anyway, what's in it for us?'

'Money and lots of it, is in it, and more, if we don't have to pay for the stock. Say… trap brumbies, most of the money is pure profit.'

They look at my lowly rig, my grizzly head and determine I must be taking the piss.

'Why would they trust you?'

'I was an army horse wrangler during the Boer War. I have a reputation, and the right contacts still in the service.'

'I see.'

'Yes, I thought we might be able to run brumbies off the D'Aguilars, and add a few cheap ones we pick up from local sales, and Bob's ya uncle.'

'How do you ensure you get to buy them cheap?'

'Leave that to me. I won't let anyone know who we're buying for, until we have things tied up. That'll hold the local prices reasonable. You guys run the brumbies. There should be a future in it.'

I don't tell them I'll lift horses from the big stations around the area, from Kilcoy in the east, to Taabinga Station in the west, and feed them into the holding paddocks. I'll work alone to ensure secrecy.

I don't hear from the Nobles. In the meantime, I've sweetened to the idea. This is an opportunity to set myself for the future. Having fled Allora and lost all the savings I'd gained from years in the Territory and Africa, I need a break, and this is it, my last chance.

At night I toss and turn, attempt to think of other ways I could pull a herd together to meet the contract, but fall short. I feel the claws of desperation and disappointment drag me down to depression. Three weeks have passed and I've resolved myself to the fact the brothers will not play. Next day I receive a telegram:

BILLY>

HAPPY TO PROCEED< MEET NANANGO TWELTH FOR DETAILS>

NOBLES>

I give my contact the go-ahead. Weeks later, he's awarded the army contract. The Nobles and I gather stock. I set out to lift a mob of Taabinga horses.

I brew-up beside a small lagoon, where I've trapped a large mob, and the mossies flog me anywhere there is exposed skin. I watch one draw blood on my wrist, attempt numerous times to smash it, but it avoids me. I concentrate, hand poised, watch it insert its straw. I suck in my breath to trap it, then smash it flat.

I see compulsion at work in that mossie. Despite better sense, and even warning, it persisted in its suicidal behaviour. I recognise myself in the pest and realise I'm heading down a path I'd begun long ago. I'd survived for years without lifting, why do so now that I'm desperate? There must be options?

I take an even bigger risk. I leave the horses in the trap and ride over to introduce myself to the owner of Taabinga Station, note that there are hundreds of wild horses on his property and offer a contract price to take them off his hands. I still stand to make a large profit. To my surprise he agrees. I drop in on other large runs, with the same deal, and all agree.

In addition, I do a deal with George Green to get paid extra for broken horses. I break-in our horses and it makes it worthwhile for me. My depression lifts. There are days it barely hovers. The war arrives and we are set up to profit.

35

THE sun flaunts its goldens and crimsons along the horizon and I'm in a rush to finish as I assist Mrs Clements, from Goomeri, muster.

In some ways, the war years are my salvation. I'm able to contribute. Many able-bodied men enlist, leaving women, older men or young children with the chores. It means I am offered more work mustering, shoeing, droving, fencing and other bush work. I receive numerous invitations to socialise or attend functions to make up the numbers. I seldom accept, but it makes me feel important.

I'm a member of the fledgling Race Club, hoping to encourage some entertainment in the community and promote the district's quality horse flesh. I've also argued for the need to have an Agricultural Show to highlight local produce, provide entertainment and promote the district for when the boys come home. We need to be ready to heal.

Mrs Clements and I are show society members. Her husband, Mervin, and their two sons, volunteered early in the war. Mervin was killed at Gallipoli within weeks of arrival, but the War Office won't let her sons return. During the war's early years, the locals believed in the British Commonwealth's power and the wisdom of Australian and British leaders to ensure victory. Now that telegrams arrive reminding citizens of the rising bloodbath, the mood has changed.

Having fought with the British in Africa, I felt nothing but dread when war was announced, and have little faith in either government, nor their generals. Food and goods are rationed, so a growing moroseness has fallen across our stoic community. Any able-bodied person, who's not at the front, is viewed as a coward. Women are known to send a white feather to that chap, hoping to shame him into enrolment.

I'm not sent a feather. I'm considered too old to fight, being in my mid-fifties, and anyone who sees me on foot understands my bandy legs prevent me being accepted on medical grounds. I also contribute to the war effort through the supply of horses.

I'd liked to have argued that being a Boer War veteran is enough, but like most aspects of my life, I have to keep my service a secret in case the police still hunt me.

The Clements had a fellow organised to look after the station in the men's absence, but he's taken up with a woman in Kingaroy and left them in the lurch. The deepening dusk makes it difficult to draft the remains of the yard, no matter how fast I try. I hear Mrs Clements call over the bellowing mob.

'Billy, you better come in now. I've made dinner.'

I see her on the yard-rails. I wave; move closer.

'I was going to draft-off the last of the weaners and head home, Mrs Clements.'

'You could have dinner, at least. Two lonely souls need some company.'

'Ah, I suppose, when you put it that way.'

I didn't think of her as being lonely. I seldom recognise it in myself these days. I can jog the old horse home later. I finish the drafting and head across to the house, rinse at the outdoor tank, remove my boots and let myself into the living area.

She's a wonderful cook, as I witnessed at lunch, and the spread tonight looks very posh. It's like something I'd see the officers sit down to, when I was on mess duty in Africa. Silver table-settings, sauce-bowls and gravy-pourers, spirits and sherry in crystal decanters, bowls of fruit and vases of flowers.

'Have a wash, Billy. I've left one of Mervin's shirts on the bed for you. He was about your size. There's a clean towel behind the door.'

Minutes later I emerge. The candles are alight, wine opened, food odours tempting; a domestic scene of my yearnings.

'Gosh, it's a long time since I've been near a flash nosh-up like this, Mrs Clements.'

'Call me Marylyn, Billy.'

'Thanks, Mrs Clements.'

She pours two glasses of whiskey, hands me one and clinks glasses.

'To you, Billy.'

'To you, Mrs Clements.'

We sip. She takes my elbow and escorts me to a cowhide sofa with enough space for the two of us.

'What's your set-up over at Redgate?'

'I have a hut. Nearly a log cabin, but with a tin roof and a lean-to out the back. Not as flash as your place.'

I nearly say palace. The whiskey has impacted.

'Well, it's home after all.'

'It is indeed.'

She empties her glass, uses my thigh as a platform to launch herself upright and pours herself another. She points at my glass.

'Drink up. I'll get you to carve the chicken in a moment.'

She pours from the whiskey decanter then sits again. She empties the next glass just as quickly.

'Sorry… I'm a little nervous. I haven't entertained for so long… Since the war began, people have stopped doing it. It doesn't seem proper to enjoy yourself, does it?'

She waits until I empty my glass, then stands, extends her hand so I can take it. She hauls me to my feet, so that our toes and noses are quite close. She giggles as she bumps me.

'Whoops, I've nearly knocked you down again.'

'Nearly.'

'Here, take this cloth and move the Dutch oven off the fire.'

I do as I'm told and she sets me up with carving knife and fork, a carving board, and a large porcelain plate for laying out the chicken portions. I carve a few pieces.

'I hope I'm doing this right?'

'I'm sure you do everything right.'

'Not in domestic matters I don't. I'm sure I'm hopeless.'

My carving must pass inspection, for she seats me and proceeds to serve. While I'd carved, she'd poured more whiskey.

She's warm and generous, and misses her family. She speaks at length about them and the love she has for her departed husband, who I learn, was ten years her senior. She asks me many questions about myself, which I manage to dodge to avoid giving too much away. I'm disappointed I have to, because I believe Mrs. Clements is one to respect my privacy, but it's too early for me to know.

When the kitchen is tidy, she pours two sherries without my noticing, and hands me one.

'Oh no, I really have to go.'

'There's no need to leave. You could sleep in one of the boys' rooms.'

My face must have registered fear, or horror, or something.

'No, no, Billy, we're grown people. No one need know you have even been here.'

'No, I better go.'

'I insist. You can't leave like this. We're having such a lovely night and we haven't had our sherry. It would be such a shame to finish it before the sherry.'

She has her hands on my chest, pins me against the sofa, where we've returned momentarily. I shake my head. She shakes hers.

'No! No way. You're not going. Here, now drink this.'

I sit and we continue drinking. An hour later and I'm dizzy; not used to wine.

'Ah, which room have you sorted for me?'

'Sleep in Jacob's. It's the one beside mine.'

I rise. The walls sway a little, as do my legs.

'Night, Marylyn.'

'Night, Billy.'

I make a crooked line to the room, find the bed and remove my boots. I remove Mervin's shirt and wriggle out of my jodhpurs, then slip beneath the sheets, still not convinced I'm doing the right thing. I hear dishes rattle, the sound of cupboards opening and closing, and smell scented soap.

I wake with a sense of dread. Something has me trapped. The shearer! Am I dreaming? Are my crickets loose? I thrash my arms.

'Don't you ever get lonely, Billy?'

It's Marylyn wearing nothing but a slip, and sitting on the edge of my bed, peering into my face. I scrutinise her features, up close. I like what I see.

'I don't any m-more, M-marylyn. Get l-lonely, that is.'

Through my alcoholic haze and my fear of situations like this, I'm determined to be gentle.

'But men have needs. Mervin always says that.'

'They d-d-do. Yes.'

'Well, women have needs too. I have needs right now. I've watched you all day… You're so manly it's driven me crazy. Being near a man has flamed a fire where coals already burned. I'm sorry, but what's going to happen to my needs?'

She stands to remove a bamboo comb from her bundled hair, lets it fall in braids over her swollen breasts, and I make out the silhouette of her shapely body through the flimsy fabric of her slip. I add to it with my lifetime of imagination. Perhaps, tonight, I'll experience what everyone else appears to have experienced. To act out the promise I made to myself in Sydney, so many years ago.

I feel excitement in my groin. My breath faster, my cock rises to lie against my stomach. I may be able to do it. My cock pushes against my underclothes, the woman's panties I'm wearing.

I'd forgotten the underwear. I panic.

'Oh Jesus, Marylyn, you've picked the last person in the world to answer that.'

I can't let her see the panties. The falsities and lies of my life would unravel. She will never understand a man in woman's clothing.

'There's just the two of us and no one for miles around, surely you can do something?'

I remain silent, attempt to look sympathetic, which I am, but my security is more important. I can't, won't, risk it.

'When my boys return, they'll watch me like a hawk. For me, there'll never be another occasion like this. I'm going to turn into a barren cow. Never feel the joy of a man's desire consume me... If Mervin had just told me he wouldn't return. If God had warned me that our last embrace was our last?'

She sobs and folds gently upon my chest. I wrap my arms around her shoulders and hold her. She continues to sob, and her soft flesh envelops me. I owe her an explanation, but what can I say? Her soft flesh weaves its magic.

'Don't you find me attractive?'

Her voice is quieter, calmer. Is there a hand grenade in the question?

'You're very attractive. It's... it's m-me.'

I both lie and tell the truth.

'Do you need a hand?'

Oh damn!

'Extinguish the lamp, Marylyn.'

She rises and closes the door, effectively blocks the light. She sits again, then leans across and kisses me in the tenderest, deepest way.

I can't remember ever being kissed. I'm sure my mother kissed me, but I don't recall. Joy and excitement swamp me, and it's many minutes before our lips part.

I'm on fire. Marylyn sits upright and removes her slip. I wriggle out of my undies and place them beneath my shoulders, to stuff under the pillow when I get a safe moment. Marylyn pulls the covers aside and slides in beside me. Her hands find my fire. She slides on top then astride me.

I'd seen horses mate and think there is no way it could physically happen; the stallion is so huge. I feel that size myself, now, but the puzzle solves itself. I'm not a man of words, but the feeling is like I'm a red-hot horse-shoe being quenched in a bucket of warm water. It is such a relief, and I hiss and bubble until Marylyn calms me.

'Thank you, thank you,' I hear myself saying.

Marylyn makes a strange but wonderful sound then slumps over me. I feel her tears fall upon my cheek where her head rests. I lie frozen.

'You alright?… You're crying.'

'Sorry, they're tears for Mervin.'

I move as if I'm about to disengage, untangle our plait.

'Don't you dare move,' she hisses.

I freeze. We lie still for a minute of two, then she moves again and from her breathing and her kisses, I know we are alright.

'Thanks, dear man.'

She cries herself to sleep and I lie awake, holding her until I, too, doze. We wake, hours later, just as the magpies start calling. She kisses me again and we repeat the performance. This time I have more confidence.

'Whew,' she says.

She kisses me on the cheek, then rolls out of bed.

'Not a mention of this to anyone, Billy.'

'Your secret is safe with me.'

She pads to her bedroom with her slip in hand. I glimpse her juicy figure in the lamplight before the door shuts.

I can't believe what has happened. Someone, a woman, finds me desirable, and making love wasn't as fraught as I imagined. It was wonderful and happened so naturally.

I lie there, mind alight. My demons have really screwed me up, but there's hope. I'm a man.

36

THE Great War is over. I seem to have healed somewhat, and have grown to accept the "damaged" me. I'm not the only one. It was the "war to end all wars" so we strive to put it behind us and I strive to start a new life, yet again. Marylyn and I continued our relationship until her boys returned and convention constrained her. We've become good mates and I'll be forever thankful to her for sorting that part of my life. The dreams still join me at night, where I sleep poorly, but the grasshoppers appear to have moved along. The Great War has given a name to my condition: shell shock. I can cut myself a little slack. It's a human thing. I'm not weak and green pick appears from the barren dunes of my soul.

It's a beautiful summer afternoon at the racetrack on the town's outskirts where, over the years, we've built facilities like a grandstand, and club rooms to trap more punters. I've had a punt, to throw more excitement into the day, given I'm too old to ride – I know my limits. I may even be happy.

Around me, bookies lay out their prices, and I examine the odds on their colourful boards. I struggled with school but never believed I was dumb, and I manage to understand the odds like it's my native language. I hear spectators urge their favourite to the line, watch punters' excited faces when they collect their winnings, feel the drama as losers explain away a loss. It's 1925 and here, the world is writ small.

For a few brief moments at the racetrack, all are soul-mates. None of us is mightier than the other, and the beautiful get plainer and the ugly more beautiful, with the booze. Owner drinks with stable-hand, jockey with punter, and it all occurs against the dusty backdrop of horses being ferried to stables into the falling, rusty sun. I crave these moments.

An out-of-town jockey I bump into at the bar, realising we are of similar height, says to me, 'You look like you may have been a jockey in your day.'

I smile at the backhanded compliment.

'Yeah, I was the right size, but I just didn't have the contacts when I was younger.'

'That's a shame, I just live for it… racing,' he says. 'I can see how disappointed you must be.'

I'm desperate to boast about my race wins at Beechworth, Benalla and other country meets, but I learnt my lesson at the shearing shed and, for once, keep my mouth shut. I don't even tell him about the time I cleared the monstrous Wangaratta railway gate.

'I'm a club member. I earn my spurs through my ability to pick good horses, to break them in and shoe them,' I say.

I don't tell him I refined those skills in Africa, trying to keep our exhausted animals mobile.

'Where do you conduct business?' he asks.

'I work in with Waldock's Blacksmith to get my shoes made and often shoe the horses in their yard, helping them out, if necessary. On other occasions I have my tools in my spring cart, and turn up at say, a property, race meet, sale yard or show, fire up the forge and within thirty minutes, I'm ready for business.'

'That's handy, custom made.'

'Yes. I'm often tempted to train a race horse, to test my ability to pick a good horse and bring it to a win, but resist the urge. It'd tie me down too much,' I add.

Again, I don't tell him I still worry my demons will appear, to wreck me. I'd have to learn to trust someone else to jockey it, but who could match my high expectations? I'm a fringe player, and I grow more content with that.

I'm about to leave but bump into Megan Wiggin: one of the town's society ladies. I'd broken in a horse for her. I break the horses with the rider in mind.

'Hello, Billy.'

I lift my hat.

'Miss Wiggin.'

'Call me Megan.'

'Thanks, Megan. How'd that mare turn out?'

'Wonderful, Billy.'

'I broke her for the side-saddle.'

'Yes, there's never been an issue. We'll show her this year. Lady's rider!'

'Oh good. As you know I've been a member of the show society since before the first show and pleased you support it. I like to see an easy bond between owner and horse... Learned right the first time, we don't confuse them.'

'Thanks Billy. It worked.'

'My pleasure.'

It's not always a pleasure. While I attempt to move the horse into the sport required, whether it be stockwork, show riding or camp drafting as part of the finished product, it depends on the owner and their riding ability.

As I spoke with Megan, I noticed another young woman being led home, all the worse for the drink.

I broke her horse last year and introduced it for show jumping, or hunting, and explained, 'No need to have a long, fast run up.'

'How long?'

'About six lengths is enough for the heights you'll be jumping.'

'Six lengths?'

'Yes, let him have a good look at the fence, then go at a measured canter.'

'Will do.'

The horse didn't need speed or a long run-up, as some riders assume. When I handled him, he could leap four-foot, effortlessly.

Come show time, I watched the lady rush the horse, in spite of my advice. The horse pulled on the bit and she failed to gather him in. His head jiggled as she tried to exert control and he baulked, pulled rails, and due to panic incorrectly measured the fence and lost balance time and again. That's the business though, you hand over the mount and your reputation is in the hands of others.

We seldom dismounted to open a gate or a fence when I rode with the Kellies, but jumped them instead, never missed a beat. It frustrated the heck out of those in pursuit. As a consequence, we learnt a lot about the skill. We jumped fences in the dark on our many night-time cross-country journeys to attend parties or horse meets, or visit family or friends. As a result, we seldom left tracks at gateways or common junctions, where the traps could check. We would appear in one town and confound all by being at another soon after, due to our knowledge of short-cuts and our ability to scale steep cliffs at speed, or to travel over country considered inaccessible. Our round horseshoe also flummoxed many a trap when we were forced to cross common areas.

Most riders are happy with the horses I break for them. Sometimes, I work three or four horses at a time.

I'm pleased to have my military experience and time with the "breaker" to call upon, to help manage the load. In fact, folks around here call me "the breaker", unaware of the connection.

Funny, but I'm contracted to keep the local traps' horses shod and have done so for years. We're good friends. Bit different to when I was a youngster.

My life is settled.

I wave to Sergeant Stern, the local trap, and he signals he would like to share a beer or two before the bar shuts. He doesn't mind a drop, the old sergeant.

I deliver a horse to the saleyard, where I pen it for a customer to collect later. I skirt the town to return home and notice a tall horseman on a large chestnut with a white face, approach from the railway station. I don't recognise the chestnut, or the rider. As we pass at a distance, something stirs in my memory. Something about the rider's seat makes me uncomfortable. He appears unnatural, feet turned out in the stirrups, slumped posture. I think *lop-eared shearer.* I swivel on my saddle to find he's swivelled on his. I shorten my rein without realising, urge the horse to extend his stride to distance myself from the stranger without drawing attention.

I hear a voice in the wind.

'Hey, Steve?'

I don't respond. I ride on. I catch a sight of him from the corner of my eye. He's turned his horse. I don't have my pistol.

I push into a jog as if I'm readying for a long trip. By now I have a three-hundred-yard lead. I rise in the stirrups and bounce on the saddle in rhythm. A hornet buzzes past my ear. I've heard that before in Africa. A bullet. Shit. I hear its discharge, a voice. 'Hey, hold up!'

No way. I need to outrun him to the hut and find a weapon. I spur my brumby-runner, so pleased I didn't bring the spring cart I've grown accustomed to driving. The horse gallops. Another hornet slaps a tree beside me. I aim for the creek and reach the security of vegetation along its bank. The wind tears at my hair. I ride Indian style along my horse's "off" side, keep the creek as protection and the horse between myself and the shearer. The shearer falls behind in the scrub.

I rise, jockey style, and dash across open ground past the Sipple's cowshed. The brumby-runner's legs pound like train pistons. I need to cross a holding yard. I aim the horse at the closed gate, gather the horse in a little, not sure if it can, or will, jump. It doesn't hesitate and a minute later clears the next gate as well.

I hear gunshots but no hornets. The shearer has to stop to open the gate. He's out of range. His magazine must be near empty. I've gained precious seconds. I hit the scrub patch that swallows my hut, let the horse pick its own path. We whizz past large ironbark and various softwood, leap across fallen trees and turkey bush, crash debris underfoot as the brumby-chaser forces a way through. He's familiar with the process, our pursuer appears less so. Sweat flies from the horse's shoulders; the hut is over the rise.

We slide to a halt at its front door. I feel the ant-bed underfoot as I race inside to where the pistol is stashed. My hands tremble, struggle to unlock the lid. I hear hoofbeats. I grasp the pistol. Is it loaded? The oil rag falls away. The steel glints in the half light. I see my birth certificate in the box, and my medals. An ominous sign?

'I've got you now, Hart, you murdering cur.'

I peek through the window to locate the shearer. A bullet whacks into the wall beside me, slivers of wood embed themselves into my neck. I know where he is. I'll bob up and take him out. I lift my head and the world caves in. Timber shutters, riding boots and the shearer, clatter on top of me. He's jumped through the window. I'm stunned but the shearer is on his back, beside me, pistol ready. I brace for the slug; for my death. He pulls the trigger. A click.

I kick out, strike flesh. Hear him grunt. Roll onto my knees, raise my pistol.

'Hold it there, you bastard.'

He prepares to attack and I shoot above his head. Phew, it's loaded. He holds steady, like a dingo about to pounce.

'You've got it wrong,' I shout.

I stand. Pant like I've ridden a buckjumper for thirty seconds.

'I'm not who you t-t-think I am.'

'You're Steve Hart.'

'No, I'm not, Martin. You've got K-k-Kellies on your brain, mate. I can understand that, given what they've done to your f-f-f-family, but I ain't one of 'em. They're dead.'

'You've changed your name.'

'Yeah, of course. You were going to kill us.'

I back up to the box of trinkets, remove the birth certificate and shake it open.

'You two ran from the shearing gang.'

'I have my own ghosts, mate. My own reasons to hide.'

I step close and hold the certificate in front of his ugly face.

'Here… look at my birth certificate. Can you read?'

He scans the page, then looks at me, then re-reads it.

'Fred Layton, as you knew me when we met… alright?' I shout.

'Maybe.'

'No, maybe. Now piss off before I shoot you, like you were about to do to me.'

'Me gun.'

I'm so angry I kick him in the ribs, pull him to his feet by his hair and point him at the door.

'No gun, mate. I'll be telling the police, also, so piss off; don't come back.'

He stumbles to his horse, which shies backwards. He makes further attempts to trap him. Succeeds, mounts and returns along the track to town. I trap the brumby-runner and follow at a distance. I watch him ride past Sipple's dairy. Think he's convinced about my identity. Return home, and unsaddle, feeling terribly weary. I move inside and sit on the edge of the bunk and shake with shock. I have no appetite and night falls. Much later I sleep.

37

SOMETHING has me by the boot and it tugs like a pup on the end of a sock.

'Okay, you've got me!'

I'm having Sunday lunch with Joe Sipples from the farm next door and young Marcel is beneath the table and has me by the boot.

'You're not supposed to know it's me, Billy,' she says, her voice tinged with disappointment.

'Oh, dash! I went and forgot. Try again.'

I look to where I've tethered my buggy and its two roan ponies to the homestead's white fence. I like the fact that unlike riding, I can dress and sit high on the buggy without creasing my clothes. My appearance, again, is important, since the shearer's gone and my crickets have quietened, and I make sure I dress well and use the buggy for social occasions.

Lunch is a regular Sunday event, and I'm very grateful for the company and fond of the family. I move my feet to make it more difficult for young Marcel to trap them. We're all on the veranda, except her mother, who's in the kitchen.

'What's for lunch, Mum?' Marcel shouts from beneath the table. Moments later her curly head pops up and she slips into the seat opposite me.

When the mother answers from within, Marcel mimes, with exaggerated mouth movement, her mother's exact words.

'Roast beef with baked vegetables.' Then mimes, 'We had lamb last Sunday,' as her mother feels the need to justify.

She's a funny mite, that Marcel.

'And dessert?' she asks.

'Bread and butter pudding, sweetheart.'

'Mum, Colin is poking a hole in the bread you baked for Billy.'

We look across at the bench where Col has a loaf in his hands.

'Col, you stop that this instant.'

'I did not.'

'Did too.'

Mrs Sipple bakes a loaf of bread for me every time, and often includes something else. Today, it's a bottle of pickles. I really enjoy her cooking. In contrast, my cooking is very basic, confined to the open fire, bacon and eggs. A slab of corned beef, a bag of flour and a bag of potatoes, last me for weeks. But I think most of all, food aside, I really enjoy the family banter.

Sunday lunch is a time to catch up on the events of the past week, and any local gossip. The children tease each other for various mistakes, or contrary opinions they hold, and the parents, especially their mother, orchestrate the conversation so there's abundant joy and laughter.

'Billy, what do you think? Should I be allowed to stay with my friend, or not?'

It's as if I'm a sounding board for them. I feel privileged to witness this. I sop-up the atmosphere like damper absorbs the gravy on my plate. I wonder how my life would have turned out had I been privy to such love and consideration as a child?

After we've eaten, Mr Sipple takes me aside.

'Billy, I've been meaning to ask if you'd be interested in passing on your leatherworking skills?'

He's aware of my skills through the Murgon Show's crafts exhibits and competition. I'd learned crafts in Beechworth Prison. Breaking rocks is designed as punishment for the lag: to break his spirit. But a broken person is good to no one.

The crafts enrich the spirit. They allow one to see the virtue of building something, rather than breaking it down. It allowed me to attempt to create something beautiful; to seek advice and assistance, when I got into difficulty; and to learn to take criticism about something outside myself, in order to correct it. To perfect my basket, pot or saddle-bag. It helped "me" work on "me".

'I've never thought about it,' I say.

'Well, you were suggesting at the Show Society meeting that the art is dying out and leatherworking would be a good skill for local stockmen to have, perhaps offering an occupation to some of the wild youth.'

'No, yeah, I did say that.'

'Well, I thought we could organise for you to teach it at the school, if you're interested. I'd like my lads to learn it. They like you, so you must have a way with youngsters.'

'I need to think about it. I never imagined myself being able to teach anything.'

'No rush. Let's have a cuppa. It's just brewed.'

We nurse our cups in silence. I look from the veranda across their ploughed fields. *Will I agree to teach? What would I ever say to children? Imagine Pa, if he knew I'd been asked. What would he say?*

We talk about poor milk prices, and the possibility of adding a piggery to the farm to bring in money, and other practical topics while my head spins. I notice the sun's position, figure it is time to leave, so I excuse myself.

Mr Sipple stands on the top step to farewell me.

'Let us know if you're interested in those leatherwork classes.'

I flash a weak smile, head along the path, then think, *What the heck, I'll take a risk*: Turnabout.

'Look, we could give it a shot, those classes… if you think there's an interest.'

My mouth is saying yes, but my head refuses to nod.

'I'm sure there is, Billy… All right, I'll line it up at the school.'

How many years has it been since I'd sat in a classroom? Sixty? Can I do it? Will the children be interested? Will they listen to me? I'm plagued with as much doubt as a softwood slip-rail full of white ants as I buggy home.

❖

'Children,' calls the teacher above the clatter and din of students scraping chairs, talking, laughing, closing desks, beating each other. 'You need to put your tuppence on the table for the course materials, and then resume your seats.'

She waits until they settle, then introduces me.

'This is Mr Meade, who is here today to teach us leatherwork. Over to you Mr. Meade.'

She steps aside with arms spread wide, like a lion-tamer at the circus. I remove my hat and step before the class, hat in hand.

'Hello ch-children,' I begin, 'j-j-j-just call me Billy.'

Perhaps I'm being fed to the lions? My mouth is as dry as a slate-cloth after holidays and I pray a willy-willy wanders in and blows me away. *What have I done? What do I say next?*

'I wish I had w-w-w-worked harder at school, but I have always been pleased to have learned things, which were useful to me, l-l-later,' I explain. 'L-l-like being able to read, or understand geography, which was handy when I found myself in Africa, for example. I was surprised how a boring subject like that came in handy. Never, in my wildest dreams at your age, did I think I would find myself in Africa,' I continue, hoping what I say is funny but, apparently, it isn't, because not one child laughs.

I lie a bit. I didn't really learn to read much. I lick my lips and look from child to child, as if I'm staring down a posse of traps about to nab me.

'Something I often use in my job, is leatherwork.'

I don't know what to say next, so gulp air. I twirl my hat. I spy some examples of my work I'd earlier placed on a side-table.

'I have a few things on that b-b-bench over there,' I say, pointing. 'I'm going to show you how to plait your own six-round, greenhide whip, like this one here,' and I hold up a small one I'd made to show them.

'Does anyone know why plaits are useful?'

Not a hand is raised. I hold a strip of leather in the air.

'Well, this thin strip is easily broken but, when woven together, becomes very strong. Strips of different lengths can be plaited-in, and despite the joins, the whole remains strong. Also, there is something quite beautiful in the pattern and is calming to make.'

A couple of youngsters nod. I think of Dan. How once we'd been plaited together and endured so much, then dismiss the thoughts in case they disable me.

'We will work on it over the next six weeks, so I can get to show you how to tie it off at the finish. If you complete your whip, you get to keep it,' I say.

Whew! I hand around some leather and sharp knives, and demonstrate on a hand-sawed piece of timber, how to cut the leather into fine strips. We spend the rest of the time on the veranda floor, each child laying out their piece of leather and cutting it into fine strips, ready for plaiting. Some sit closer to watch what I do. One young lad stands beside me with his hand on my shoulder before gathering confidence to do his own. We unconsciously weave into a group.

I appear each Wednesday for the next five weeks and all complete their whip, I'm pleased to say. It's one of the few things in life I'm really proud of.

This little mare reminds me of Greeny's mare all those years ago. I kept her back from the sales for just that reason. Her owners mistreated her as a youngster and she was headed for the knackery for being difficult to handle. I find if I treat such outlaws well and gain their confidence, I can use their wild spirit and bravery to my advantage.

I'm slow to saddle her. I need to thaw my bones, unravel my old muscles. I reflect on a recent story in the local rag noting I've been with the show society for longer than a decade. There, the president described me as "a solid citizen". Said folks are used to seeing me in my buggy, with my roan ponies and my big hat.

I guess he's correct, I just blend into the background. And, while I still lead a very private life, it's probably the only life available to me. But now, I'm not an outcast. I belong. Something, except for a few crazy years as a teen, I craved most of my life but was denied. That's life, I guess.

I face the bay and gingerly lift my beat-up leg into the stirrup, swing up on her and a feed-tin blows over with a racket behind her. Oh, my Jesus. She shies away and it's all I can do to stay close. I slam into the saddle; her head drops low and I lean back but my foot has not found the off-side stirrup. She rears then swings offside as she drops her head. I'm in trouble. I've lost my line with her muscled neck. My body skews to the side; I notice a yard-post fill my vision…

38

Wondai Hospital, 1938

'AND there you have it, Matron Drinkwater: The truth and I'm of sound mind. It all started with borrowing a horse.'

'Well that certainly is interesting, Mister Meade.'

'Billy, just call me Billy.'

'I never would have thought when they brought you in here, Billy, that you were such a fascinating character.'

'Strange what happens to you.'

'Did you ever catch up with Dan?'

'No, I tried a couple of times. I hear the drink got him. He moved on from Allora. Heard he was living at one time near Ipswich. There was a newspaper report of him living under Toombul bridge in Brisbane. Each time I chased the sighting down, he'd shifted.'

'That's a shame.'

'Yeah, I hoped he might track me down, but he never did. I had to accept that the plait had unravelled.'

'Mrs Gardiner's prophecy came true.'

'I guess, but not quite in the manner I imagined. I lived and there is no need to keep the Kelly secret if I'm about to die. Australia needs to know the truth. I hope you writ some of it down.'

'Well, I never said you're dying, but Doctor says you've been hurt badly by that crazy horse.'

'It wasn't his fault, was circumstances. I don't bounce like I used to. Especially with a horse on top of me.'

'I guess not.'

'As I said, it's not the life I thought I'd have. Not the "short but merry life" I set out to have with Dan. But I lived. That's an achievement in itself.'

'You're nearly eighty, Billy. That's quite an achievement.'

'I'm gonna close my eyes for a moment, Matron. I think I hear Danny calling. He's just around the bend of the river.'

Billy Meade was buried in grave 323 in Murgon cemetery, 1938.

ACKNOWLEDGMENTS

A debut novelist is in debt to numerous people. I'd like to thank Carolyn Martinez and her dedicated team at Hawkeye, first, for showing confidence in me and my writing; second, for the technical support to transform the idea to reality; and third, promoting Queensland regional storytelling. Of the Hawkeye team I'd like to acknowledge the role Nicole Kelly, author of *Lament*, played in recommending my manuscript.

I'd also like to thank Maria Simms who, having edited a previous novel-length manuscript, *Identity*, came out of retirement to undertake a structural edit of *Steve*.

Thank you, brother, Gary Long, for your flamboyant rendition and introduction of the *Steve* legend. The story never left me. In turn, I'm appreciative of Murgon residents Col Sipple, and Ex-Mayor, GW Roberts for their recollections of Billy Mead. I'd like to acknowledge the valuable contribution the courses offered by Queensland Writers Centre and AVID Bookstore have made to my technical writing capability. Thanks to my *Aspiring Authors* writing group for urging me to seek publication for my writing. I'm also in debt to the reviewers who read the manuscript and provided comments within these covers. I appreciate your generosity in providing insights for prospective readers and promoting writing.

This is a fictional account, a work of the imagination, but I owe much to various source materials. Apart from the published histories, I appreciate and make special note of, the depth of historical material in the Ironoutlaw.com and would have loved to have yarned with the site's editor.

Kelly 'buffs', history purists and gang family members, may be concerned where I have taken liberty with the truth in areas where there is little known about Steve and the Kellies. I acknowledge that some facts are contestable and, in some cases, facts of convenience are used to support the narrative.

Similarly, when dealing with indigenous matters, I attempt to weave a path of respect, yet remain relatively faithful to the times. I have been privileged to work with many indigenous elders and privy to much knowledge, some of which is sensitive. But cultural matters mentioned in this work are sourced from the public domain and may not be relevant to particular nations or clans. I hope, however, I have managed to transfer the awe I feel living beside the world's oldest refined culture, redolent with symbolic knowledges beyond my comprehension.

Was Billy Meade, Steve Hart? I find it difficult to believe someone who'd lived a respectable, though isolated life, would confess on their deathbed to being a notorious criminal and destroy that social credit. It piqued my interest and I went backwards to see if dates lined up with legend. Certain reports of sightings appear credible. There are, however, a number of individuals who have claimed to be Steve, but dined-out on the notoriety, where Billy didn't. (Harry Thompson died in Wallumbilla, and Jack Day who reputedly died at Thargomindah, believed they were Steve Hart. Source: E. Navarre).

Most published work concentrates on the Kelly story: *Dan Kelly Outlaw* (Ambrose Pratt), covers Dan's life up until Glenrowan; and, *Game as Ned Kelly? His Brother Dan Was* (Vince Allen), explores how they were whisked away from Glenrowan. *Ned: Knight in Aussie Armour* (Eugenie Navarre) interviews sympathisers' descendants who explain how Dan and Steve were rescued. Newspaper articles refer to Billy Meade and Murgon locals made promises to use DNA testing of his remains, to confirm his identity. Testing has not been undertaken.

The legend continues.

Peter Long

ABOUT THE AUTHOR

Photo by Mark Crocker

Peter Long is a Brisbane writer with an interest in regional and historical fiction and any other topic that attracts his fancy. He attempts all forms but appreciates short stories for their variety, discipline, subtlety and colour, and novels for their ability to provide a platform for extended ideas.

Peter has worked as a stockman, public servant, consultant, researcher and academic. As a Rotary Graduate Fellow, he studied in Canada and holds degrees from University of Queensland and University of Toronto.

His poetry has been highly commended in the 1980 and 1981 McGregor Literary Competition and a long poem published in *Paper Children*, an anthology from that competition. He has been long-listed and published in both The Stringybark and Sydney Hammond short story competitions and his collection of short stories long-listed in the 2020 Hawkeye Manuscript Development Prize.

Peter has been a QWC committee member since 2021 with a focus on support for regional writers.

Steve Hart: The Last Kelly Standing is his debut novel.

BOOK CLUB NOTES

1. Was the Kelly Gang a pack of violent criminals or homegrown revolutionaries?

2. What does the novel contribute to the notions of mateship, gender, heroism, violence?

3. Why would Professor Stephen Torre suggest the novel is a post-modernist love story?

4. What do you think of the novel's characterisation?

5. What could the metaphor of the drover's herd imply?

6. What could the various waterholes represent?

7. Have we learned the lessons of the past in terms of youth justice, diversity and migrant inclusiveness?

8. What role does landscape play in the novel, if any?

Book reviews can make or break a book. If you liked what you read today, please do consider posting a review on Goodreads or your favourite forum.

Steve Hart: The Last Kelly Standing is available at hawkeyebooks.com.au and all good bookstores and libraries.